Direktorin Elke Kriemhild

Mr. Gil Jackson is the author of this, An FBI Agent Charlie O'Hare series of crime novels. The first two, The Seventh Gift and The Sentinel Mother are available as paperbacks and ebooks. He has also written an historical fiction novel, A Barrister Phileas Cluff Novel. The first in the series of these, The Tinners Hut is set on spooky Dartmoor, home of 'The Hounds of the Baskervilles'; and is a time travel hostage siege adventure. First written as a television script, it still awaits the taking up by an agent.

In another life, he is sole proprietor of Hiram B. Good Professional Book Production and Allied. Following on a professional life in the printing industry since God was a boy, he formats ebooks and paperbacks.

Married with three children and two grandchildren, he lives on Dartmoor with his wife. He runs on the moors. When he can, he wild swims in the sea.

DIREKTORIN ELKE KRIEMHILD

AN FBI AGENT CHARLIE O'HARE NOVEL

GIL JACKSON

DEDICATED TO

Christine and John Pead

BEFORE 39 BILLION YEARS

AHRIMAN SLIPPED INTO A PAST. To a time of his inception. Where he was to go unnoticed, further beyond 13 billion years. A place he was familiar, for it was here he first sought the Equation for Creation. A set of data of math calculation formatted by God; and only for Him. Here Ahriman began again his equations. In this place he would try to understand and mark the universal constant of the data; ever-changing drafts, each in its turn becoming obsolete, to be replaced with finite changes for improvement; remaining long enough to become valid and uniform before obsolescence.

Using the backdrop of oncoming cosmic microwaves, Ahriman worked through these calculations that would one-day become apparent to Newton, Friedman, Schrödinger and Einstein, hoping for a random equation that made sense, break the code. Billions of years was of no consequence. For here time did not exist, here he worked until coming close to his objective, where permission from God, no longer in the picture, were to be ignored. Equations from the beginnings of time itself were written across his blackboard. For these were calculations chalked up, miscalculated, before being discarded only to begin again, to combine with the chalk dust of time.

Until the Equation for Creation,

$$-ds^2 = a(t)^2\, ds_3^2 - c^2\, dt^2 \text{ [∞]}$$

came into being with a BANG. Inaccessible to him and other spirits; only by man in his turn. For only then would there be a vacancy for another creator from the destruction of His universe. Then the force holding them would be opened with another, BANG.

THE DAY BEFORE HESS LOST $50K

DR. HERMENBERGUR ALOYIOUS had returned to attend O'Hare. He needed to bring him out of the cataleptic state he had induced him in, for he was close to never coming back if it was not soon. His one overriding concern was the man's untimely awakening before lapsing back into a coma, mark his end. He had put the man into his current state with drugs, and drugs were to revive him. He stethoscoped his heart. Not great. Heart rhythm was showing signs of arrhythmia, tachycardia, which he fully expected the age he was. He listened to his heart once more. Steady now. He wired him to an electroencephalogram. Switched on. Major brain activity showed to a level no man should survive. With no clear cause for the activity, was there a fault with his equipment? He checked connections where they were meant to be. Then run the test once more. Levels were exactly the same. With signs the patient was at the crossroads of life and death, he decided to inject rapamycin. Waited. Too late. He was convulsing.

SENTINEL MASTER–EVT hit into the brain of the human. In a trillionth of a billionth of a second it had run through eighty billion neurons of this human brain. Finding the nucleotides holding the stored analogue information for creation it attempted to download them back to its own time before the man was back in the land of the living. It hit a brain lock threatening the invader with a crash to its own neurons making them irrecoverable.

An unknown myth was in the data.

SENTINEL MOTHER immediately disengaged SENTINEL MASTER from −EVT setting −EVT adrift. SENTINEL MOTHER attempted to pull the 10^{124} bits fragmenting for a lack of Space−Time of creation of the current universe into semblance of order. Universe−Verse−Time threatened to crash not only their Verse, others also. A mathematical collapse in natural data was at hand. For the gateway holding this onslaught of data in check, threatened the collapse of all space and time in all verses, bringing on a cease of entropy for all their ends. The ten thousand trillion years to the power of eight's span of creation's existence, threatened to end, were downloaded in a trillionth of a billionth of a second, prevented and saving this Creation Blueprint from being destroyed; likely take its host with it.

O'Hare moved forward into an upright position, clutched his head. Aloyious steadied him, waited for his first thought to occur. A cerebral hemorrhage was in the waiting room. He immediately checked his concerns and placed his hands on O'Hare's head. Warm. Looked into his eyes. No swelling to the man's optic nerve, no seizures, no hand tremors. What he first feared had not materialised. Aloyious helped O'Hare to his feet. Standing, looking bemused, O'Hare shrugged, opened the palms of his hands and asked, 'What's all the fuss about?'

before falling back into an unconscious state once more. Speech normal then.

There was fuss though, for the man showed all symptoms of having had a massive overload of energy to his brain, that would kill him for sure, if it occurred a second time. He returned to the electroencephalogram, this time setting different parameters for recording. Opening a metal case, he took out another set of sensors and began replacing them with new ones. The human brain was a complex structure, containing enough neurons to transmit 1 000 electrical impulses per second, a phenomena he was keen to obtain out of this man's head whatever the outcome. For it was clear, his brain held a vast amount of information.

All the time he was attending O'Hare, Daniella Scripps stood beside him looked on, with all the anxiety of a nurse, instead of a mortician assistant. She was at a loss. The doctor asked her for assistance. Having watched O'Hare standing up before collapsing back down, she was at least relieved he wasn't dead.

Since first being admitted into their establishment back in New York she had taken sole responsibility for him. As a licensed mortician and cosmetologists, her job was to make him appear the age he was, and not what he appeared to be. A challenge for her in O'Hare's case, for to make the dead appear younger was easy. To make them older, not so. In those endeavors, she had succeeded. If he had risen from the dead state he had voluntarily been put into, walked out of her parlor, she would not have been surprised, for he looked now more sixty than a hundred and eight. She readily agreed to assist the doctor with whatever he had in mind for his recovery.

Aloysius pointed out the positioning of each of the sensors for her to attach them to his patient. He wired them into an alternative, and more up-to-date device. Connected one through his laptop on to another separate hard drive, then switched it on. They did not have to wait long. The tracking needle went off the scale as it came into life, hovered, stayed in position for a full second, then swung back to zero. Curiously, he looked for any downloads onto the hard drive. There were less than seven kilobytes of data displayed in its properties. He ignored it. Hardly enough to store a name and address. Analyzing such a trifling amount of data was not worth the time or trouble. And certainly not with a man so close to death as to make no difference as he was. He was this man's original doctor of death, knew what he was about. He stethoscoped him once more. The man was peacefully asleep now.

Neither Dr. Hermenbergur Aloyious or Daniella Scripps saw those results, for as soon as O'Hare came around, in the quietness of the room he had been left to sleep and recover from his trauma, he removed the newly downloaded hard drive from the doctor's briefcase. The key to opening the other half of the hard drive, never having been secreted away in his coffin, from the half currently in the hands of Elke Kriemhild and the Order, had been returned to him by: His seraph, cherub, sword-wielding avenging angel, or whatever guardian name she went under since being unpossessed from on high, had obviously done her part.

O'Hare placed the hard drive into a case. Put the case into his brief case, then wondered who in hell was going to come for it now? As if he didn't know. For although the keys were with the

Order, the data Hess was in possession – wherever the hell he was now – would be their priority to open those files. A criminal organization such as they were, its connections to a government department, so far unknown, was something else. For trust, unreliably speculative, had been his nemesis since the first. He saw no signs of change on that front.

DAS BOOT

———

DETAILED INFORMATION TUBMAN OBTAINED was immediately passed to Jean Ronstandt. She used the electronic mailing system Johnson and O'Hare set up some time ago for each to communicate with the other. Although hopelessly out of date, the Department of Defense system from the late sixties, an email device of sorts, was its inability to be hacked. What enemies of state were going to be aware such a system existed, let alone still being used by FBI operatives in the field, was further reason for using it.

Kriemhild was a dangerous woman. The one person, despite her having come across some of the most terroristic criminals doing the rounds since working undercover with Homeland Security and Counterterrorism, she feared most. It was always a dangerous game trying to soften the consequence of action meant to harm, while at the same time keeping up hundred per cent loyalties with the criminal organisation you are part of. Fortunately, the woman was not always here, preferring to conduct business from the nerve center of their operation at Drogstadt Castle.

She herself had visited the site to see why Kriemhild needed to be there as often as she was. Soon discovering it was a highly sophisticated operation requiring a level of technical equipment to hack into many of the hundreds of government departments and agencies the United States has going for it. Homeland's anti-cyber teams worked day and night, tried to keep a lid on breeches in their systems through her efforts to keep them informed. So far the Order had limited access, the result of Ronstandt and O'Hare setting up fake companies and websites, having these redirected leaving the original URLs showing if the Order hacked into them. There was no paper trail linking it to them. Getting information to Ronstandt went through Johnson and Son's (as she fondly referred to them), and *that* antiquated electronic mailing system.

She had successfully organised the contract killer, Coxly Hess's operation into Ireland for the Order. It was her job. His introduction to the Abwehr group under Kriemhild's cousin, Roisin. A woman seriously and historically connected with the IRA in County Wexford. Coincidentally close by Castle Rose, the ancestral home of the O'Hare's. From there, Hess was on his own. Assuming circumstances permitted. Supernatural and creatures from other worlds, where messages and information came down the wire from not only Johnson; Kriemhild herself, were reported reasons. As was the horrific killing of her cousin, Roisin. A killing Kriemhild took personally, vowing to seek revenge against those responsible. Castle Rose was put on a yellow terror threat notice by US Homeland Security, the result.

Information gathered was Kriemhild's family, descended from German aristocracy, worked closely with both the Abwehr and the IRA during the second world war in Ireland. Records also showed from National Archives Elke Kriemhild herself had murdered both her father and mother. The father for impregnating her after years of abuse, and the mother, for allowing it to take place. There were no record of any issue.

Tubman organised a German submarine to pick up Coxly Hess with the hard drive. It was to be passed to a waiting German submarine off the Irish coast. Hess thought he was going to be picked up along with it, but Kriemhild had other ideas. After his had bungled assassination attempt of O'Hare at the Wells Fargo bank, he had to go. She arranged for him to be shot as soon as he delivered the hard drive to the German boat.

Tubman spoke to the organisation charged with carrying this out. A background voice from a telephone operator, barely audible, gave the introduction, *Guten tag*, and the name, *Reichsbürger Movement*. A name she was familiar, although Kriemhild had been at pains to keep the name at a distance, never mentioned where the Order and its dealings were concerned, overheard Kriemhild discussing policy and her assistance for them in that regard, for the dissolution of the Federal Republic of Germany in favor of a New German Reich.

They arranged for an old East German submarine to be used. There's one for Charlie, she thought. She was to give a time and position for the rendezvous. A German submarine. Any submarine, turning up off the coast of a Nato country was bad enough; turning up off the coast of Ireland, with all implications of the second world war, England's suspicion of the country's collaboration with Nazi Germany during that conflict, was going to ring alarm bells. How she was to pull the mission off while at the same time informing and expecting O'Hare to handle the situation, she had little idea; not her problem. She was having to rely on Johnson and his infernal electronic mailer to get information to Ronstandt, since her previous mail dropping activities for coming and going were more and more being watched by the Order's security. She wasn't being singled out, all staff at Malaka's Corner were. Communications were to be kept as they were and Tubman's arrangements, set in place, were now to be passed to O'Hare for whatever he could do to put a spanner in the workings of Kriemhild's plans.

O'Hare didn't waste time. Within a day of receiving Ronstandt's relay message he made a call to an old friend of his, from a time past, in Russia's Federal Assembly.

Ex-President Sergei Bezukladnikov, the man responsible for authorizing shipping to operate outside Russian territory, readily agreed. He knew how close the Order had brought the world to the brink of an apocalypse before, politics aside, there were emergency protocols responsible countries took when nuclear war brinkmanship loomed, while at the same time keeping everyone safe and content. This was one such protocol.

Good as his word, Bezukladnikov gave orders for a submarine in the port of Severomorsk, home of their Northern Fleet on the Barents Sea in the Arctic Circle, to be readied.

Commander Jürgen Poske read the order. He was to prepare his boat and crew, go to Ireland. There they were to intercept an old East German submarine organized by the Reichsbürger Movement. *Das Go!* would come as soon as they got authorization from Nato and the Federal Government. He wondered what authorization was needed but was not going to ask. Preparations for a nuclear strike with a Nato state was not his business to know. Involvement with the Reichsbürger Movement could only be guessed at. *Vielleicht, um etwas klarzustellen.* Making points for a German Reich over the Federal Government, likely possible, was to be taken seriously.

O'Hare was contacted by Ronstandt. President Ryder wanted to know what credible reason could be used for boats from organizations of opposing ends of the political spectrum being close to combat battle stations on the open seas. He asked if he had any suggestions?

O'Hare thought a while, then said, 'Ah. I'll have a word with Bezukladnikov, shall I?'

Direktorin Elke Kriemhild, hearing, ordered the East German boat to evacuate this 'potential theatre of war' they found themselves, in favor of a Russian submarine alongside the one belonging to the Reichsbürger Movement. Worldwide news reached her. A Russian boat was having problems with one of their torpedoes playing up. Jammed in the tube, apparently. The old German submarine having no authority to be in Irish waters was too close. If the Russian was to go up, then it would take them with it. Not wanting to draw any more attention to herself or the Order, she was left with little choice. The mission was aborted.

She immediately called up Commander Poske, told him to recover Hess, then move away from the Russian alongside. For his part, the aged commander, 'Ace of the Deep', wearing the uniform of a vice admiral of the Kriegsmarine from the Third Reich, anxious to carry out Kriemhild's first order to collect Hess from the sea, delayed. With no sign of the man as yet, delay became threat to the Russian, who fired several rounds from a light machine gun over their bows. Poske He having no valid reason for being off the coast of Ireland in the first instance decided it was time to leave, without their man. He would leave this theatre of war, quietly relieved, take the old boat back to its museum in favor of the Russian, torpedo up its tubes or not, still with enough fire-power to make food tins from what would be left floating should he disobey.

Taking matters out of the hands of her security communication techs (she would deal with them later) she wanted to know how Drogstad's network had been compromised. 'I want Hess's whereabouts, and I want those responsible for das ficken operation being leaked?'

A RUSSIAN ENIGMA FOR MCCLUSKY

O'HARE WAS GETTING READY TO LEAVE Castle Rose confident Kriemhild's plans to have Hess picked up by one of her submarines had been thwarted. The hard drive being returned to America by Hess via a Russian intermediary was particularly pleasing to him. To have seen the look on Hess's face, dropping from a helicopter into the Atlantic, expecting to be picked up by a sub with Kriemhild's name on it, only to discover it was Russian, was something he would have paid good money to see. He laughed gently to himself. His trumping Kriemhild with an ex-president of Russia card, against an East German naval admiral exceeded even his abilities. Although, he was now expecting an outfit of misfits connected with Roisin Kriemhild's Abwehr to have another go at taking him out before he left Ireland. The sooner he left Castle Rose and Ireland for America the better. He would speak with Sin O'Hare and Clan O'Sullivan and fill them in on what he had been up to. Prewarning them in case further trouble came from his actions. Repercussions and vengeance were not only the Order's stock in trade, but also those of Elke Kriemhild. Not that they couldn't handle a developing situation, but forewarned as they say, is forearmed.

And with Fitch sunning himself in Istanbul, waiting for the Russian submarine to make its delivery he would have the hard drive back in his hands. He had not informed McClusky fully of what he had done, keeping most of it between Ronstandt and Tubman. For although he had good relations with Bezukladnikov, politics between America and Russia not being in a good way (when were they ever when it came to both powers), in particular those of the ex-president of Russia may not go down well with McClusky. Keeping rescue plans for the hard drive between Ronstandt and Tubman; not to mention President Ryder was prudent. He did not want to make them worse putting more on McClusky's plate than he had already.

Oh, for the days of the second world war when the old Soviet states were in alliance with America and Great Britain under Stalin. 'Uncle Joe', the Russian murderer of his own people, we've certainly shaken hands with some dubious characters in the past. Although, thinking about it, neither he nor Hitler matched Chairman Mao Zedong when it came to mass murder. What was the saying,

Kill a man, and you are an assassin. Kill millions of men, and you are a conqueror. Kill everyone, and you are a god.

To his people Zedong was a god.

God and psychopaths, there's a thought. We're not above having dealings with psychopaths, though less for some reason he was not able to understand than with God. History will once again be disregarded as no more than,

It's not the same as then; history will have taught us differently for next time. Will it bollocks, came an answer inside his head. History repeats itself. The good ignored; the bad continuing to remain unchecked in some forlorn hope those doing the checking will live to see them seeing the light beginning to behave better. Lessons of the past are never learned by those choosing to ignore them for their own self ends. And this old, yes, it is old, Order of the Most Divine Third Circle, had Satan infest the soul of Marco Giuseppi as its front man to finance an operation to bring about the downloading of data from God's secretary the first-time round; using child abduction and slavery to finance the science to do it. Ambitions are the same as they've always been, and the Order is no different on that front. World domination and subjugation of the masses using force. In this case, the power derived from data programmed into its software the ultimate physics to achieve it. This New Order . . . this . . . World Order of Neuropa, whatever name or any other related to its past they choose for it, will bring a wrath of God down on mankind for good and all unless they can be prevented. The consequences. The reasons few will acknowledge, learn or remember will save no one.

'Phone, Charlie.'

He was awoken from his preamble thoughts and talking to himself with a start. Castle Rose's gatekeeper, Ned McCoy, a particularly useful man when it came to security was shaking him awake. 'Thanks, Ned.' He took the phone from him. 'O'Hare.'

'Agent O'Hare? Agent, Charlie O'Hare? Can you confirm your identity, please?' It was a magnetic and tinny voice asking. Probably a robot or some newfangled artificial intelligence monkey product. He answered with an affirmation for they had used an agent title instead of plain mister, which gave birth to the seriousness in his mind of who he was about to be hooked up to online. A pass phrase came to mind. One with bad memories. He sighed its name.

'DAEMON CRUSH.'

'Thank you, agent O'Hare. I have a call from the Whitehouse for you.'

Mm. Not a pre-recorded voice after all. 'Of course.'

'Go ahead, caller.'

'Charlie, Joe McClusky. Been waiting. State of play please?'

'Still in Ireland,' he said.

'I managed to figure that meself. The hard drive? Where is it? Can I tell the president you still have it?' McClusky asked.

He was going to have to fill him in after all.

O'Hare took a breath. And began his explanation and why he had not involved him.

'I see. But really, Charlie, running America as an assistant is not as hard as some people imagine. Moving on. Where is the hard drive now? I take it Hess has it with him?'

'Well on its way to Turkey,' O'Hare said relieved McClusky being kept out of the loop in this particular piece of skull doggery hadn't taken it personally.

'Turkey,' McClusky echoed casually as if Turkey was the safest place on earth securing such a valuable item. 'Tur-key! Turkey!' He reiterated the word as his mental capacity for further more things to go wrong went up a gear. 'What's it doing there?' A semitone lower demanded an explanation. 'What's going on, Charlie? Who said it should go to Turkey? Weren't the Irish Naval Service happy enough arresting Hess in their waters?' There was silence. 'You still there, Charlie?'

'Still here, Joe. No, there wouldn't have been it's —' he added casually the method of getting it out of Ireland by way of intelligence from Tubman would cause problems for them getting its return if he contacted the Irish Naval Service. 'Fitch will liaise with the sub in Istanbul. The hard drive will be back in our hands shortly after.'

'You've allowed an East German boat belonging to the Reichsbürger Movement to pick up our man, an assassin, with the hard drive in his possession. And why will they go to Istanbul, they're not under our jurisdiction?'

'Ahhhh. Russian actually. The boat is Russian. Friends of mine.'

McClusky, his forehead furrowed, had missed a trick here. He wasn't aware of any arrangements being made by him to transfer the hard drive back to the US via the Russians. Had the information passed to Ronstandt from Tubman been misconstrued. Had they misheard East German for Russian. He was getting older, he wasn't senile. Yet.

'Run the part you spoke of about Russia past me once more will you, Charlie? Only I was under the impression arrangements had originally been made between Ireland and Ronstandt for Hess to be allowed to take a flight out with the hard drive. Where does Russia come into it?' McClusky asked.

'Tubman got the information to Ronstandt. With have intelligence Kriemhild was planning for Hess to be picked up by helicopter taken to rendezvous with a German submarine from the Reichsbürger Movement. I organized a Russian sub to pick him up instead. Hess taken to Turkey. Hamilton Fitch will liaise with the Russian sub when it arrives there, Hess will be arrested and taken into custody by the Turkish police, all under the auspices of the American embassy, and we will have the hard drive back. Easy. No worries, Joe. All in hand.'

'No worries, eh. Charlie. Wish I had your confidence. Ruskies and Turks. What a mix. Promoting international friendships are we? All you have to do now is convince the White House Cabinet how you managed to get a Russian navy boat to be at your beck and call without being arrested for treason. And when you are, I'll put the manacles on.'

'Easy. Hired it from 'em.'

A NICE DAY IN ISTANBUL

FITCH WAS SITTING AT A TABLE OF A BAR overlooking the Bosphorus on the Turkish Straits. A fug of cooking kebab was already in the air, a tad on the early side even for him; with his liking for Turkish cuisine. A park to one side of him had exercise machinery going full out. He was surprised at the number of older men taking part in daily exercise routines. Something he could do with. He patted his stomach. A waiter came out from the open-fronted café to his table. He was wearing a pair of well pressed gray pants, a clean white shirt, polished black leather shoes and a leather apron. Fitch felt underdressed. He was wearing an English Manchester United football tee shirt, tartan pants, and a pair of old leather open toed sandals. Not a good look, but then he was supposed to be a tourist. When he got dressed that morning he had to admit it was not a good look even for him. But then sartorial elegance was not his middle name. To look more a tourist than a terrorist, even a spy, or whatever other person passed through this place was his intention and in that regard he considered he looked the part.

'Kahveniz efendim,' the man said.

'Teşekkürler,' Fitch replied with a smile.

'Your coffee.' He placed the tray with his Turkish on the table alongside of him. A plate of small cinnamon biscuits, he guessed to dunk in his coffee was next to the cup. The man moved across to customers at other tables, while he himself settled to enjoy the morning view overlooking the sea. He took a sip of coffee and pulled a face. He took the cup from his mouth dabbing grains of coffee from his lips with a napkin before continuing to drink. The flavor hitting his tongue was pleasantly surprising, though the residues of coffee grains at the bottom of the cup was off-putting. Mindful not to tip the cup too far back he stopped short at the bottom. Next time he would ask for an Americano.

He was to meet an officer from a Russian submarine on exercise duties cruising from the Black Sea to the Mediterranean. He shielded his eyes from the sun and looked across the water. He just about made out the silhouette of a submarine. It was in the process of finalizing a mooring. Was it the one he was to meet? Time will tell.

He was here to collect a hard drive. And if that was the Russian he was to meet then they were the courier. Of course there was also their kidnapped CIA agent aboard. The man with a secondary job title of assassin, and the bastard coming close to murdering O'Hare. Coxly Hess. Why was O'Hare entertaining such a man? Now there was a question if you like. Did he have some ulterior motive for having him arrested so far from home? There's never anything simple when it comes to O'Hare and what's ringing around in his head. And if that involved Hess, well, he only hoped he wouldn't live to rue the day with that man's acquaintanceship. Fortunately he wasn't handling him personally. A member of the American embassy was standing by with two Turkish police officers ready to make an arrest. Standing off-screen in the shadow of the café, trying to look innocuous, he had he doubts of their being up to arresting a bag-snatcher in the resort let alone an assassin of Hess's caliber with the man's reputation being what it was. How O'Hare managed organising the arrangement he was at loss to know. He had got the call and his own family connections with him over the years: he was more than willing to continue helping. For none of those problems had gone away. If anything they had got worse. Kriemhild and the Order had notched up a gear and the sooner he took possession of that hard drive and got it back to the States the better for all concerned. He took sip of his coffee. But then as with all things about the 'honorable agent for the FBI', as he styled himself, he wouldn't hold his breath.

There was movement across the Strait. A motorboat was coming across towards where he was. The state tricolor of the Russian Federation on its stern mast. Three horizontal bands of red, white and blue furling from the effects of the north easterly wind blowing across the Bosphorus from its Asian side were in tune with its choppy waters.

An ancient port, Istanbul was well used to intrigue, espionage and murder running through its veins, was once more a subject for further intrigue from the house of O'Hare. A major trading port between Europe and Asia it was still a network of spies and informers passing information between east and west as information demanded. For what had once been Byzantium when the Greeks held it, and Constantinople when Rome invaded, was now Turkey. Whoever was the commander of the Russian boat across its waters had no need to worry, for they were allies with Turkey despite the latter's membership of Nato going unhindered about its business.

A mooring rope was tossed from the boat as it came alongside the jetty. A crew member tied it off while at the same time helping his passenger ashore. He then stood to attention, brought his right hand, palm down, almost touching his right temple and saluted him. This then, was the Russian officer to greet. The man stepped onto the jetty and adjusted his jacket. For some reason he was not wearing the uniform of a Russian officer as Fitch would have expected. Instead, he wore what looked to him to be a badly made three-piece suit. Gray. One that could be typically bought at the cheaper end of a Kowloon market for eighty dollars. Less even. He guessed he'd paid the latter, for it had the look of having been cut and stitched together by a tailor who was either bad at following a chalk line, was drunk, blind, or close to all three.

He came towards him in a manner suggesting he knew exactly who he was and where he was to be found. He was not carrying anything resembling a hard drive though; neither had he any assassin with him for the Turkish police to arrest. Fitch turned in the direction of those charged with making such an arrest and shrugged at them. All the Russian had with him was a brown envelope. Perhaps Hess and the hard drive was still on the submarine. If it was, then this was going to make things more awkward than expected. The thought came to him that perhaps the Russians, knowing the importance of such a commodity demand a ransom for it.

The attended crew were watching proceedings closely from the deck of the motor launch no doubt for signs of trouble. Although no guns were in evidence that he could see, he'd bet his life they packed enough fire power to shame a gunfight at the OK Corral would be close to hand should it become necessary. He subconsciously felt for his own weapon in the bum of his trouser belt.

The Russian came into the café and seated himself at a table behind him. With his back towards him he gestured the waiter. He made no introduction, instead ordered a coffee. Fitch guessed he had been here at least once before judging by the bottle of vodka the waiter brought out as an accompaniment to the coffee. Fitch turned slightly to one side. The Russian saw Fitch, smiled at him.

'I am afraid you have had a wasted trip, Mr. Fitch.' He unscrewed the top from the bottle of vodka pouring some in his cup of coffee. He held the bottle to him. 'A little refreshment?'

'Thank you, no. Wasted trip? What do you mean?' Fitch said not altogether surprised at this as a normality when it came to O'Hare's world.

The Russian officer didn't immediately answer. He was looking at the two Turkish policemen standing in the doorway of the café, accompanied by a member of the American embassy here in Turkey. He would no doubt recognise the three of them and why they were here for.

'Your country certainly employs some slippery customers, Hamilton Fitch. We could have made use of Coxly Hess ourselves. Too late now, I guess.' He laughed then stood up to leave. 'Your Charlie O'Hare certainly has friends in high places. An ex-Russian president, no less. They are not two a ruble you know. However—'

He passed him an envelope. A coat of arms of the Russian

Federation. A golden two-headed eagle on a red background was displayed as a logo in its corner. Fitch took it as he continued the conversation. 'Tell me about it.' He unpeeled the flap from its sticky and removed a sheet of paper. It was a bill of cost. Required in dollars by all account.

'Your comrade still has the ear of Bezukladnikov though. Tell him we're sorry we lost the goods he required to the Irish sea. We don't suppose his assassin fared much better. He would not have survived the swim ashore. That's his invoice for services rendered. Hiring Russian submarines doesn't come cheap you know.' Fitch read the statement. 'Only our new president is not as condescending as the older. The Russian state is no longer a charity, tell him.' He turned to leave. 'It's a nice day in Istanbul, Mr. Fitch, no need to get up. Warm. Plenty of culture. Enjoy the sun while it lasts won't you. Do svidaniya, Hamilton.'

Fitch stood up to shake his hand. The Russian didn't reciprocate.

He was gone. For all the man's dress sense, or lack of it, he was convinced he was Commander Oskar Chirkov from the Russian Federation's Black Sea fleet. In his way, he felt he had been regarded by the man.

'Call for you, Charlie.' Sin O'Hare passed him the phone. 'Why don't you move your office here while you're about it?'

'Hey, old man. Howya doin'?' the caller said.

O'Hare thought about it. It was not a particularly good line. He guessed it was coming long distance as in, *This is Voice of America relayed from Tangiers*, far away. He laughed. An old phrase he used when the phone system went into freefall.

'Your newspaperman is still in Istanbul, it's plokhiye novosti,' the caller announced laughing.

'SERGEI?' O'Hare queried the owner of the caller's voice he thought he recognised.

'Your package was lost at sea along with your gangster. Try and keep better company, Charlie. Come over to our side. We'll look after you in your dotage. Anyway, you know our newly unelected president doesn't operate a no result, no fee policy. Those goods nearly cost the life of one of our top naval commanders, and one of our submarines in . . . I was going to say British waters, only the Irish government give us more of a consideration than they do the Brits, probably the reason we managed to slip away from their navy before a shot was fired. By the way, when you get the bill, pass it to President Ryder. Ax. And a bottle of decent Irish for my granddaughter's grandfather while you're about it for all the trouble you've caused me. Ha, ha.'

'Do svidaniya, President Bezukladnikov.'

HESS COMES ASHORE

HESS CRAWLED UP THE BEACH OF BRANDON BAY, for it was the tide was pulling him in and out over sharp rocks partially tearing the immersion suit caused it to leak cold water. He had been close to drowning from exhaustion only an angry sea can bring than lack of fitness. Pulling himself up out of the surf he noticed the waterproof case containing the hard drive had come along with him for the ride. By a quirk of fate, the cause of all troubles was casually floating back and forwards in and out of the waves caught in a Walmart carrier bag. Luck was on his side. One minute he was wrestling with a Russian in the sea and the next he had fought him off escaping capture. On top of which he still had the hard drive. Or nearly. He went to reach across the sand to take hold of it without plunging back into the sea. As it was, unlikely. For it was beyond his reach.

Fuck.

For a man in his fifties, bordering on being overweight he was pleased he had managed to get away from . . . was that really a Soviet-class Komsomolet, not meant to have been German? Hess hadn't stepped off into the blue sea quietly, he had taken an officer off the sub, into the water with him.

'Da svidaniya, Mr. Hess,' the Russian farewell wormed in

his brain from a crew member as a repeating tape as he swam from the sub. No doubt words extenuated by cold sea water sloshing around his inner ear when he shook his head. The advice from its commander from the conning tower through the boat's hailer, 'Seven nautical miles to shore. You'll never make it. No more than you succeeded in shooting dead, Liberty Valance.'

He heard the name Commander Oskar Chirkov shouted down from the conning tower of the sub while he was fighting for his life. A name he had heard Elke Kriemhild use in reference to O'Hare. One he supposed the hearing of was supposed to surrender his fight. The man he was fighting was already beneath the waves. Drowning. Before he had need of using his knife on him. This hard drive was turning out to be an as much needed and valuable commodity by the Russians as it was for Elke Kriemhild.

Another notion entered his head. One he had put on the back burner of his mind. A figment of an over-ripe imagination was cooking.

Aliens.

Back in New York. An alien cast member filming outside the German Consulate at the United Nations Plaza killed one of Kriemhild's people engaged in a similar activity as he was himself. Transferring the other half of a hard drive system back to her. As everyone else, media reports for what was seen as a real alien by people witnessing the scene were suspect, only after witnessing Roisin Kriemhild being torn apart limb by limb by an Alien; a priest having his head taken from his shoulders by another, did the truth dawn, that was no Disney film being made back in New York. Any more than it was here in Ireland. Those stars of the silver screen . . .

Those Aliens . . . were the real McCoy.

The penny dropped.

O'Hare. Nobody would use a name in passing if they didn't know what was going on. You gotta wonder who you're really working for in this line of business.

An arrangement clearly having gone tits up for both Kriemhild and whoever was supposed to make it; instead of which an interception had been organized by someone else. Perhaps it had not gone as tits up as he had first thought, more a case of a misunderstanding on Kriemhild's part or one of a conflict of interest from another source. Whatever. It was clear she had tried to rid the world of him. His attempted assassination of O'Hare to recover the hard drive along with a membership list the US Government were keen to secure, not forgetting his subsequent funeral, had not been orchestrated, for a rare act of good nature he was responsible and paying the humiliating price for his failure. Dispatching O'Hare with a bullet to his ginger head when he had the chance at the Wells Fargo bank had cost him dear in bucks and reputation. For reason he had been unable to fathom he had faltered in shooting the man in the back of the head. In a single moment, he had broken the first rule in the Boy Scout Handbook for Assassins.

When you have to shoot, shoot, don't falter.

Not that it made any sense. He reasoned the man returning from the dead, was the result of his gun having been loaded with blanks; not the supernatural. Convincing the world he was dead, having his body moved box and bones to his God-forsaken Isle, taking the hard drive with him, was a masterful stroke coming close to working. If he lived half as long as O'Hare, with his abilities for survival, he would be more than pleased. No matter how lucky an assassin might feel when it came to his job, making old bones was to be pushed to the back of his head. Kriemhild aside, everyone seemed to be wanting that hard drive. He was going to have to get it out of the sea if he was to get his money. He was exhausted. Wet, cold and fucking miserable he was none-the-less having to go for it. He stood on the shoreline and considered how he was to achieve this without drowning in the process. Given the distance it was beginning to move away from the shoreline, time was not on his side. He shuddered with the thought of the cold once more.

Bollocks. This will not get the better of me.

He waded into the sea to a depth where walking precluded any further advances and began swimming. He felt the effects of the Atlantic immediately. A tingling in his hands told him as much at least and if he didn't get this job done and get into a warm and dry place soon, never mind Aliens, dying from exposure was on the cards.

Fuck. Fuck. Fuck.

With his feet barely touching the bottom he reached out to grab at it only to touch it before it escaped his grip. An ineffective grip as it turned out. Waves were annoyingly slapping into his face, and the saltwater getting into his eyes was beginning to burn. The hard drive was infuriatingly close. Reaching out he grabbed for it. It was as if it had its own propulsion unit taking it back out to sea. He was not going to be beaten. Barry Manilow was worth more than that. He chuckled to himself. How he would like to be warming himself at that hottest spot north of Havana. Get this done, and he might well be. One last desperate bid, then back double-quick ashore before he froze to death.

He was cold, so cold. His hands were as ice, and the salt from the sea was irritating his eyes to the point he was losing focus. He pulled himself out beyond the hard drive as it was about to sink. Now that was all he needed. He was on the wrong side of the incoming tide and the waves were hiding it from view. As a particularly high one passed towards the shore, it came into view. He put one last effort in. Closing his eyes, he swam forward to where he thought it was as another wave broke over the point momentarily causing it to disappear. His heart raced with excitement. The closure zip of the waterproof bag was showing a grin, and it was beginning to sink. Did he have it in him to dive down for it. He lowered his head, closed his eyes then pulled downwards with his arms. Too late. A freak wave had broken over the bar in the bay. It was already coming towards him fast and high. It took him somersault fashion towards the shore and dumped him unceremoniously onto the wet sand. A surfer's wipe-out without a bodyboard was how he finished up. He didn't have the hard drive; but he was lucky to be alive after suffering exhaustion and cold. And now, staring up, he had more to contend with.

An early morning audience of people and dogs stopped to watch, seeing him lying there, they helpfully laughed at his dilemma, then walked on. Thanks for that, folks. He was going to have to remove himself from this exhibition of early morning swimming. He had done enough. Barry Manilow, you're out at sea for all of eternity now, he thought and smiled.

Getting to his feet he assessed the situation. He was a wanted man, an assassin, having been chased across a large part of mainland Ireland in a helicopter, dropped in the sea. Left to fight the crew of a Russian submarine alone was not part of his brief. The boat was supposed to be German, not Russian, suggesting switching of nationalities had been planned. Options included Elke Kriemhild, pay back for not killing O'Hare; or the section of the government first threatening him for an allegiance for the recovery of the hard drive. His bosses at the CIA knew nothing of any such organization when he queried their existence. That's what you get for involving yourself with hard drives for money, Hess. Of course, when he thought about it, there was another possibility, or was there? . . . No, couldn't be. O'Hare. Surely not.

Whether any of that mattered now was all academic. He had not been able to get away from this damned country. Whether the Abwehr knew he had not been taken, and was still in Ireland, was of course possible. They were his only option if he was to find his way out of Ireland and return to the States. He heard voices once again.

He turned. This time it was two groups of early morning runners coming towards him from further along the beach. They appeared to be no more than what they purported to be. Runners. He began exercises, something he was not particularly fond, but what the heck. Once they passed he could stop. In full naval survival suit he dropped down onto his hands and knees began press-ups. A marine keeping fit was not out of place even if they had not seen him before. Up down, hands outstretched into the wet sand, he began his warming-up exercises. He was knackered, and the suit was catching him in places uncomfortably sore around the marital region. Rubber creasing between legs with the combination of sea water and sand thrown in for good measure was chafing his skin sore. He needed to keep going, the youngish crowd of runners, he guessed from a military barracks somewhere close by, watched on as they passed. He considered they would look on him and his age as inspiration. If they only knew. They all ran by waving and bidding him good day until the last one, slowed to a walk. Using the Irish comedic vernacular of:

'A top of the morning to you, sir.'

He nodded back at him, smiling between bouts of grimaces, he struggled to contain. The man in his early thirties, approached him asked,

'Smart survival suit, mate. Where'd you get it?'

He was given it by Roisin Kriemhild's people when he was being dropped into the Atlantic from their helicopter. But he wasn't going to tell him that. With no further thought, he gave the first stupid answer that came into his head, 'eBay.'

The remainder of the running party he was with carried on their run not wanting to get involved with a complete stranger and his conversation.

'Interesting. As it happens I'm a specialist instructor with a unit of the Irish Naval Service in the base around the other side of the bay. I'm assuming you're connected with the service, but for the life of me I don't recognize you though. What's more, your suit's a dead ringer for several that went missing a month or two back. We suspected at the time it was IRA, but seeing you wearing one, well, you're either a member or an opportunist thief. What's it to be? For as sure as hell, you didn't buy it from eBay or any other similar outlet. So where did you get it, and who the hell are you?'

The rest of his recruits ran on leaving him to speak to this stranger doing press-ups on the wet sand. Staring into faces of their wrist watches, more interested in PB's than their instructor. Hess stood up smiling. He was at last relieved the crease had stopped pinching. Having to think on his feet no doubt having some bearing. An eBay reference was going to fool no one. For a professional assassin on the run in a country where knee capping was a job description he was relieved he was not one of them. As an answer to buy time or get a person to shrug and walk on by was crap. More a hot dog dropped out of a bun from a greasy vendor's stall onto the sidewalk in New York on Independence Day, stupidity. Now he was in trouble. Now he needed a reason, an excuse even, for the action he must take for what he intended. His diving knife, still in its sheath strapped around his ankle so far not blooded came to mind. One last ploy, first though.

'I represent NauticExpo. We're testing them out for you lot.'

Both men stared into each other's eyes. From Hess's point of view it was not going to wash. He was not wrong.

'I doubt that, matey. You're IRA, aren't you? If you were listening, I'm a naval officer instructor up the base—'

Hess was not listening. He had a decision to make, kill this man where he stood or . . . or, he looked around for a weapon to take the man out without killing him. He knew his chances of getting out of Ireland and back to America were slim if he was arrested by this man. Getting caught as a wanted criminal was not good. Getting banged to rights for the murder of an officer from the Irish Naval Service would bring a whole lot more problems to his corner than he had already. The man could see he was armed. That was his job. Hess made a play of ignoring the weapon in the hope of diverting the man's attention. If this man was a naval instructor, a trained killer as himself, an Ontario navy knife in its sheath around a potential enemy's lower left leg was easily seen. The consideration for this man using it to attack him would be at the top of his mind. Watching for any movement to use it. He had to make a determined move away from any intent on his part using a diversion tactic. An illusionist's ploy. He tipped his right foot over and began to rub the side of it in the sand as if he was trying to alleviate an attack of pruritus.

'Salt water and rubber certainly brings on itches to your old skin, don't you find?'

He didn't wait for an answer. Going down to his foot while at the same time watching and grinning at the naval instructor, he gave the side of his foot a good scratch for relief. Before the man realised what was happening, Hess picked up a rock from the beech. He stood up and came forward and hit him in the side of the head. The blow, not enough to kill him, nevertheless put him down and out. He was quick. As normal professional training demanded. Over in an instant. Blood was pouring from the strike and his eyes, open for a second, glazed over, then closed. Too late for any preventative measures the man was unconscious before he hit the wet sand. A sea weeded piece of green stone the size of a fist smacking him to the side of the head took him into unconscious oblivion.

An action the instructor was later to recount to his superior, being the last thing he expected from a stranger he had given the benefit of doubt as to his being either a sales rep for NauticExpo or a member of the IRA. The latter not likely to risk such an encounter for the risk of stirring up a hornet's nest.

Hess looked up the beach. The remainder of his club runners were no longer to be seen. Their footprints, impressed in the wet sand were fast disappearing from the tide washing onshore.

Fuck. Fuck. Fuck.

Despite having no choice in knocking this man out, this had not been what he wanted. He was not being paid to take out innocent people. But the questions being put to him by the man came close to catching him out. Being taken into custody was not an option. Interrogation and the ultimate discovery of his real presence in Ireland, would put his relationship with Elke Kriemhild in jeopardy. If his earlier relationship with her cousin weren't bad enough; her connection with the Abwehr following her demise; there was the US Government and the CIA to contend with. An American accused of stirring up trouble with the Irish Government, or his own government with sensitive policies when it came to the Abwehr, politically sensitive. There was also his own standing to be considered. As if a licensed assassin with the American military wasn't bad enough, working for a section of the CIA stroke FBI was going to mark him out for deletion from the service if who he really was became common knowledge. For his occupation crossed overlapping boundaries. Sometimes appearing to work for law and order, other occasions not so. Putting his trust in someone up there, or over there, or around the corner even. Being used by political heads constantly turning for other ambitions before finally coming to rest facing in a direction good for the people was a long time coming. He needed to concentrate on saving his skin in the here and now, worry about speaking to masters' after. And Direktorin Elke Kriemhild wasn't one of those masters.

In this instance it all came down to a hard drive floating out into the Atlantic wrapped in a Walmart bag. He'd heard it contained data valuable beyond dollars to both man and beast. And with a Barry Manilow track playing out from it, someone must have got it into their head he was a fan. Getting Copacabana repeatedly playing as he journeyed along would take music appreciation one or two ways. You liked it or loathed it. A first in the annals of music history, while at the same time adding service dollar value. Not a bad way to make a living for Mr. Manilow.

His greed concern was being paid by the woman for its return. After wrestling in the sea for its recovery; had it not been for a group of runners, he might have recovered it on the shoreline when the tide came in. Unlikely now for it was lost to the Atlantic, though not necessarily for anyone else beachcombing in the early morning sun. The group of runners discovering their instructor hadn't caught up with them was going to set alarm bells ringing. Returning to discover him lying face down breathing grains of wet sand up his nose was going to set the dogs out. They could easily later identify him to the police. He needed to be gone from here, get dry, eat and drink before contacting what remained of Roisin's band of desperadoes to make another attempt to get him back to

America. While doing all of this, keeping an eye on the shoreline. An incoming tide may well return the bag. Fortunately an old plastic shopping bag wouldn't be picked up by anyone other than a conscientious litter picker. He may be lucky.

He shuddered. Hypothermia was on his horizon; he needed to shed this suit that was turning into a tomb of ice. He looked up the beach to where the shoreline sloped to the headland and spotted a cottage. Partially boarded up, possibly empty. A holiday let, perhaps. A change of clothes, too much to hope for, Hess? You never know you're luck.

He pushed at the door. It swung open. Fortunately, not having to break an entrance wouldn't alert anyone. He quietly closed it behind him.

Mailman. Anybody in? Need a signature.

His voice echoed back from the hallway. No answer. Not that he had any mail to give anyone if they came out to greet him. In case they did. He bent down and picked up an old mailshot envelope to be on the safe side. He listened. Still no echo of a voice, just the sound of his own anxious breathing. He relaxed and brought it back to normal.

Way to go, Hess.

He stepped away from the front door to begin an inventory. Ground floor first. Soft furnishings with a two-person settee and a single armchair in one room. A bookcase, a table, a television in the corner with a radio balanced precariously on top. He went up the stairs, his suit was leaking seawater through a tear onto an old threaded carpet. He really needed to be shot of it. There was a bedroom off the landing.

A single bed and a chest of drawers was showing in the reflection of a long mirror of a wardrobe. The chest was missing the second of three drawers. It was lying on a bed. On top of it was a pullover and socks. Do for starters. He opened the wardrobe, empty. There was another door next to the room he was in. A second bedroom. He stepped in. Better furnished than the other, a master by the size of the double bed. Two sets of drawers in here. He opened the first. Ladies' brassieres and knickers. He quickly closed it and opened the second. A pair of jeans, three more pairs of socks, a couple of thermal vests, a shirt, not folded properly, guess recently worn by a man. There was a wardrobe in the corner. Opening it he found an old sheepskin coat, a fisherman's raincoat and a waterproof hat.

No, siree. No boots, shoes. Pair of ladies' low heels. Won't pass muster in those.

He got down and looked under the bed.

Holy moly. The luck of the Irish has walked in the door.

A pair of man's boots. Stout. It looked as if they might fit where they touched, assuming he could get this damn suit off. He began tugging at the zip, his hands cold and soft from immersion in the sea were not going to do the job alone. He knew how Harry Houdini must have felt attempting to extricate himself from a strait jacket now. Ridding himself of this damn survival suit on his own was not turning out to be as easy as he thought. Putting one on when you were dry; not close to exhaustion as he was now, was awkward enough. Cold, wet and fatigued was close to impossible. If he had all the time in the world, he could manage unaided. When was that ever an option in his profession?

A casual view out the window showed business as usual.

For the man he had assaulted, had come round and was being attended by good Samaritans out for a morning stroll. He needed to be gone from here and desperate measures were called for. A sharp diving knife. He went down to the sheath around his ankle and pulled out its eight-inch stainless steel blade. Holding the pointed end steady at his chest he began cutting the material away. His hand was shaking as he did so. He was going to have to cut hard and deep to impress upon the rubber without cutting the hairs from his chest. Even worse. Awkwardly mishandling the knife, what with his manhood being only nine inches from the lower end of where he needed to cut was a possibility for a nasty accident. He concentrated and slowly went for it. The front fell away with barely a nick to his chest. He struggled with what remained. Straining sinew on sinew then the whole suit fell away. A heap of wet, black rubber lie on the floor smiling at him. He kicked it towards the corner of the room. It hardly reacted. But his big toe did. The one with a touch of arthritis.

Whoa, whoa, whoa.

There was no point in his trying to conceal it. Finding somewhere to hide a survival suit would take more time and energy than he had. He roughly dried himself down with a bed sheet and dressed himself in the pair of jeans, woolen socks, the thermal vest (he puffed out a breath from its odour of an unwashed body), then it was the shirt's turn. He looked in the full-length mirror of the wardrobe door and shuddered. Like a fucking hobo about to jump a box car in mid-thirties' American depression. It was going to have to do. He sat on the bed and pulled on the boots. Standing up he put the sheepskin on. He might smell a touch, but he hadn't been as dry and warm for an age. He wouldn't look back in the mirror for any self-indulgent approval this time. Food and water was uppermost now.

He clonked his wearing boots down the stairs and made his way to a kitchen. A Formica cupboard was coming away from the wall, its door hanging from a hinge threatening to fall away if it was moved. There was half bottle of water on its shelf. Or what might pass for water, for a brownness gave the impression it had been drank the night before, passed through someone's kidney, then pissed back. He removed the lid and sniffed, went to the sink to discard the contents then hesitated. If that faucet didn't work, whatever was in the bottle was going to have to be drunk. Uhgg. He turned it on and prayed for salvation. There was a gurgle and a spurt of air, then fresh water gushed out. He ditched the contents of the bottle and rinsed it out. Filling it he drank the bottle in one go. His primary body function sated he went through the remainder of the cupboards. A loaf of bread, stale and green; a tin of tuna; another tin, this one without a label. All there was. The key for the tuna was broken. Finding an opener in the cutlery drawer, worked it, elevatored its lid, then smelt the contents. He shivered. Not fond of fish, let alone tuna, it was going to have to be his meal. Taking a fork from the drawer he ate the fish between large draughts of water. Finished, he picked up the other tin and opened that. Putting it close to his face he looked at it and sniffed.

My luck, Macaroni. Tuna and maca-fucker-roni, what a meal.

He retched at the thought of the mix that would be lying in his stomach. Rinsing his fork, he dug in and consumed the whole tin, trying not to breathe as he did so, for the gag he had never got used to from his school days, was memory budded in his brain. Ending his excellent lunch, he cleaned up the mess, taking care to wipe his fingerprints from everything he had touched. Finding a carrier bag, he put the empty tins in. He needed another bag to carry away his rubbish. As luck had it, one was hanging from a hook in the hallway, the screw holding it barely attached to the wall.

Fuck me. But this place could do with some screwdriver action.

A black shoulder holdall. He put the carrier bag in. Now he needed a toilet. Finding a closet on the ground floor, he checked the flush system. Nothing. No water. Passing bowel movements into the carrier bag was his only option. No evidence of a personal nature was to be left on the property. He went back to the kitchen and urinated down the sink. Then ran the faucet to wash the urine away. Satisfied everything was as it was before he entered the cottage, he took up the carrier bag and dropped it into the holdall putting it over his shoulder. He was ready. Opening the front door, he gingerly looked out. Clear.

He allowed his eyes to get used to the sea mist coming down then studied the beach for anything the tide left behind. There was nobody about now. Should he go down and beachcomb for it? Probably not the best of his ideas. It was gone, along with his money, live with it. He closed the door behind him quietly leaving Brandon Bay to tourists and trainee naval officers.

Glancing back from a distance at the beach. A crime scene of his own creation, was playing out. A square of crime scene tape, with accompanying footprints in the sand being all there was for the forensic police workers. They would be able to do nothing with an Atlantic tide coming in fast.

He would make his way inland. He needed to locate Roisin Kriemhild's group once more. His first thought being the hotel he had visited when he first met her. The Jigging Leprechaun was as good a starting point as any if he was to make contact with them.

He had been walking six hours. There had been several Garda cars heading in the direction he had come. Fortunately, none were interested in a ragged individual walking the roads. A change into warm clothes, making him look more the . . . fucking hobo he was looking obviously worked.

A football match was in progress as he approached the park. A game between young men instead of schoolchildren meant decent clothes and money was hanging up in the changing room. Stealing then getting caught was chancy, but there was no other way if he was to get back to the Jigging Leprechaun. He went in and made his way to where the match was playing; then mingled in with those watching. Leaving it five minutes he asked the guy next to him where the gents' toilets were.

He came away from the changing rooms looking a lot smarter than when he went in. He'd had his piss, now he would leave the park without running, giving the impression to anyone watching he was one of a crowd. All he needed now was transport. A billfold inside the pocket of the hooded jacket he was wearing with the twenty- and ten-euro bills inside would sort that. He hurriedly counted them. A hundred odd. Enough for a travel ticket. He couldn't be too far from either a bus or railroad station. Needed a definitive direction.

He did not have to wait long. Chancing upon a woman he stopped and asked her. She mentioned she lived close and that her husband would take him if he wanted. 'Where were you going?'

He was reluctant to give any destination, although, difficult to see how he could answer the question without doing so. A railroad station though, in itself was indifferent to any destination. Useful if the authorities put out a search asking people if they had seen anyone they hadn't seen before, or who appeared suspicious to them. Assuming the railroad got him to County Wexford. Problem was, the naval officer he assaulted would put any stranger seen locally, informing the police. This was bandit country where any stranger was regarded fair game in that category. For sure, the ticket clerk would need to know where he was going, there was no way around that. If the train from the station he needed didn't go to his destination he was stuck, and if it did, the man on the run was going to . . . a single please.

'County Wexford. I have relatives there.' The word, relatives, used would give a sense of his belonging to this place.

'Well, it's a way, at least 150 miles. Not direct, but a train goes twice a day. Takes about two hours if you take into account leaves on the line.'

He had forgotten he had gone from there by helicopter. The flight had taken about three quarters of an hour, but they were being air chased by a Garda helicopter then. Seems like an age. 'The station will be a great help, ma'am.' He smiled.

Her husband dropped him off. He thanked them both, went inside the entrance and bought a ticket costing fifty euros for the journey. He had forty euros remaining. He was going to need more than that. For how long he was to be on the run was a question he tried to put to the back of his mind. Experience told him police sweeping the countryside for a dangerous man was unlikely to have a good outcome for anyone hoping to avoid capture. He considered himself in that category. If luck was on his side, then time wasn't.

Wexford Gas and Food. Last Petrol & Diesel Before Ferrybank.

No customers, apart from a young boy assistant, shuffling between and behind a security counter and food shelves in the main store unpacking boxes. He thought of his knife as a weapon, one of persuasion rather than killing, for he was of no age. He was an assassin, not a murderer. The appearance of terror on the young man's face when confronted by him gave an immediate response.

The cash register opened at the sight of the knife in the hands of a demon was enough. The young assistant handed a large wodge of notes ready bound and enveloped for the bank night safe, thrust them into his hands.

CCTV later showed a camouflage of shrubs over the robber's head and shoulders to the Garda officer. He had to admit his face and bare body was smeared with a residue of some description or other did give an impression a demon had carried out the robbery. The petrol station attendant passed the footage over to the officer.

'A demon. No demon. He's wanted in connection with an assault of a naval officer over at Brandon Bay.'

Coming out from the station. A two-mile, and direction sign in its leafy-green car park, gave a location, for of all places, the Jigging Leprechaun. Too late tonight. He was tired and needed sleep. The steak and kidney pie, along with the tin of lager he had taken from Wexford Gas and Food on his way out from robbing the place was dinner. A barn on the edge of a field, his restaurant and hotel for the night. The only living creatures seeing him going in were cows. He was up and left before milking.

He arrived at the hotel shortly after and booked himself in for one night. With any luck it wouldn't be necessary. The landlady recognizing him, asked how he was and whether he would like breakfast. He was sure news the American staying back here before returning would soon reach the ears of the Abwehr. All depended on the gossipy landlady as to whether it would be them, the IRA, or those he transgressed at Castle Rose. He hoped against hope it wouldn't be the IRA. Being in bandit country without Abwehr being around to reinforce his credentials was chancy. Having his knees shot off for spying for any other side filled him with dread. And here he was, a professional killer. Going soft, Hess?

Halfway through a bowl of corn flakes he was approached by a woman. She whispered in his ear. He responded that he was indeed Coxly Hess needing to return to America. He didn't get the welcome he was expecting for a gun was placed at his temple. A woman with the determination to kill had him. She had a hand around the back of his head tight against her shoulder. So close, she was exuding too much body odour. He guessed the confrontation she found herself was exciting her; that or making her anxious of any potentially deadly outcome here, whether she would escape its result. Either way, if he tried to pull and twist away the opportunity to kill him was assured. He was in a jam.

'Compliments of Direktorin Elke Kriemhild, Mr. Hess. A small prayer. Du bist verdammt nutzlos.'

The gun clicked. His heart missing a step, told him he was still alive: the result of her fucking the job up. Her gun had jammed for want of professional maintenance. Hess took one of those rare opportunities afforded once in a lifetime. He hitched the table up under his assailant's chin sending her crashing into a trolley of chocolate fudge cake, crockery and cups of coffee on it.

'You can take your German, *fucking* useless, and shove it where the sun don't shine, lady.'

He was up and out the door in a shot, knowing his luck wouldn't last the gun jamming a second time. Running across the public house's car park he muttered to himself, 'N-n-n-noo,' straight into the side of a gypsy caravan, complete with horsepower, temporarily knocking himself out. Stunned from the bang to his head sustained on one of its wagon wheels he slowly came around. He looked up. One of a company he hoped to avoid were there to wish him a:

'Top of the morning to you, Mr. Hess.'

The wagon driver was looking down on him, a shotgun across his lap.

'Ohhh, fuck.'

'Sin O'Hare. You didn't get far, Mr. Hess. Please. My home is your home.'

He put his hands in the air deciding if it was worth making a run for it a second time. Another stepped down from the back of the caravan. A weapon primed with the catch off, leveled at him from a man he had seen fleetingly before; who he knew to be a professional as himself, dissuaded him of any folly of attempting to escape either of them.

'So there's no misunderstanding, I'm still Ned McCoy at your service, and I still ride shotgun for Mr. O'Hare. If you don't want the Garda arresting you for attacking an officer in our military, you'd better come along with us.'

He sighed, 'Okay . . . you win. I've had it here.'

McCoy levelled the shotgun at the woman running out of the hotel towards them. A magnum in her hand, her finger pressured to the trigger. Opening both barrels, the man he knew as McCoy shot her dead, a single bullet from her gun whistling, passed between them, after she hit the ground.

'Russians. What are they to do with any of this?' McClusky asked. 'Have you taken leave of your senses, O'Hare? Though thinking on, you never did give much attention when it came to your choice of friends, certainly not all anyway. There are still those eager to take you out and have you shot for previous acts bordering on treason. Involvement with our cold war enemies of state will do your cause no good at all. Now the hard drive. Where is it? Don't tell me at the bottom of the sea with Hess. Or did your friends manage to collect it on your behalf?' McClusky asked cynically.

'As it happens, I've organized its collection from Istanbul. Soon as I get a call from Hamilton, I'll let you know.'

McClusky's implications of him committing treason were over the top, but thinking further forward he was playing a dangerous game involving the Russians, for they were not what they once were when allies of the west against Germany's Third Reich. Then again, any more than they were in 1939, when a non-aggression pact between both countries was signed off between Starlin and Ribbentrop. Funny old world.

Politically a deal of changes had taken place since Sergei Bezukladnikov was president, none of them in America's favor. He had banked on the man having influence when it came to the west as he had been in New York where they first met. The future Russian premier (as himself) were much younger then. Those were the days. They played backgammon, drank whiskey and generally despatched troublemakers taking the piss out of them for engaging in games in a bar still favoring poker over brain workouts. Bezukladnikov being an exponent of the Queensbury sport of boxing; enjoyed sending dullards sprawling headlong onto the sidewalk outside Donheny & Nesbitt's, in the anticipation of furthering their education.

O'Hare put the phone down confident the Turkish police will have arrested Hess by now; having him shipped back to America. He was staring out of the window as he replaced the phone. He did not at first take in Sin O'Hare's run-down bow top wagon being pulled across the gravel drive of Castle Rose by a horse. Not until Ned McCoy opened the back doors and pulled a man out, his wrists cable tied together, down the steps did he realize his escaping had come to an end.

The captured man turned to towards the window. Hess seeing O'Hare put his tied hands to his chest and gave him a two thumber with an accompanying smile. McCoy cut the cable ties from his wrists as O'Hare came out.

'Found a friend of yours,' McCoy said.

O'Hare put his head in his hands. 'Oh-h-h, boll-ocks. What've you done with the hard drive, Hess?'

He was going to have to give McClusky both good news

and bad. The bad being he had unnecessarily compromised American–Russian relations beyond a worsening situation; the good, his plan to have a Russian submarine pick up both the hard drive and Hess and deliver them both to Fitch in Istanbul, where Hess was to be arrested was not going to happen now. Delivered of the one, without the other.

In its Walmart carrier, the waterproof plastic bag with its contents, containing electronic keys to open medieval files in its other half, was being pulled out into the Atlantic Ocean. A tiny blue light, accompanied by a bleep, bleep, bleep inside became active from the re-coded data deep within its software, continued to pulse a millisecond hour on hour. Barry Manilow was drowning in, ♫ *It Never Rains in Southern California* ♫.

UNDER THE SPHERE

A SHIP OF THE LINE from an invasion fleet of two ExtraVersialTerrestrialist's attempted to come through the Time–Portal into Area 51 before applying their version of brakes from the scientists beneath before tipping over one of the side wall trusses where it came to rest. Suspended in space, defying laws of gravity without the aid of any propulsion system to hold its position, hovered. Half-in half-out from the Time–Portal, it looked to all on the ground staring up it was lodged. The Donut construction expanded tenfold its original diameter freeing it to allow this enormous spacecraft through. A spacecraft had travelled from earth's future using earth's Time-Tracking footprint through the Universe bringing it to a present time from where they were under the directive of – EVT CHRIIKUN was followed by a second.

The truss supporting the top roof beams in place with its attachments of steel rods buried into the concrete base of the temporary building caused extensive damage to AG-MX-960, the Order of the Most Divine Third Circle's electromagnetic field force and mind penetration machine as they came crashing down. By more luck than judgment no humans below were either killed or injured.

As the first of Alien craft came through, it did so slowly,

testing the amount of access space available. To operations director, Professor Kurtz Konig, a Post-doctoral fellow for the FAIR Accelerator Project at the Helmholtz Centre for Heavy Ion, lately of CERN, and advisor to the United States Government, concluded an observation to President Howe as follows,

A textbook example of a manouvre, if such a craft possessed side view mirrors, so tight was the gap between ship and hangar, it would have clipped them off, Mr. President.

The second spacecraft following on had no such trouble, coming through cleanly. The cameras around the site recorded an increase in velocity from both spacecraft from five mile an hour to an estimated light speed in less than three seconds after breaking free from the hangar. The multitude of flashes of lightening and thunderclaps from breaking earth's atmosphere was a boom comparable to Krakatoa blowing its top.

What came next was horror turned to incredulous humor. For those scientists had been sent to Becland when the Time-Portal first appeared, seeing the carnage acted out on the US Marines sent to prevent the threat to earth from Aliens, were relieved it wasn't turning its attention onto them. An Alien followed both ships.

An attempt by an Alien left behind by its peers, morphing before their eyes from a Belgian Malinois to a half robotic grandfather clock, resembling a human being blindly trying to manouvre through iron trusses and girders the spacecraft brought down. The last of this comical display by the Alien and their ships, having killed occupants of earth in such a degrading manner had gone.

Earth's Impact Monitoring system, SENTRY, cataloguing close encounters of asteroids threatening earth didn't show on its computer trackers. Opinions differed as to the reasons for this. Konig was sought for a definitive answer. As a scientist he offered none. Pressed by President Howe he reluctantly took a hypothetical supposition as to where these aliens had come from. Taking him from his field of known science, into the world of unknown quantum physics for possibility best guesses, he broke them down into two categories:

First event: The Alien ships' had not come from our universe.

Second event: They had come from any number of multiverses of which there was no current scientific evidence for any such existence. He went on to say anyone from an infinite number of multiverses would find it impossible to ever calculate, such were time variables for their existence placing one of them (a world) into time part 247 zeptoseconds based on a single particle of light passing through a molecule of hydrogen past and future, since the beginning of time.

Howe fully understood first event; fell hopelessly confused when it came to the second.

Operational base of choice. 40°00'00.0"N 50°00'00.0"W. A starting point for their search in this primate community. The Creation Blueprint was coming across the ocean aided by their tractor beam. Once in their possession, they were to leave this Time–Verse leaving earth to an ultimate ending of their own making.

–EVT CHRIIKUN had come through with no hindrance from the inhabitants of earth, and although it and the crew carried the same DNA as humans in those parts of the cell nucleus and mitochondria were not machine, they were intellectually superior up against their ancestors. For they were the offspring of wealth and technologies outreached ordinary people providing the work and intellect to allow this to happen 120 000 earth time years before, only for those managing to vacate earth, which were not evaporated by an asteroid then.

The difference between them and those they had arrived among was striking. Only the contrasted time-span of five million years between primate and homo sapiens being their only relationship from an event never to occur again. From homo sapiens to this race had taken no longer than a thousand years due to their understanding of Time-Verse physics. For despite evolving from part-machine and -human, with the ability to move through Time and Space with impunity, ExtraVerseTerrestrials' evolvement demanded constant fast changes for life existence. This was critical for their survival. An evolvement they were fast losing. Creator Blueprint was their last chance before extinction.

Information leaked from a source they had no knowledge, informed them Creator Blueprint was in this Time–Verse. For its complexity as a universe within this Time–Verse, a requirement for one was a necessity. Problem for them was evidence showed earth was on a collision course for a world war bringing on the ultimate and final complete extinction of the human race this time. A time event perishing those remaining, not so much from the effects of the nuclear blast, for basic survival of food, warmth, shelter and health from a weather system partially blocking sunlight for two years or more, marking their end. They needed to be away from earth with the Creator Blueprint before then.

Two truths fundamental to species in all universes, multi– or otherwise, was known to them. If a race fails to keep up with technology, they will perish. If a race fails to prevent nuclear war, they will perish. A double-edge sword for all science and evolvement for moving a super race forward to the next level, demanded the opening up of further physics, not for basic nirvana, but for the survival of any species. A Creation Blueprint for all survival across the whole spectrum of the universe with all its verses an ultimate answer. A belief such a plan existed common to all. For physics and architecture demanded its presence. Without a Creation Blueprint there is no universe. And it was clear they were not alone in this thinking. This inferior human race had stumbled across it. Word had reached SENTINEL MOTHER it was here on earth. They had reluctantly killed to get among their inferior human ancestors to access it. So far it had alluded them.

The human ancestral species currently occupying this Time–Verse had no understanding for the full potential of its possession. Their assumption being it was a path to its author. An ancient book was not an answer as certain inhabitants of this planet assumed it to be, being no more than writings of faith over truth. ExtraVerseTerrestrials’ were not inclined to myths, for they were content for physics to show the way as it did when it came to their ability not only to discover how to move from time travel to shift Time–Verse. This discovery brought its own problems when they had crashed headlong into other Terrestrials with problems of their own, went with their advancements of science discoveries.

A war of verses ensued with circuits being burned on both sides before the adversaries crossed back to repair their machines. They never returned to the battle. Discretion from them showed neither side surviving a war of world's with no winners.

For themselves they were fortunate they had robot technology programed with advanced engineering to rebuild their systems. It was later when SENTINEL MOTHER was going through the smashed and burnt-out enemy programs, their MASTER COMMANDER confirmed the unknown source knowledge evidence of a blueprint existed. Only then did they understand what this enemy's mission they had fought so hard to win before quitting the field of battle was for.

With his experience as a soldier of the SENTINEL, –EVT CHRIIKUN had been delegated and sent to investigate. He found a connection between two spirits difficult to disseminate. For a powerful spirit seemed linked with one lesser; who determined to possess the Creator Blueprint for a means that would condemn the universe, physics, creation, and Creator for all of time. While the Other: the writer of the code, repossess it.

Information passed back to the SENTINEL MOTHER through the SENTINEL–MASTER COMMANDER SYSTEM confirmed all of this. Opposition on this planet did not entirely come from primate ancestors. An unknown and powerful force was driving it. For there were creatures in this Time–Verse more powerful than its inhabitants. Information logged and at first overlooked by the SENTINEL–MASTER SYSTEM indicated a super race named only as MYTHS. Of human form with extraordinary powers. Who they were and what they were alluded SENTINEL MOTHER for the time at least, their best chances of seeking them out lay with the one they had already logged into their system. They concentrated on the human known as Harley Hare, for he seemed to be the standard model primate with extraordinary strengths, whose links to at least one of those MYTHS, had on more than one occasion successfully manifested themselves, preventing their obtaining the Creation Blueprint. –EVT CHRIIKUN had firsthand knowledge of Harley Hare and his links to one of those MYTHS. Attempting to send an extraction dart into his brain to seek it out, failing time and time again, striking into his brain, having to pull away. For whatever prevented his extraction, the attempt of it threatened to destroy the whole of their SENTINEL–MASTER SYSTEM. This one coming through was similar. The downloaded data displayed a mix of information, none of which was interpretable to aid any defence.

Scanning showed barriers being employed needed caution on their part. For even they were having to conclude they had been buried under their own arrogance in their quest for this Creation Blueprint for too long. For although they were ExtraVerseTerrestrials, masters of Time–Verse–Morph, those abilities were becoming ineffectual. Attack and destroy attributes had given them an edge over their enemies, were being superseded from a source they had no knowledge.

The scanning commenced. The Alien crew picked up a signal. Their Identity earth computer system showed a file picture program of a woman. Elk Kriem. With their Time–Portal rapidly corrupting, no longer fully operational, they were not able to show the possessor's location.

ATTACK | DOWNLOAD | SENTINEL MOTHER DATA PROGRAM INCOMING | –EVT CHRIIKUN INACCESSIBLE FROM SENTINEL MASTER PROGRAM | PREDATOR MYTH CLOSING IN | ALL SYSTEMS LOCKDOWN | UPLOAD INCOMPLETE

–EVT CHRIIKUN needed SENTINEL MOTHER to assimilate the data for there was too much for its own system. Morphing had taken a mass of energy and –EVT CHRIIKUN was being overwhelmed. SENTINEL MOTHER downloaded once again, reinterpreted the coding where necessary, deleted all unnecessary data, then passed the information required by –EVT CHRIIKUN on to continue.

–EVT CHRIIKUN possessed the information it needed. The names streamed through. Marseppe, Frederik Spannared. The last, Ahriman. Data bits sent their system into freefall closing the MYTH link. Elk Kriem with it. A reverse Time-Shift was employed back to the Elk Kriem link causing a lockdown in their system. Restored SENTINEL MOTHER sent –EVT CHRIIKUN out to obtain the data using the information gathered. Data copied from the computers of Elk Kriem gave them data with files needing a key second part. Data once again in the possession of Harley Hare. –EVT CHRIIKUN was to be sent on its way to recover.

–EVT CHRIIKUN came port 40°00'00.0"N 50°00'00.0"W. In an explosion of water hit an obstacle. –EVT CHRIIKUN came away from its edge as if unsticking itself before becoming suspended in the sea void to ascertain what had happened.

–EVT CHRIIKUN moved upwards slowly seeking out what had hit them, then came across it once more. It had not caused any damage. It moved around the obstacle seeking a gap. There was none. Searching for a way through without success it sent for an analysis from SENTINEL MASTER–EVT for further information. The returning information came back:

DOWNLOAD | SENTINEL MOTHER TRANSFERRING DATA PROGRAM | SENTINEL MASTER–EVT PROGRAM RUNNING | –EVT SINGULARITY ISOLATED | SENTINEL MASTER–EVT PROGRAM ACCESSIBLE | SENTINEL MASTER–EVT PROGRAM FUNCTIONING | MYTH PREVENTING MOVEMENT | BEACON ACTIVATION | STANDBY FOR BATTLE AUXILIARY PROGRAM

White Bear's Angel came away from a sphere of water. A Satan Ahriman bifacial blended soul had returned to earth to infect another soul, she did not have the power to take on Ahriman at the same time as creatures from another Time–Verse alone. Their master programs had been infected. She remained guardian over the spacecraft to earth's end in order to protect it from any further invasion.

The hard drive had arrived at its destination in a plastic food bag with the wording Walmart. The signal tracker inside had enabled the alien ship to reach out to it 1 500 miles across this ocean of water towards their ships and no closer. For lying 12 000 feet below the surface, three Alien ships settled into the sediment unable to move up, down, or sideways.

–EVT CHRIIKUN sent on a mission for recovery of the first part of the Creation Blueprint asked for an analysis from SENTINEL MASTER–EVT, was buffeted between the swell of the sea on the sphere and the ship. This was passed back to the SENTINEL MOTHER who returned the answer. A force field of water had them trapped they could do nothing to free themselves from. A response –EVT CHRIIKUN was aware. The next request was for –EVT CHRIIKUN to return to the ship.

One ship accompanied by two others were set immobile side by side in a sphere of sea water. Their tractor beams no longer functioning, SENTINEL MOTHER was unable to give aid. –EVT CHRIIKUN was vulnerable.

NASA DETECTS SIGNAL

ONE WEEK LATER | 40°00'00.0"N 50°00'00.0"W.

THE NASA RESEARCH VESSEL FRONTIER was despatched to the North Atlantic by McClusky, firstly in response to what O'Hare had told him about Hess losing the key data hard drive to the sea, and NASA locating an unexplained signal bleeping for a millisecond on the hour.

The signal was detected by the Ballistic Missile Early Warning System out of Thule Air Base in Greenland. Tracking monitors showed the signal were not coming from enemy missiles being fired from a submarine. Sinister events were at play in the middle of the Atlantic Ocean. Earth being on the cusp of an invasion, the result of aliens at Becland, was the probable reason. An immediate investigation of the Atlantic was set in motion.

Before any wrong-footed response raised concerns with other countries, McClusky double checked with O'Hare. He needed to know if Daly had installed a signal pulser in the software of the hard drive.

'Matter of urgency, O'Hare. Don't be all day about it.'

O'Hare only took an hour to come back to say:

'She said she was good, but not that good.'

Which question set O'Hare on his inevitable chain of thought, seeing as he had been inadvertently carrying the data in his brain put there by the White Bear Angel. Had she installed one for reasons of her own; to do with humans, or Aliens, even McClusky?

NASA received reports of mysterious objects coming in from earth's galaxy daily. Asteroids sufficiently large enough to cause deaths in populated areas such as cities were detected by SENTRY. With regard to Aliens ships there was not a trace. Nor when they first arrived on the shores at Becland. Which was not surprising, well not to Konig and his team from CERN, who reckoned they were from another Verse or Time and not from a star system in a remote part of the universe or galaxy, at least. Aliens coming in from another Verse or Time under earth's radar. The likelihood gave cause for concern to both McClusky and the White House. For a War of the Worlds confrontation from such a quarter was less preferrable than one conventional. McClusky made the point enemies of the United States want us to bow our necks to their yokes, at least they were earth's enemies. We know how to deal with them. When it came to Aliens and extraterrestrials it was a different story. He was not overly impressed with the thought we were ducks in a row waiting to be annihilated.

'If we have to, we can fight Alien life threatening us, not ghosts in time.'

An early warning function in the conflict-response timeline was nonetheless issued by the Secretary of Defense, General Abital Pereira, to all branches of the armed services. For this was not the first time Aliens were suspected of hiding at the bottom of earth's oceans and seas for such an invasion. In this instance, as in all other, this was a game of chance in a game never played out before. A toss of a coin. Heads or tails for a first strike scenario against earth by Aliens. In respect, McClusky gave a heads up to the Russians and ordered a ship to investigate.

Coming under the directive of the chairmanship of the US Government's Joint Chiefs of Staff, Admiral Clement Butler, McClusky decided the person already familiar with events at Area 51, who had overseen searches for the signal, and where it emanated. Professor Kurtz Konig was to be the man overseeing the operation. Butler being hands-on admiral to accompany him. Despite Alien ships coming through the Donut, destroying part of the roof housing, it is showing no sign of any attack at this point in time. McClusky ordered Malstrom air force base in Montana to be put on standby, their missiles switched from their usual tactical footing for other countries' aggressions, to part of the Atlantic the signal was coming from. Another reason the Russian's were informed.

Butler had said all along the killings of those marines, bad enough as they were, did not constitute acts of violence for violence's sake, more for their own defence. He went onto say there was also the possibility they arrived on earth more by accident than good judgment.

They were Aliens with a capital A, as opposed to aliens with a lower-case one, we are already having to live with and deal with, as in, terrorists and the unhinged.

Butler was skeptical. Reserving judgment to those not wanting to ideate too deeply about the consequences of such an invasion. All of which was overlooking the problem in hand, the other half of the data program was wanted by Aliens and humans alike. He expressed no further view other than the one he had heard from past odd sources, change his view, one, despite being questioned and listened to; but having no concrete evidence that such an organization existed in seeking its possession.

On the subject of creation, coined by a band of unhinged scientists involved in bringing it to earth in the first instance, ignored the consequence of another, prematurely closing the universe down without a moment's notice, before its natural time of 20 to 30 billion years if Higgs field of vacuum decay was to go by, allowing him to begin a new universe in his image.

'Has he the power and the glory?' Butler asked.

'Why not?' O'Hare muted. 'He was created at the creator's first appearance. He will have creation's equation for starters.'

McClusky understood O'Hare's interpretation of those downloaded codes and what they were at a Whitehouse cabinet meeting when they discussed the Alien issue,

For creation's codes, you'd better read, a program for resetting the universe, was one Butler and Konig approved. For Konig was a man of math who daily saw known physics being turned on its head at CERN. Konig's view was the creation of life within the sphere of a chaotic universe, was not possible without data based on math. Whether this data built into a software program could be read by our computers was, for him, another matter. The government had listened carefully to Professor Kurtz Konig who had liaised with O'Hare in its potential for scientific investigation before concluding,

'Opening those files with a possible result in world's end.

Was it worth the risk?' Having said so, his thinking now, the Manhattan Project had taken one.

Captain Alex Foskett commanded MV Frontier. A man hailing from El Dorado had the eponymous name, Mississippi, after the film. They had been at sea two days when he discovered all was not well. Butler and Konig were engaged in conversation on the deck when a crewman came over.

'Gentlemen. The captain needs to speak with you.'

The sea was beginning to churn up while making their way to the bridge. Neither man was feeling particularly well from the rolling of the vessel. A crewman opened the door and Foskett greeted them.

'Come through, please.'

'You got a problem?' Butler asked anxiously.

'Yeh. Look at this,' Foskett said.

In front of them, the sonar screen was showing a quadrant of the Atlantic Ocean the signal was coming from. Butler studied the scanner screen. He double checked their position. They were 700 miles out and the blip pulsing on the screen was being accompanied by the sound of a motor.

'Surely not an engine.' Butler concentrated his hearing. 'It is you know.'

'Why I called you in,' Foskett said. He was looking at Konig.

'Two signals.'

Butler looked closer at the scanner. 'A hard drive with a motor attached. And I've been assured O'Hare wasn't responsible for any installation.' He looked back at the screen. 'Eighteen fathoms, speed 15 knots. Whatever's powering it, we can't detect what it is.'

'All we can do is continue tracking it and hope whatever is powering it will eventually stop it or run it into a reef. Though judging by the way it's moving it's going to do neither of those things. It knows exactly where it's going. Should we be following it? It could be taking us into all manner of troubled water.' Foskett said with an uncertainty in his voice. The responsibility for the vessel and all those aboard was to the forefront of his mind.

Butler saw Foskett's anxiety. 'We need an executive decision to continue,' he said to him. The relief for the decision to be taken from him was plain. 'Get me a line to Vice President McClusky?' Butler asked the first mate.

Butler called up McClusky, the line went quiet. After a second or two he asked if anybody was there.

'Wait, Admiral. I'm thinking and consulting at the same time.'

McClusky's consult took him on a simultaneous phone journey to Ireland.

'Charlie, I asked earlier if a tracking device had been put into the hard drive by any of your people . . .'

'You did. And I said, as far as I was aware, one hadn't been. Although we do know it has one.'

'Could you be a little more explicit. Far as I'm aware, is kinda on the wooly side. An electric motor, perhaps?'

O'Hare took the phone away from his ear. Was McClusky asking if he had installed one. The world was mad enough as things were. Now, America's vice president wanted to know if he'd installed a motor in the Seagate hard drive. Come back Howe, all is forgiven.

'A motor. Huh. A Ford Mustang, perhaps?'

'Yeh. A *fucking* motor. Does everything I ask you necessitate an Irish smart-aleck remark on the side?'

'Well, what'd you expect asking me dumb questions? How in God's name was I supposed to have attached a motor to a hard drive? How was I supposed to have invented and organized technical engineering for data to respond for a forward movement? Apart from which, Hess was the last person to have handled it, why don't you ask him?'

There was a momentary break in their conversation. It sounded as if McClusky was speaking in company while carrying on conversation with him as he seemingly disregarded the Irishman's reply.

'Okay. It's definitely coming from it, thank you. Charlie. You still there?'

O'Hare didn't answer.

'Only the ship is picking up a signal similar to a missile being launched against us. Could it be from one of your Alien friends? You know, like the one tried to rip you from your coffin. I accept it doesn't have a motor to drive it forward, are you absolutely sure it doesn't have a signaling device fitted?'

He carried on a more relevant conversation to the man's inquiry hoping a more sensible conversation might throw light on what he was actually seeking.

'What kind of signal are we speaking of here, Joe?'

'One going bleep, bleep, bleep,' McClusky said feeling he'd recited a nursery rhyme. 'Did you notice?'

'No, definitely not.'

Butler was listening to the conversation the two men were having. Trying to keep it together without cracking up. McClusky then asked for him.

'I'm listening, sir.'

'Can the captain maintain speed with the object?'

'Can we, Captain Foskett?'

Foskett looked at him. He was weighing up a question from the representative of the Whitehouse a few minutes before. 'Long as we have permission to stay on the surface.'

Butler was not going to repeat that answer. 'I'm afraid not. Unless, whatever it is, decides to go as far as the coordinates 40N 50W. We don't have fuel for the return.'

'Don't worry about returning, Captain, we'll send another vessel out to you when you get there. Our job is getting the hard drive back as soon as possible.'

McClusky rang off. O'Hare put Castle Rose's phone down and shook his head, wondering who was manufacturing motorized plastic bags.

Captain Foskett became aware of the engine's revolution counter from the bridge after sailing no more than half an hour. He hadn't had to call down to the marine engineer, he was already alongside of him on the bridge. He was checking the vessel's readings to confirm what he had seen on the engine room's computer. They did. The ship's engines were increasing revolutions to the propellors, fast becoming overheated.

'Everything's okay now, Captain, except . . .'

'What?'

'There's no water resistance to the propellors. Sure they're under the water. But the water is acting as air, the ship is no longer propelling itself forward. Unless we cut engines they're going to overheat.'

A plastic bag with an earth company logo, Walmart,

emblazoned on it floated tantalizingly out of reach of the SENTINEL MOTHER ship. Coming to them without the need of their tractor beam, the Creator Blueprint they desperately needed for the survival of their species mocked them from the other side of the Sphere. The SENTINEL MOTHER, unable to bring it on board one of their ships and return to their own Time sensed another alien, one it had noticed before.

A PREDATOR GUARDIAN was in the field. One familiar. Locked into their systems through SENTINEL MASTER into their −EVT PROGRAMS when they had first entered this Time−Verse. No sooner had this PREDATOR GUARDIAN locked into their system, than it immediately logged out setting −EVT CHRIIKUN free from the SENTINEL MOTHER and the SENTINEL MASTER from the MASTER PROGRAM. And as before, it recognized this Alien as one from a Creation Controller, keeping SENTINEL MOTHER secure from whatever was to come next, or again.

A WAKE-UP CALL FOR O'HARE

O'HARE TOOK A CALL FROM JEAN RONSTANDT asking him to cast his mind back to 1997. O'Hare considered the year then thought back a further fifty to the 1920s when this all started. Clearly not for others, but for him, friends, dying or worse, the consequence. Oh yes, there was a worse fate than death. Suffering torture being one of them. He had in mind his friend, Father Michael Riley, the man was to officiate his marriage to Sarah Weinberg. Found in the Church of Magdalena, chained to a stone pillar by his wrists. A bloodied silver candlestick on the stone floor testament to having his bare legs beaten and broken before having his throat cut. His penis transposed for his tongue; the latter pushed up his rectum with the aid of a pillar candle. An example to O'Hare and his lieutenant to back away from their investigations into child abduction and sexual slavery from suspected and corrupt government officials. He was convinced they were something to do with the FBI, or the CIA. He had no intention of backing off. Neither did Lieutenant Frank Weinberg, his boss, murdered in the street after an FBI bust.

Nineteen fifties New York was when Satan's shit-cohort, Frederik Spannocs ruled supreme. A man financed and aided by the government to manage post-war expansion in the dockyard. There was a lot going on those days. He remembered everything, not 1997 though. He'd a touch of the,

What did you have for breakfast this morning syndrome, O'Hare?

prompting Ronstandt for a memory prod as to what he had in mind.

'Your criminal attempt to leave America with data destined for possession by the United States Government, that's what. Remember now? The data you said was key to opening files the Order was locked out of.'

'Oh. . . . Criminal attempt,' he replied.

'Funny how you can remember somethings when the fancy takes you, Charlie.'

He had good reason to decide what to remember and what not to. Who to trust not being the least of them. He suspected the jury was never to be allowed to return their findings when these people were all lined up and held to account. A division within the CIA in league with anyone getting their hands dirty, or otherwise, witnessing the downloading of data from a ghost using memory loss being mightily useful when it came to defending yourself, if it ever came to court. He had tried to get away from the security services of the CIA and fly to Ireland for other reasons, not for those of committing treason as suggested. He had been convinced there was a section of the CIA involved with the Order under Frederik Spannocs back in the day, directly in league with the department. Which begged the question; from the 1920s. Who in government had been controlling security services then? There had been too much information and disclosures about him, and his boss being leaked while they were still working for the NYPD, which put into question their promotion. Get them out of their hair. Pass them on for brain-washing. Now there's a science from the CIA's Book on Project MK-Ultra if you like. He wouldn't put reinstating those methods past them. Information needing to be passed up the line to their superiors had evaporated time after time. Though not all of them were corrupt, they wouldn't have had to have been. A word here, a whisper there, was all it took to keep a lid on their investigations. A hard drive coming to the attention of the Order from a source emanating from one of the security service. Whispers from shadows.

A doctored hard drive for tracking.

He had flown the USA in a private jet accompanied by his IT Queen (as he styled her), Miss Kayleigh Daly, taking the hard drive with him. Webb the pilot. If ever there was evidence of whispers from shadows, then it was then. Airport authorities refusing them entry into Ireland after landing, then as quickly changing the arrangement. An order had been sent to the Irish authorities for them to be arrested and the hard drive, supposedly containing terrorists plots against the US was to be confiscated until collected by a member of the CIA arriving on a flight the following day. So much for his thinking the hard drive was as secure in Ireland as America.

They got to Webb.

In the process of re-fueling the plane for the turnaround when other arrangements were being enacted. Webb had been ordered to remove the plane to an area where it was to be impounded and searched for contraband. An excuse and delaying tactic, not to mention a mistake on their part for we were still aboard. Webb, quick off the mark. Smelling the proverbial rat (he had a rather good nose when it came to sniffing out rodents), re-twisted the plane's rubber band back up and we all fucked off. Traffic control crackling radio instructions from the tower on the lines we were not authorized take-off. Too late we were gone. Lear jets don't hang around in the skies.

Treason was on the card then. Unfortunately, the Henry Clancy Montgomery III's of this world are rare species when it comes to recognizing the innocent from those being hung out to dry. President Howe was not so inclined. Returning the hard drive back to the US authorities in the name of the CIA was not on his cards. O'Hare had asked Daly if she might be able to divert attention away from any speculative examination of the hard drive before they landed back at Kennedy. She studied him as if to ask what she was supposed to do inside a Lear jet rocking around in the skies at this speed? He tapped Webb on the shoulder. He removed his earphones while O'Hare put his argument.

Webb put the Lear onto auto flight mode, got up out of his seat. He smiled at him. He knew exactly the right place, sat back down, took control of the plane sending it into a hard to starboard roll before straightening up and carrying on as if this was routine for him. He lit a cigarette from a pack in the well beside the rudder stick under a sign reading, NO SMOKING. A brand added to his name. Baxter 'Spider' Webb. A black Japanese cigarette pack with the picture of an arachnid on its side. Not everybody's favorite insect.

We landed at a small airfield that didn't ask questions.

Close to Newfoundland. She would see what she could do. Whatever that was. He didn't ask. Anything that turned the hard drive into something else, where it would be cast aside as being useless.

Daly sat on a box waiting to be picked up at the side of the runway. She tried to work but kept complaining of a musky smell coming from it. Webb laughingly said to her it was probably marijuana, looked around,

Don't take any notice, ignore anything you see here.

She took a handful of screwdrivers, an electronic device of her own invention, opened the hard drive wired it up and began searching its files. Not an easy task on her part, for only later did we discover those medieval files,

Those could, oh so easily have been corrupted in the process, she later remarked to O'Hare.

Job done she reboarded the airplane and Webb took off.

To O'Hare, Secretary Daly was one smart cookie when it came to things abacist. He smiled at his memory of asking Webb what he was listening to through his earphones on their way to Kennedy. He had given him his usual old-fashioned look as if to ask what the hell he was up to before answering,

Copacabana. And do you have a problem with Barry Manilow, Agent O'Hare?

Daly overhearing his reply smiled. She had not only downloaded Copacabana, but also installed a transmitter device going through to Webb's own music sound system. She had done what was asked by the tin.

'Daly managed to download a music track? Triggered whenever anyone tries to open those files? Get out of here,

O'Hare.' Ronstandt went into scramble mode.

'And where did you get your information, Jean?'

'From a man, his wife and son. They had been gone over with an acetylene torch for the information the files held. A hacker from a company by the name of CORASK Tech. Kriemhild employed the services of this man and his company to crack those files. Files any self-respecting hacker could've opened. But these were not any old files as you know. Of course he couldn't tell them what he didn't know, despite burning up his family in front of his eyes. A child finding the dreadful scene in a children's playground in the early hours called the police. He was alive when we found him. He mumbled the people responsible. Elke Kriemhild.'

'Most bless'd, Mary, Mother of Christ.'

'You might say that. But there's more. We've had intelligence from an insider to the Order. They have issued a live curse on you and your associates.'

'A live curse, eh? And what is one of those when it's at home?'

'A live curse in this particular case is being burned alive with an acetylene torch. The kind of intelligence best ignored, Charlie,' Ronstandt said.

'That's not intelligence gathering, those are threats from deranged criminals. I've had them before, and I'll have them again,' O'Hare replied.

'Have them. You've got them.'

Live curse merchants could get to him through those closest to him. Hamilton Fitch and Annie Carter. Number two was Nathaniel Johnson. He'd been in the same job since the 1920s, a career move for him would be wise.

'Enough of that for the moment. We've got clearance from the Irish authorities for you and Hess to leave Ireland. Well, with Garda's permission actually, so no chasing off north if Hess decides to do a runner that way. Garda have also informed us they have intelligence of a contract out on him to blow his kneecaps off. No doubt instigated by the man whose home you're currently residing. We're not particularly bothered about Hess . . . so let him go if he does decide to take a chance on freedom. Let's try and keep it tight just this one-time Charlie. Right—' Ronstandt reiterated.

'Right.'

Although he was not keen on putting his relationship with Clan O'Sullivan on the line when it came to protecting Hess, seeing as he was responsible for putting the life of his daughter Mary in jeopardy, neither was he going to follow close orders when it came to that branch of his family.

O'Hare trusted few people. Especially those involved with either the CIA or FBI, although there were others, Hess possibly knew of. If he was ever going to get to those involved in government sponsoring of the Order and their ambitions, keeping Hess on side was key. His minus one concern was to take apart the Order, whoever was running it, and he was thinking Kriemhild here, before injury or death to anymore of his associates that happened to be standing in the firing line. Two more friends he considered trustworthy were to be added to his list. Madeleine Tubman and Jean Ronstandt.

'As long as you consider what I'm about to tell you. And in light of those files, assuming they're one of the same, being in the Atlantic Ocean. . . . Are you listening Jean?'

'I'm all ears.'

'If either of those two medieval files are opened then it curtains for all of us. Two sets of data coming together in a mix will create a black hole that will flip itself before annihilating all animal, vegetable and mineral on earth leaving a clean whiteboard for another to formulate his version of creation on it in a new universe. And Kriemhild has the padlock, the key and the sea, in which to do just that,' O'Hare said.

Ronstandt remembered the conversation he had with O'Hare previously.

'If it's not news to you, then it's news to one of our listening stations. A signal, with a lyric. Copacabana. Barry Manilow. Tap any feet, Charlie?' Ronstandt asked nervously.

Ronstandt came off the phone. He had been hit by an enlightenment of monumental proportions, not altogether sure as to how he was going to use such information. He had been listening to O'Hare on the phone. He could have been sitting next to him in the same room, such was his presence and power of argument. He was going to need a whole lot more information about Charlie O'Hare before he made any permanent move into the man's corner of belief. The creation of a black hole taking earth and everybody on it into its void was not something they had thought about.

He was going to have to go into records. New York 1920.

Hess was sitting in an armchair in the library of Castle Rose. He was reading Dickens' Bleak House. A glass and a bottle of whiskey on the table beside him. O'Hare looked at him. When it came to making oneself at home he recognized himself in Hess.

'Comfortable?'

Hess turned away from the page and smiled at him.

'Did you notice anything out of the ordinary while you were dragging you and the hard drive around in a shopping bag? You did lose it to the sea, didn't you?'

'Wasn't sure if I was imagining it at the time. It did occasionally bleep though. Thought you were something to do with it? And on the subject, it emitted a tiny blue light corresponding with a heartbeat. Mine, not yours. Thought at the time . . . that Charlie O'Hare fellow, well, he's one clever bastard. For his age.'

O'Hare considered Hess's remark. A blue-colored heart monitor. Daly hadn't mentioned that him.

'That it.'

'Isn't it enough?'

'It'll do, but don't get too comfortable, Hess. I've orders to take you in.'

'A simple assassin, that's me,' Hess replied shrugging his shoulders as if he considered himself no more than a motor engineer for a profession.

'Worthy of a good fifty-year stretch in the Florence facility for what you've done.' O'Hare poured himself a glass of whiskey from the side cabinet holding the bottle towards Hess, in a manner of asking if he wanted a top-up.

'Not happening, Charlie,' Hess said tapping his glass against O'Hare's in respectful salutation.

'Don't take my word for it, confinement could be the ticket. You mentioned your employer promised you $50k for the recovery of the hard drive. You know she'll charge you for failure.'

Hess shrugged, 'Don't forget, included killing you. Vacant heart, hand and eye, easy live and quiet die. That, according to my literary studies of Walter Scott, if memory serves from my high school days.'

'Never put you down as a student of literature, Coxly. Nevertheless, my lord, I'm grateful for your incompetence. Perhaps I could reimburse your losses.'

'There you go, you never really know one's enemy, do you? Reminds me. Thank your relative for saving my life outside the Jigging Leprechaun. Shooting a woman assassin right through the chest, both barrels. Very impressive.'

O'Hare made enquiries. McCoy had called the incident in to Bleachtaire Ard-Cheannfort Patrick Polkinhorne of the local Irish constabulary, who asked him to come to the police station to report it officially, and wind up all necessary paperwork. Polkinhorne, in the meantime was to call the landlady, an ambulance and a police investigation team with forensics, to the scene. She told him there had been no such incident, only that one of her patrons had been taken away by Sin O'Hare and his side-kick, McCoy in that old Gypsy wagon of theirs.

SPIDER, ZAC & SKIDMARKS

O'HARE AND HESS HEADED out across the apron of Dublin airport towards the plane. They were accompanied by two-armed airport security officers. Hess looked at the plane, turned to one of the security guys said:

'Better shoot me now. I'll have a better chance surviving a round from an automatic weapon than I will getting away in one piece in that sky-junk.'

O'Hare had to admit, as far as passages home went this one was unusual. The pilot came down from the cockpit to greet them. '*Fucks, sake.* As I live and breathe the clover—' O'Hare said, who immediately recognized the pilot.

'Hi Charlie. What'd you think?' Webb asked.

'What do I think? I think first world war aviators had guts. That's what I think. This however . . .'

Ronstandt had said they were sending an officer from Critical Response to bring them home. Was he possibly thinking a plane crash in the middle of the Atlantic would solve their problems at the Whitehouse.

. . . 'I'm not so sure they had Critical Response officers in mind when they sent you over with this, heap of junk, Spider.'

O'Hare walked around the plane as if he was making an

engineer's report as to its airworthiness. 'A further thought comes to mind.'

'And what's that, lord of the skies?'

'If you get this back home with all of us in one piece, it'll be a miracle.' He continued his mock inspection, poking the fuselage with his finger trying to make a hole appear as if to reinforce his argument.

'And we all know about miracles, don't we, Charlie?' He did. As for lightning striking in the same place twice he was not sure if such a miracle was to happen to save their lives a second time round. 'More bad news, Charlie. My co-pilot. All the way from Marthas Vineyard after repossessing a large yacht from a Russian oligarch short on rubles, my able co-pilot, Mr. Coleman.'

His co- came out of the door with a jerry can under one arm, the other bandaged to the elbow. 'Bastard shot me off the coast of Cape Cod. Don't you know, the man was having a shower while I was carrying out an exercise of piracy on the buccaneer. He smiled. How are you, boyo?'

Both men were in the business of repossessions of aircraft and boats for banks and finance houses; moonlighting when not working full time for the FBI.

'Wasn't your lucky day, Zac.'

'As it happens, I knew his girlfriend. She whacked him around the back of the head tipping him into sea as he was about to give me another round from his assault rifle, turned out it was. Got the girl. Made 50k from the China Merchant Bank. Piányí huò.'

Hess was startled by Coleman's bargain pay out remark, 'Fifty thousand dollars for repossessing a boat—'

'You're in the wrong business, Hess,' O'Hare said.

'Exhibition-experimental. Nineteen fifty-four, and as solid as the glue holding it together. This . . . my friends of small faith and no wings . . . is a Grumman HU-16 Albatross I grabbed from the United States Navy before they mothballed it and sent it to the Museum for Natural Disasters. You were in a hurry, short notice,' Spider said proudly. 'And kindly cease prodding it about. It won't get off the ground with holes in its wings, Charlie.'

'If it's all the same to you, O'Hare, I'd take my chances with your family and the IRA. Better still, wait on the shore at Brandon Bay for a passing Russian sub,' Hess came in.

'Ah, up speaks the infamous assassin General Coxly Hess,' Spider said.

'The same . . .' O'Hare replied.

'The one who tried to murder you in a Wells Fargo bank?' Spider asked of O'Hare.

'Leaving me for—'

'Dead. I remember. He shot the sheriff, missed the deputy. Pleased to meet you, Mr. Hess. Never met a real assassin before,' Spider said offering him his hand.

'Making you fortunate indeed,' Hess said wiping a dab of oil transferred between the men's handshake.

'Decided to save the price of a bullet when you saw how old Charlie was did you?' Spider changed his expression and turned to O'Hare, 'Are you really trusting this man?'

'With my life. Probably not. In all other respects, he'll do until a more capable assassin comes along to take me out. Seriously Spider, this plane—'

'Seriously. If we ditch it won't sink, what with it being a

seaplane and all. Not unless a Russian sub decides to surface under us. Ready, Mr. Coleman?'

'As you are, Spider.'

'All aboard for a skylark,' Coleman announced cheerily.

Dublin Airport's control tower flight operation's director of the day was coming on shift. As usual, he hung his old sheepskin coat on the hook on the wall behind banks of computer screens lit with lines of planes coming and going, walking to the window, he picked up a pair of binoculars. He knew all about planes and airports. A former Royal Air Force pilot during the cold war, he had been forced to land a Vulcan bomber during a blizzard after an operation of hand-waving salutations to Russian pilots doing the same job for their side. It hit the runway, he braked, it lost grip on the ice, went sideways at a rate of knots, leaving those watching to hold their breaths at the inevitability of a fire ball; putting runways and hangars out of service for weeks.

For Vic (Skidmarks) Hall was no backroom boy when it came to flights in and out of Dublin. His assistant, MacLeish got up from his computer, took up his own binoculars to join him in this early morning ritual for what needs doing and who needs doing it. To Hall, MacLeish was a man of infuriating habits when it came to airport safety, and although driving him to distraction on occasions, a good man trusted and true, with a little more experience and learning, will put him among gods along with himself.

Among the assorted passenger and tourists planes, baggage handlers, and plane parkers with their signal boards, Hall spotted the seaplane. Removing the binoculars he wiped his eyes. An apparition. He replaced them. Nope, he was not imagining a scene from Tales of the Gold Monkey. It *was* an old sea plane displaying a United States Air Force decal on its fuselage; one having not been used since, what, the mid-90s if his memory served. His mind was immediately cast back a few weeks when another aircraft, one displaying the Seal of the President of the United States of America emblazoned on its fuselage, had landed unannounced. On that occasion he was asked to remove it to hangar W14 where they were to unload a coffin from it. He put the binoculars down. Once again he had been kept out of Dublin Airport Authority's special loop of a need-to-know arrogance, and once more kick arse.

Henry. Is there a reason the Yanks keep bringing their dead to Ireland?

Hess had to be careful returning to America. But then he didn't have any say in the matter. Far as he knew he was still contracted to the Order by proxy. A question always bothering him: was Kriemhild also proxied. O'Hare had never been sure about Dr. Nathaniel Johnson and his allegiances when it came to which side of the fence he was sitting. In Johnson's case, a special operation unit of the CIA would have difficulty getting another as close as he was without Kriemhild being in the loop. Nor the woman she had appointed media operations director for Star Birth.

The Albatross touched down at Kennedy with applause from plane spotters at TWA's rooftop pool overlooking runway 4L/22R. Seeing a vintage flying boat coming onto land was a rare treat. Hess was handcuffed as they disembarked and was at once arrested by the CIA officer's waiting for him. Despite

O'Hare's protestations he had been granted an executive order by the President's office for a clemency conviction, and was to be kept in his charge, he was taken away in one of several CIA black limousines lined up alongside the plane.

TWA's rooftop was becoming overcrowded with more than plane spotters.

In all his years with the FBI and his liaising with America's government elite, O'Hare had never come across this treatment before. He was not given any details or any forwarding address of where Hess was to be taken. Apparently it was to follow was all they said. He only hoped Kriemhild was not involved with these people, for he would be deaden and cremated in one fell swoop if she was. A thought not dismissed. A knee-jerk reaction ran through decades of mistrust he always held than a secretive government department knowing more than they were ever going to let on linked to Direktorin Elke Kriemhild, the current CEO for the Order.

As Roswell and the UFO question had been kept from the public, so also had the exploits of the Order of the Most Divine Third Circle, having nearly brought the world to oblivion, been. With Aliens coming to earth, the government will have to adopt a different policy when it comes to dropping hints about Disney films being made in future.

HESS IN FORT LEAVENWORTH

FORT LEAVENWORTH WAS AN ARMY CORRECTIONAL FACILITY. He had Hess back in the fold. Ronstandt was not in the business of interrogating, he was thinking prisoner, though technically, Hess hadn't been arrested. And yes, he knew members of the security services were not above the law, their activities considered wobbly at times, not always within the bounds of national interest, with clemency deals being made by the sitting president as and when, in Hess's case, working for the state he was involving himself too much with Kriemhild for monetary gain. Bad enough in itself, when other parts of the service where agents were concerned assassinations were strictly out of bounds. For God's sake he was sent to assassinate O'Hare by her.

Despite being held on charges of being a double agent, his connection to the Order, surprisingly assisting him in Ireland, his arrest was nonetheless necessary. He had orders. O'Hare had tried to play the clemency card, getting Hess released as soon as they arrived back in America. Ronstandt tried to convince O'Hare into thinking he was special within the security services. Not enough. And certainly not with Counterintelligence.

He had heard O'Hare suggest he belonged to a department of the CIA involved with the collection and processing of the hard drive. I only wish someone tell me. O'Hare had no evidence such department existed. All his paychecks appeared to show they were from another department, one no longer in operation, probably defunct, for those having been around longer than most didn't mean to say it was CIA. He was in his fifties. His own inquiries couldn't find any pay office belonging to the CIA for older staff except the one indicated on his bank statement. He was not connected to any phantom organization as O'Hare kept insisting he was, other than an old US government payroll department showing on his paychecks coming his way monthly from them, saving $48 000 a year for the US taxpayer ceasing gave some kind of credence to him being one of theirs.

O'Hare had breached data protection for salaries seeking clarification with Internal Revenue. They discovered Hess hadn't paid a penny in tax through those pay checks.

You inform your Mr. Ronstandt, financially speaking, there is and never was any Coxly Hess on the books of Counterintelligence. If there had been we'd had picked up on such a long time since. We don't miss data breaches when taxes haven't been paid to this department of Internal Revenue. He pays taxes on his army pay. . . . Far as we're concerned, he's an enlisted soldier.

No records. No names of employees. No departmental address. No field of operations. Unaccountable sources of paychecks showing no tax had been paid. Without which, IR were hog tied. Hess was an army officer.

An enlisted soldier. That's it. The reason he was being

entertained in Leavenworth. The attempted assassination of Fidel Castro being one operation, although the excuse his weapon had jammed did not exactly pass muster. His going over the top with methods considered too dangerous and provocative for purposes of assassination. His penchant for poisoning the end of bullets with low-grade plutonium and chilies being two of the methods he was renowned, had not gone down with his other officers. Where he had got plutonium was anybody's guess. He knew all about chilies causing blood poisoning, if the shattering of vital organs was not enough to finish you off then plutonium finds its own way, showering conversation particles over all those close by.

All of this until Messrs. O'Hare and Hess came into his field of work; and not so much Hess (he was about to question him for all the good it was), also the Director of the Central Intelligence Agency, D/CIA Adrian Browne. He had only been in the job since he was appointed by the President a year since. If he knew (and he did ask) if he was using it as the reason to keep shtum. Giving the man more credit than he deserved for not going into details of phantom departments, assuming phantom was another word for substantial existence. As for President Ryder 'Black Dick' Howe himself, with their being more departments of security in both the FBI and the CIA than anyone can shake a stick at, it was no surprise he was unaware of any phantom department, 'involved in special operations' other than a department of the CIA paying salaries. Administrative departments involving personnel president have no dealings. Which was all well and good, but why didn't the regular payroll people of the CIA wedge Hess up on a yearly basis if he was working for them.

Ronstandt couldn't exactly say there was a conspiracy surrounding this phantom outfit, not unless one considered O'Hare's belief in one or other of the security services' existence, for conspiracies rooted to the ground were difficult to remove once spread. This conspiracy never took wings. Not a whisper. He had even tried working out if CIA initials were used elsewhere other than Central Intelligence Agency. Cairo International Airport, Culinary Institute of America; even Central Indiana Academy of Wrestling, none of which seemed to fit the man officially known as, Lieutenant Coxly Hess of the United States Army Sniper School at Camp Perry. Which brought him back to the criminal organization, the Order of the Most *fucking* Divine Third Circle, who had employed Hess to take out O'Hare, get the hard drive and the membership list of the Order. The last item: list of members of the organization, had a names interest if it hadn't gone missing.

O'Hare made an interesting point, unique and possibly to Ronstandt's way of thinking before O'Hare dismissed the idea as ramblings, telling him to forget it. For lack of concrete evidence. Or he thought deeply about his relationship the two men had, and wondering if he, can be trusted.

His idea a person working for a legitimate group, the CIA as an example, without knowing they worked for them or for another legitimate group at the same time pushed the boundaries of possibility. This was not a new concept when it came to counter espionage, double agents, undercover agents, cloak-and-dagger or whatever. A blend over of black and white into gray; continue in this way until questions of where their information was coming from were irrelevant, only the field was becoming blurred enough for them to no longer question people engaging them, for they were no more special than any other 'special operations' unit so divisive, buried so deep in the government's psyche to give an impression orders issued were legal; having the authority of people also deep in the department. Not the government of the day (he stressed the point), greater than life itself incorporated in the ethics, in this case, laid down by America's founding fathers.

And who wouldn't wanna subscribe to such high ideals?

Hess was a killer using the CIA as a front for his trade. A hired gun and a loose cannon.

The door opened. Hess was wheeled in. His face swollen and blue with eyes sunk back into their sockets were surrounded by overlaps of his brows and cheeks bones. His lip was cut in one corner from a punch his assailant hadn't removed any of his rings from his fingers before hitting him first. There were no other cuts of a similar nature on his face giving the impression two men had gone over him. One working on his face, while the other had viciously punched into his ribs and stomach for there was heavy brown bruising showing through his shirt, torn in the assault.

The army guard left him where he was and attempted to close the door before Ronstandt stopped him, in wanting to know who was responsible for this outrage. This man was to be questioned by a Whitehouse Cabinet member of the Howe administration.

'Who authorized this treatment on this man?'

He smiled. 'I'm a civilian. Medics. I don't work for the army.'

'Get me the garrison commander.'

'I'm afraid she's not available, sir.'

'Get me the garrison command sergeant major then.'

'I will pass the message. Can't do any more, I don't work . . .'

'I heard you first time. You seem to know a lot of what's going on for a medical orderly though.'

'Who are you?' Hess asked in a voice surprisingly lucid considering his condition.

'Jean Ronstandt, CIA. Who did this to you?'

'Ah. I've heard of you. Fell out of a plane, didn't I,' Hess replied.

'Fell out of an airplane. Well, makes a change from falling down stone steps I suppose. Come on, you can do better.'

Ronstandt looked at him. Hess shook his head, smiling.

'Get us a bottle of beer. Bud'll do. Homeland Security can run to a bottle can't they?'

Ronstandt tried to imagine how he was going to manage to drink with his lips looking the way they were. The man was treating his incarceration and ill treatment with the casualness of being in a dentist's chair. The porter medic left leaving him alone with the prisoner. Surely his position in government didn't qualify him as a guard. He needn't have worried. The door was immediately opened by a military policeman.

'SIR.'

'This man needs a drink . . .'

'Can't leave you alone, SIR.'

'Do you know who I am, soldier?'

'Yes, SIR.'

'Get me two bottles of Bud then. How far is he going to get in his condition do you think. I'll take responsibility while you're gone.'

'SIR.'

'Ice cold.' Hess called after him.

'SIR.'

'So, who did do this to you, Hess?'

'I tried to kill O'Hare, what'd you think was going to happen to me in this place? He has friends.'

'He wouldn't have ordered any mistreatment.'

'I've always had respect for Mr. O'Hare doesn't mean to say he's above dealing out violence.'

'SIR. Two bottles of Bud. Ice cold. Caps off . . . SIR.'

'Good. Leave us.'

The MP hesitated.

'Go on, he's not going to escape this place.'

He took them, gave one to Hess, took one for himself. 'Who are you working for?'

Hess put the bottle of Bud between two bruised and closed lips and began to sip. Swallowing a healthy mouthful he then took the bottle away, licked his lips then wiped the back of his hand across his chin, removed a trail of liquid about to run down the front of him.

'Now there's a question, I'd like an answer for myself. If I was to say the army would that suffice? He took another sip.'

'We have a partial record of you. We don't subscribe to your remuneration. Now there's the rub.'

'It's about time you people got up to speed,' Hess said smiling. 'It's called intelligence for a reason. You cover counterterrorism for the government. Technically you have no right to question me.' He studied him. 'Why are you here, Ronstandt?'

'Your relationship with Elke Kriemhild. We know she sent you to the Apache branch of Wells Fargo to steal a hard drive, remove a list, kill O'Hare. I suppose we are grateful you succeeded in two out of three, not all to do with her though is it?'

'And what of the two of the three are you grateful for, Jean?' Hess said smiling. 'As to the rest, my relationship with Kriemhild, I'm at a loss to know what you're implying. I'm an army assassin working for the government when I'm needed along with any other operative called on for special duties. I don't work for anybody. The operation I was involved in was for the CIA. For all I know Kriemhild works for the CIA.'

Was this man convinced in what he was saying? If it was true it was not impossible. Government bodies involving security and national intelligence were not especially open to those responsible for the running of them. Reason being heads and members of the government were only passing through on their way to more ambitious occupations. If that wasn't the case, office leaks, breaches in security, would be more regular and consistent than they were already. He shook his head in a negative manner.

'You didn't know? You have an informant on the inside of their operation, and you don't know who these people are.'

'Who are you talking about?'

'Corrine Diaz. She works for you or O'Hare, and if the Order is not involved with the CIA, Kriemhild knows who is, and who planted her in her employ. Diaz's career as Deputy Director of Operations for Star Birth would soon come to an end if she was unaware.'

Ronstandt left Leavenworth leaving Hess to his fate. He

was not going to approach the president seeking clemency as O'Hare wished. He had no time for professional assassins whether they worked for the government or not. After his shenanigans in Ireland had caused diplomatic embarrassments with their authority, leaving him in a military prison for the foreseeable future was an ideal and applaudable arrangement.

Hess was wheeled into the room. This was part of the garrison not used by the Army Military Police Corps, for it was a dedicated area for the security services of the FBI and the CIA. He got up from the wheelchair and sat down in the barber chair. A woman already in the room came over and began unpeeling the prothesis and blood paint make up from his face. Slowly unsticking it, mindful of his eyebrow hairs, she carefully removed the remaining glue and putty using floss and face wipes. She dried his face off. Thanked her.

'Your car is outside, Coxly.'

He nodded at the driver. He was gone.

TUBMAN & JOHNSON

FOR REASONS SHE DID NOT FULLY UNDERSTAND, Madeleine Tubman was at times inclined to forget her birth name. She had broken her first rule of using the same name for more than one operation.

Occasion was White Bear. On this second, she decided to use it for O'Hare's sake. His failing memory was beginning to cause concern within the inner circle she was part of. His lapses of memory have occurred since Hess attempted to assassinate him. Although the closeness of the gunshot to his ear could be a discernible factor, the lapses she noticed would not have been a loud and pressured explosion of an explosive. Neither did his ability to control events, for he continued to play them with all the skills of a chess grandmaster. Just something about him was different. People still alive and around to link the old with the new, when earth took a bad turn on its axis, threatening everybody with man-made obliteration might be the answer, for he was in the midst of the chaos when it occurred. For better or worse, she was forced to stick with what he said had happened; a time stop and shift in the universe, being the reason.

She was not alone in her thinking.

Another. A man O'Hare had known for years, and one she had never been able to bring herself to trust. She knew he was in contact with Charlie through his messaging system they had devised, even though he was not as free with her as she expected seeing the situation they were in. If he was working for a department of the government he kept himself within the Order's camp. Trust never came easy in their line of work if they were to last long to see a completed and satisfactory outcome. He was a strange character whatever field of operation he worked. She supposed he could say the same for her, she was on the Order's payroll.

She always thought he was the double of actor Lee Van Cleef. His curled pipe at least. It was the way he knocked old ash from the bowl (or was it saliva?) on the outside brickwork of the building on the odd occasion. She had watched him do it when Elke Kriemhild was passing. She shook her head smiling at this simple act common to pipe smokers around the world. A state of humanity still within her.

She had wondered about the pension she had with them and guessed Nathaniel Johnson had the same employment rights. As Deputy Director of Operations for Star Birth (USA) she had pension rights. An irony considering the building was once known as, administrative (annex ii-38) section gov.pen, one of the United States government's own civil service buildings. Her pension in the name of Corrine Diaz as opposed to Madeleine Tubman, unlikely to mature. Either her job would finish, or the Order would finish with her before she had the chance to cash it in. When they finally discover her financial dealings with the mercantile bank she worked; supposedly robbed, purported to be all lies, would be the end of the line for her. One way or another. The likelihood was no less remote now than when she had first come here under the Tom Dorcas regime. Her boss now, Kerstin Hartmann. She knew all about intrigue having overseen the demise of Tom Dorcas and the security team he had put in place after a bungled attempt to fill the vacuum of the company after the demise of Frederik Spannocs. Fortunately the two women were close enough to be called work colleagues which suited her.

She was mindful of the direction she promoted Star Birth for the Order's direction dictated it was not her own. American people in the main were religious, and with the Order moving towards atheism, she had to manage the country's youth without involving religious faiths they followed. A message program had already been developed by psychologists and other professionals in manipulating ideas for forwarding into the social media channels by the Order. Her job was to counter any difficulties when it came to controversial issues. These easily ironed out by teams of celebrities they had working on their behalf. Their influences to dispel and give argument for them from parents, and schools, and ultimately religious bodies. When it came to issuing statements, she was the front. Here she employed professional writers from its hierarchy at Drogstadt using pen names. Her responsible was to keep them on track as she saw things with editorial compromise and advice to the writers on the grounds they, unlike her, were not American, doing better to listen to people who were. Her only sway away from the evil program of Star Birth was limited. Ineffectual even. Until the whole damned organization was dismantled, it was all they had.

She thought about her acceptance letter. Bearing the name Heinrich Stein, of Graf & Mayer Recruitment Consultants, personally signed by Stein himself in a hand a third of the page in size. She laughed. It was a pity Tom Dorcas hadn't researched who he was employing to act for him when it comes to his own security arrangements. Graf & Mayer not only managed the Order's administrative paperwork, but it also handled their security arrangements. Dorcas was doomed from the get-go. She hoped she had not overlooked similar when it came to any future well-being.

She passed Heinrich Stein's name to Jean Ronstandt through her own 'drop-letterbox'. The reply hardly touched the sides. She needed to get out. Kriemhild's security teams were becoming suspicious information was being leaked. They suspected Johnson. Which was, well, not all well and good, once they had Johnson in the frame for working for the government, it was only a matter of time before they came knocking at her door. He had been called in to answer questions which did not bode well for either of them. He seemed to have answered their questions satisfactorily for they allowed him to continue his duties. Of course, being in Austria, Kriemhild was not directly involved, their report and findings sent to her for an appraisal of the people working for the Order. No trouble there bringing them in before shipping them back out to Drogstadt Castle for closer examination; torture them in comfort.

For the time they seemed satisfied with Johnson's answers. She was ignorant of what they were, only her imagination of the questioning over the leaks gave her any idea. Of course, she had no idea what those leaks were about in particular. She guessed the hard drive. Then the first of the terrors came.

'A matter of formality, no need to worry, Miss Diaz.' So the Order's team of professional interrogators stroke torturers said calling her in. They wanted a clearer understanding of her previous employment. Her explanation for what she did before she took up duties on their doorstep; and after further checks she *was* indeed the financial wizard caught taking the merchant bank she worked, for several million dollars (O'Hare had done a good job there). They nodded their satisfaction, and after a few more days of looking into a few others' activities, they cleared off back to their chambers of horrors, leaving her and Johnson continuing their jobs. It had been a scary time. The brutality inflicted on people falling out of favor with the Order beggared belief; not relishing such treatment being inflicted on her worst enemy. The security incident when Dorcas had attempted a take over the Order, convinced her Direktorin Elke Kriemhild gave psychopathy a bad press. Both her and Johnson were going to have to call it a day.

Calling it a day meant years of hard work going down the tubes now. What alternative did they have? Tortured to death by the director of the Order, the psychopath Elke Kriemhild was not to be looked forward to. She and Johnson needing to be got out of here would not be easy. The last time anyone came close to the building, arresting everyone before closing it down was what became known as the great FBI bust. All agents involved sworn to secrecy for what they witnessed. Disclosure to conspiracy theorists by those wanting to make a fast buck were sacked from the FBI on the grounds of mental instability. Ostracized. For a man to pass through a solid wall was hard enough to take on board, but who was going to believe it was a ghost, a spirit, a demi-god, the CEO of the Order of the Most Divine Third Circle even. No one, for it was David Copperfield being employed privately.

The first of the Order's administration with its aims, the involvement of a list of its names leading to members of the Oceans International, Frederik Spannocs's own Aryan Farmers Association, an organization appealing to a particular breed of human dross. The pedophiles of this world. All of them right-wing gun-toting wealthy whites not giving a damn for blacks, Asians, Muslims, Catholics, Jews, Native Americans, or anyone not fitting their brand of white supremacy and arrogance. There was more to come.

Ironically O'Hare getting Dorcas established for his takeover of the Order with the intention of finding more revealed less. Or rather, reams of intelligence apparently disclosing more about the founders, shakers and breakers of the Order was all quietly put to one side, denied, then disappeared into banks of libraries inaccessible to all, she assumed except those with motives yet to be established. Waiting. A further assumption on her part, none of it finishing up in O'Hare's hands. She assumed taken from him. Or so he said.

What was not in doubt, according to O'Hare, was dangerous knowledge to know, better denied knowing. And again, when she asked O'Hare before her own establishment into the Order that her mandate could be compromised by leaving matters she considered important out,

Concentrate on relevant counterintelligence, Madeleine. Leave it to me and Jean to sort through the rest. Forget everything else you uncover. It will only bring despair and misery.

For the first time in her life as agent for the government the penny was dropping as to how dangerous a position she and Johnson were in. Two hands of the village clock were fast approaching midnight. She remembered why she was inclined to forget her real name now. For she might never be heard of again.

RONSTANDT & MCCLUSKY

'WHAT HAVE YOU GOT ON THIS WOMAN?' McClusky asked. He wanted all the intelligence on Kriemhild there was. 'And while you're about it, where is O'Hare? He seems to have gone to ground since bringing in Hess.'

Ronstandt was more concerned with his undercover operative, Madeleine Tubman, than O'Hare at this moment in time. Since his interview with Hess, there was reference to Tubman, made as a parting shot which caused him concern. She had been there far too long for his liking. Okay, she was still sending out intelligence. He was looking at McClusky.

'There's also a matter of a request from Secretary of Defense Pereira. Remember him, Jean? The President has asked all departments to work together.'

Never going to happen. His own department for Homeland Security traded intelligence and generally cooperated with other departments, in their case, a need-to-know basis. A trait common to the FBI and the CIA, in this case though, under the order of the president. As to Kriemhild, all they had on her, apart from being head of what was being referred to as the Bavarian section of the Order closely linked to the Reichsbürger Movement.

'Apart from her German aristocratic links to Prince Ernst II of Saxe-Altenburg, and granddaughter of the SS Colonel Rauf Kriemhild . . . of course you know of the Irish connection . . .'

'Yes, yes. It's what intelligence we have for her future plans when your people are brought in from the cold concerns me? Can we take the risk of continuing as we are? Are you sure the intelligence you have is reliable enough to say . . . Tubman has been compromised?'

'Not a hundred percent, no. Even so, I'm not prepared to risk a single minute longer on taking the chance you're suggesting,' Ronstandt argued.

'Long shot, Jean. Have you thought of contacting the German police?'

'Too risky. We don't know how heavily anyone outside of our own sphere of intelligence were involved. They openly admit they have intelligence on the Reichsbürger Movement; having to tread carefully when it comes to day-to-day investigations. Currently there is no intelligence on who to trust. Of course we cooperate with their Federal Intelligence Service, the Bundesnachrichtendienst. And they won't talk about either the Reichsbürger Movement or what's going on at Drogstadt Castle or the people running it. Word has it, top-level intelligence is being divulged to enemies of the west by people working for our own security agencies.'

'So they are aware. Put pressure on them?' McClusky asked.

'However. It gets complicated,' Ronstandt said, the source of his information reliable, not being altogether acceptable.

'I'll buy it.'

'The SS Colonel Rauf Kriemhild I mentioned. The grandfather of Elke Kriemhild,' Ronstandt hesitated as to whether this information was particularly pertinent to the situation at Malaka's Corner in getting Tubman out of there. He feared such information being out there. Whether it was for the Vice-President, the President, whoever, was dangerous to any operation he planned.

'You've said as much already, Jean. What about him?'

'He's an obscure minor. One of a host of Prussians claiming they had lost their ancestry after the German Revolution in 1918. Rauf Kriemhild joined the National Socialist German Workers' Party in the hope Hitler reinstated their family's ancestry. Unfortunately his ancestry went the way of the dodo, the result of der Fuhrer shooting himself in the head. As it was Mossad, tracked Kriemhild down to south America, to Chile. There he changed his name. Nationality, etc, becoming a monk in a small-town monastery. Mossad found him tending fruit trees in an orchard when they arrested him. They demanded of the abbot a register for the remainder of the order. When the man refused on the grounds they were all Brothers of Jesus Christ His Blood, saying he had no knowledge of a person's previous life, and didn't wish to know, adding a simple message of hope for them.

'The Mossad agent in charge shrugged his shoulders, took out a pistol, ordered Kriemhild to kneel on the ground, then shot him in the back of the head. He then asked that the rest of the community be brought out. Then they were told to kneel. One at a time shot in the head. It was the abbot's simple message of hope,

What a man does for the remainder of his days for the love of God, than past sins for Satan, being more important for him than asking questions of what made up their past lives, that did it for the rest of them apparently.'

'And who told you this again?'

Ronstandt went on to say O'Hare had accessed information from his grandson-in-law, Clan O'Sullivan. Common knowledge put out without any consequence. For ramifications following the killing of Roisin Kriemhild did not enhance the Kriemhild family connection with the IRA and her hierarchical standing with them, nor any involvement with pre-war Germany.

'Sounds a typical Irish shaggy dog story,' McClusky said shaking his head doubtful of any sincerity in it.

'Well, I wasn't going to take Charlie's account as gospel. As he said, it was all a long time ago, not even he guaranteed its truth word for word—'

'Makes a change. And you've no idea where he is now?'

'I expect he got the hump after you arrested Hess and threw him in the slammer.'

Ronstandt continued. 'Well I can go part way to substantiating what you said about Mossad. A Chilean online newspaper, *El Expreso de la Costa* and a story from its archives from the days it was a regular rag. The story was taken down from its website edition, I guess from threats from Mossad if they didn't. Visits from Mossad were never good news. Apparently there was an incident involving a monastery in a rural region of Chile. Fifteen brethren of an order were summarily executed as you stated. The CIA approached Mossad on the matter. They neither denied nor confirmed responsibility. As they operated in south America tracking down Nazi war criminals at the time, it was taken as read they had done the deed. No one was going to question, no one was ever going to be brought to justice for the killings.'

'Strange. Wonder why Mossad didn't come out with a straight-out denial?' McClusky said.

'Probably because none of the fifteen were Nazi war criminals. A simple message to war criminals hiding under stones in south America. None were safe from capture. None to be given a trial. Fair or otherwise,' Ronstandt replied.

McClusky hummed. 'Can't blame them. They had some catching up when it came to justice. So it appears the granddaughter of a German aristocrat, brought to book by Mossad, is seeking revenge on the rest of us for his execution.'

'Some of us, certainly. She also wants the hard drive to achieve world domination to underline her objectives. Her firm grip on the Order with her band of right-wing, anti-Semitic, anti-Islamist, anti-fuck-knows-what-else policy propagandas on a world stage to people carrying their right-wing views to a world of listening power-hungry thugs and misfits, will add egoism to an already psychopathic murderer. With the intelligence Tubman has been providing this last year, a picture is slowly emerging. Kriemhild is using persuasion in true Joseph Goebbels's media style to get the Order's message across. The future of world youth culture and safety lies with Star Birth, not their own governments and elders. And we are not helping in that regard. The west's freedom of information adds fuel to the fire,' Ronstandt said.

McClusky was aware Mossad were looking into the Reichsbürger Movement. Kriemhild will know this. Put her on her guard. Consider there would be secret agents working within Malaka's Corner, putting not only Tubman in danger, O'Hare's man as well. Although, to be fair, Nathaniel Johnson was as enigmatic as he himself. His involvement with the Order of the Most Divine Third Circle, suggested and went back to O'Hare when he was a beat cop in the 1920s New York Police Department, where no real evidence existed as to Johnson's true allegiance then, and who really pulls his strings since. An allegiance O'Hare had never been able substantiate. Or so he says.

'Then we can do no better than keep Mossad in the loop with anything we believe can help them,' Ronstandt said.

'We can do that, certainly. But let's keep this between me and you for the time, eh Jean?'

Ronstandt possessed a box of tools in its armory to counter and engage false and fake propaganda and media bias. These methods organizations set up for such emergencies were the result of wars still having a relevance across all manner of propaganda coming from home and abroad. White propaganda does not hide its origin or nature. Black propaganda does. Those two, indeterminably used to confuse fact or argument, were to Ronstandt dangerous and difficult to counter to a public beginning to read fake news websites. His own baby was the department's affiliation to the CIA and its various modus operandi with the FBI, such as its officially terminated, COUNTERPRO. A dirty organization in its day, its methods still relevant in these times. Ironically used to counter Tubman's Star Birth's language to prevent the corruption of young minds.

Of course the Order, as any other organization, country,

or pariah state operating similar mind games as America using them against their own people, putting them on a war footing. This was Ronstandt's inherited East and West game played since the Cold War.

'Are you suggesting the rewriting of the Fifth and Fourteenth Amendments of the Constitution. For it will be a slippery slope too far where the American people are concerned, Jean. Removing the phrase, "due process of law" you are no doubt thinking defeating these people is a hot potato worthy of risk. It is not, and one I cannot back you on,' McClusky said.

Ronstandt was having his hands tied. The Order was exampling North Korea and China as countries offering freedom and atheism to those wishing to leave the west to survive a nuclear apocalypse that would rain down on America and the West. Young Americans were already leaving and plenty planning to. In the case of North Korea, they were sleepwalking into a country operating supreme leadership rules, using forced labor and execution for dissenters to keep them in power. While at the same time China, offering and extolling their freedoms of religion, Buddhism, Taoism, Islam and Christianity, not particularly to the Order's hierarchy liking, were being done down by Russia. The Order was offering two countries as a choice of freedom when the apocalypse came.

'Kriemhild is playing a cunning game here. Did you know she studied philosophy and theology at the Vallendar University in Germany as a young woman?' McClusky shook his head, no. 'Well she did. All the while, China and North Korea, devoid of thinking, cannot see her true motives. For the

Order to base themselves among those two countries, offering scientific data yet to be found, they're welcoming her with open arms.'

McClusky was seeing this woman in an entirely different light. Not one he would sympathize, for she and her kind were still murdering bastards, it did bring an entirely different complexion to the problem of the Order and its CEO. 'Are we so sure?'

'I'm sure. Freemason, Illuminati, Intelligentsia, even God's own Knights Templar,' Ronstandt said. 'Were all at one time or another sympathetic to Germany's National Socialist Party. Hiding. Under stones. All in waiting. Along with Kriemhild's order of aristocratic Nazi families. The remainder. A world order of idiots bent on putting God to the rack in order for Him to break to reveal His creation and furtherance of His laws of physics.'

ELKE & BATHILDA VAN DIJK

SEATED AT HER DESK in her mountain office. An imposing fairytale fortress high above the town of Weinberghöhe, Drogstadt Castle was also home to the Bavarian Illuminati. A medieval building from the 14th century, Direktorin Elke Kriemhild had added her own features. Her administrators insisting she continue with the present occupants associated with the Order, the two having control over the world and its financial institutions. It had been a surprise to her they considered themselves part of the Order. She was not so sure, favoring instead her ancestors' own baby, the Reichsbürger Movement. All this was confusion to her. Where once she held firm ideologies she was no longer sure.

Elected to take over the Order from the financier Frederik Spannocs, successful for almost half a century until a bizarre happening, none of the people controlling the Order will admit to. Pedophilia from a membership of followers to finance the Order had dirtied their gravitas. Spannocs had made money, no question. More than enough to finance experiments to eventually build the machinery to download the data they sought. A successful conclusion to ambitions over two millennium.

His birth name was Marco Giuseppi. Changing it to Frederik Spannocs for no other reason than an egotistical idea of fancying himself as a new Satan. She laughed at the idea of his inventing the nomenclate for himself. Prince of Darkness, she thought. Forget anagrams, consider a phrase memorable for a public's consumption they will never forget. Try Prince of Wankers. Did he think aligning himself with Satan would have given him power on earth alone?

She came into the Order through connections with Nazism, being a follower of the Third Reich, and the Reichsbürger Movement.

The mystery over his disappearance from the world stage, coincided with an event rumored, bringing the world close to dust was weird, if true. The history had been erased, for there was no factual evidence for any such thing happening at a town with the name of Becland. Close by to Roswell said it all.

Since she had taken on Drogstadt castle she had added a dome. Closer scrutiny below or above gave the impression it was a planetarium, it was neither. A sophisticated network for world-wide communication. A four-inch-thick metal door kept it safe from all except the Chinese and North Korean scientists managing it.

ChinKor were adept in their understanding of what she was about. A vast hall containing search engine server fan units, and water cooled from a mountain stream kept them from overheating. A crew of twelve engineers serviced these on three shifts around the clock. The floor below hers held the organizations World Operations Center. Programed to eavesdrop on the USA as well as Europe, it was run by a further five high-tech engineers had cut their teeth as interns working for Microsoft and Google before being head hunted to an organization promising science for the Creation of Universes. From here they had access to one of the first face recognition systems in the world. Their undetectable scanners continually hacked into the United States drivers' license offices of state, territory, extending to Washington, District of Columbia.

From this vast network she had control of the politics of the Order along with social media platforms established and those emerging. On those the Order put out political conspiracy theories, fake news, false and counter political messages across Europe. Working alongside QAnon writers they were kicked out into the ether aided by Russia's media networks of RT and Sputnik. For this was where people to be indoctrinated with propaganda and false information were to be found. And the Russians were masters when it came to misinformation and lying.

She had managed the Order's computers and ancillary facilities of telephone companies in America. The list ran to facility-based wireless service providers as well as AT&T, Sprint, and US Cellular. From an array of keywords, the computer running the system locked into all providers and callers isolating their locations to within ten feet anywhere on earth. Such was the intensity of operating these systems the staff responsible were replaced at six-week intervals keeping them from burn-out.

The Reichsbürger Movement alongside the Order, sought more than world domination, for the second part: the key to unlock unfamiliar files, were eluding them. Her masters were becoming impatient. She desperately needed to prove herself.

She knew there were obstacles and what they were.

Religion was first and foremost. It had to be taken down, for it had no place in their new world. The weakening of Islam, Judaism, and the destruction and elimination on earth, the Roman Catholic Church, along with the orthodoxies of Russia and Greece had no place. Christianity's Jewish origins along with the Old Testament were, as in her ancestor's Nazi past were also to be rejected. Her religion. Her true religion was Protestant Reich Church. Her true Hero of God was John the Baptist. She recognized his association with water and repentance, while Jesus' was with the Holy Spirit and fire going against the Order's beliefs in bringing to earth a spirit vessel possessing the entire knowledge of the universe, and what they had sought for the last 2 000 years to obtain. Ideas and myths had gone the way of the dinosaurs, the physics expounded by coincidental accident. Screaming spirits being laid on for dramatic affect rather than a scientific method having more in keeping for those making such a discovery wanting to keep the knowledge to themselves . . .

Until FBI agent Charlie O'Hare came along and removed it . . .

She was wandering in her mind again.

He and his associates. The special envoy to Pope John Paul II, advisor to the United Nations' Ecumenical Society of World Religions, Annie Carter being one such meddling individual. The *New York Post*'s, Hamilton Fitch, another. He and his family had been on the Order's hit list for years, for reasons she knew not why. She knew these people were in her way. It was as if they were possessed of special powers donated to them by Charlie O'Hare. For as far as she knew he was the one in possession of the key to open those, *verdammt* files of hers. The agent whose faked burial in Brooklyn, grave currently vacant, will not be for much longer.

One of her conditions of employment as CEO of the Order, O'Hare was to be her priority for elimination. Her faith in the man failing to carry it out in CIA custody, was a black mark against her. Indirectly it was her failure, and his abilities to keep one-step ahead of the Order was becoming tedious in the extreme. The misery and heartache inflicted upon him with the murders of his close friends down the decades by Frederik Spannocs had not fazed Agent O'Hare. Hess had the best chance if anyone had, an assassin of worth, even if he had failed. She was going to have to go for him personally. Even she, with her psychopathic tendencies, was at a loss to know as to how to move forward. Assassinations of the Order's enemies were paramount and clear. Burying such people was a justifiable cause. A mind inherited from a noble past. Her grandfather, Prince Artur. Using the defence he was firstly a soldier of the Wehrmacht, secondly a German aristocrat excused. A myth soon debunked following the execution of several villagers by the 2nd SS Panzer Division under his orders. Found guilty at Nuremberg, he was hanged at 1.52 am in the gymnasium of the Nuremberg Prison by an American Army master sergeant. She shrugged her shoulders. History. Lessons. Forgiveness. Not as far as she was concerned. Not in their world.

'Was sein wird, wird sein.'

She sighed. All this gave her an appetite. She needed sex.

She picked up her phone. A soft voiced woman answered.

'Prince Artur Kriemhild of Prussia here. I need your services. Dress appropriately, *mein Schatz.*'

Stasi had created a secret police network before their agents had joined forces with the KGB after the Berlin wall came down. Van Dijk was one such operative. Offered work with the Russian Foreign Intelligence Service staying on with Stasi to become a double agent infiltrating Baader-Meinhof. Here she learned denunciation, provocation, psychological warfare, psychological subversion, wiretapping, bugging, aiding and assisting autocratic states in the formation of their secret police. And assassination. Although Stasi was no longer in existence ex-members still held important positions in Germany and Russia. Van Dijk was a wild card. An intelligent and capable ace of spades to any country or organization buying into her. Ahead of the game, her credentials were so impressive to Kriemhild she snatched her from one group of bad boys into another.

Bathilda Van Dijk came to her wearing a suit of gray. A Stasi business dress best description. A tight skirt with an open blouse jacket showing a hint of a black bra. She wore her hair in the traditional plaited hairstyle common to German women from the 1930s. Direktorin Elke Kriemhild approved.

She ran her tongue over her lips in anticipation of work achieved. She showed her into an anti-room of her bedroom. She knew what was expected of her. Kriemhild removed her skirt and laid herself across the vaulted spanking bench. Van Dijk fastened her wrists into the handcuffs, pulled Kriemhild's knickers down around her ankles. She went to the wall taking down a rattan rod from the rack among others swishing it through the air laid it on her buttocks. Her heart was beating at the thought of the rod.

Van Dijk began gently at first, building to a pitch bringing beads of sweat to trickle down off the skin of her shoulders. When Kriemhild had taken as much as she was to endure, she raised her arms. As a condemned aristocrat giving permission for an executioner to bring down his axe, Van Dijk ceased her whipping. She removed her Stasi business suit and took down a strap-on dildo from the shelf and fitted it about herself. She came into Kriemhild, going at her as a donkey on steroids. After a breather they changed role positions. Now with Kriemhild in the dominant, Van Dijk began struggling from her advances. The woman was out of control having her hands about her neck, her fingernails digging into her throat. She was choking and Kriemhild was taking no notice of her predicament. She attempted to struggle off the bench, her wrists had been attached to rings at the front. With a gasp she screamed at her,

'Elke, stoppen, I'm not your mother. You're ch-ok-in-g me.'

Only then did her assailant recover her sense as to what she was doing. Something was getting into her, and she knew her soul about to be turned inside out was close at hand for her achievements.

Kriemhild stood in front of the full-length mirror in her private quarters. For an ex-German light welter-weight boxing champion she still had it. She was wearing her grandfather's uniform she had retrieved from his home after he was hanged in the gymnasium of Nuremberg Prison. The uniform of a Nazi officer of the Third Reich he had not been allowed to wear as a last request. She looked at herself once more, turning first this way then the other, admiring herself, imagining a world under the Third Reich. A realm suited for those of a higher position and learning. A world she was about to re-establish, one by the people having influence, money and means, was not going to be difficult to achieve. She looked at its black material and fine tailoring. Its makers label, Hugo Boss, still in good condition.

The uniform itself, although having taken the odorousness of a wardrobe it had previously hung was pressed and clean. She was proud of her ancestry and her bloodline. She had taken the Order of the Most Divine Third Circle from what once was under the entrepreneurship of Frederik Spannocs to become a single world government. Her Order would run with the Reichsbürger Movement and the Bavarian Illuminati until she no longer needed them. She tried for an alternative to divine, for the word indicated the existence of God, and as mythical an understanding as all others from the ancient world given ignorance and faith over true understanding needed another expressive.

Star Birth was to be the bright colorful packaging wrapping around the Order as so much Christmas tinsel. A para-social media platform tapping into young minds, promising fashion, cosmetics, cars, and lifestyles following *der Rattenfänger von Hameln*-style of Saxony legend. Star Birth would instill into followers beliefs of trust not found in religious faiths. For she was qualified to say religious ideologies were an anathema to her now, the pied piper would lead them blindly onwards.

But first she was troubled. She had part lost control. Her sexual tastes had come close to killing Van Dijk, a substitute transference seemed to be taking her body and soul. She had cut her own mother's throat with none of those feelings. How long before she repeated the act on Van Dijk, thinking she was her also?

She kept her grandfather's uniform on as she made her way around the castle, something she had not done before. For her ambitions for the Order were not those of promotion of a Third Reich, even though the Reichsbürger Movement was keen on the Order's ideology, no doubt having similar ambitions for themselves, were immaterial to her. She knew a re-introduction of a Third Reich was easily countered by Holocaust organizations operating internationally keeping the regime's history live through education. A massive campaign of false history and fake news was to be mounted to counter it.

She walked the workings under the dome. A cupola recently installed for a working planetarium, open to students at the University of Sax Coburg for research and no further. For steel riveted doors to other rooms around its perimeter were out of bounds. The sophisticated network for communication where massive cabinets containing search engine servers were kept. Alongside of which were air conditioning units to keep them from overheating. Here a workforce of twelve computer engineers serviced them on three shifts around the clock. Concrete steps at the end of this room took her to the Order's World Operations Center where listening devices were programed to eavesdrop on America and the world. All maintained by five of her high-tech staff involved with the founding of Microsoft and Google, for there were no interns cutting their teeth here, only people directly involved with the formulation of artificial intelligence for computer programs circumventing regular information input for dissemination to companies, in favor of those freely given up by the ever-increasing number and popularity of subscribers to what traditional press and television news editors described disdainfully as social media platforms.

The speed of this operation was phenomenal. The first facial recognition system outside of any government department was to become one of their most powerful tools.

Engineers looked up at her as she passed by in astonishment. Not daring to comment on her dress as she perused their clipboards of new development ideas and their progressions. The scamming operation was particularly interesting to her, for they were currently attempting; close to finalizing the hacking of America's offices of state through the eastern seaboard to the District of Columbia. For this had been a particularly difficult operation for her people; one they had cracked wide apart.

All of this information coming out from the government of the day, both for internal and external publication were being disseminated for the Order to act upon. They were currently working on European elections. Giving thought to an ultra-right-wing media the loss of an opposition party had suffered had been rigged, causing destabilization and loss of trust in the country's electoral system. In all of this she was being assisted by the Democratic People's Republic of Korea.

The computers and ancillary facilities accessed all telephone companies in America. The list ran to facility-based wireless service providers as well as AT&T, Sprint, and US Cellular. Such was the intensity of operating these systems, staff were replaced at six-week intervals, to keep them from burn-out.

Negotiations had been established to bring totalitarian states as DPRK and Russia and were flourishing. They had shown an interest in this technology and what it was capable. Three autocratic regimes and two others, currently democratic, signing on the line, with the promise they would enhance their reputations and influences on the world stage. While she, interested in one world, not of the Order or any other countries, hers were of concern for her own failure and of the Order's.

Her concerns put to one side as being of normal human frailty. As to the other, she was in the final stages of moving their whole operation from Malaka's Corner here to Munich. Her peers not wanting to risk a second time closure of their operation by the FBI. Regarding the thick dossier of signal traffic between Madeleine Tubman, Nathaniel Johnson and Jean Ronstandt of particular interest, she had enough. She was more than one step ahead of the US Government on score.

Fortunately there were still those with old connections to the United States Government who were still sympathetic to the founding principles of the Order under the name of Frederik Spannocs. Those not doing prison time for their past involvements with him, and pedophilia that is. So complacent with 1920s New York tolerance criminality and corruption thinking to get away with what they had, beggared belief. There were still those free, in positions of power continuing to abuse those trying to dishonor the name Frederik Spannocs and his Order in favor of her own. Believing him the true disciple of Satan. Her directive to keep the holding name a low profile in favor of her own and Star Birth as opposed to his Order re-directing opposition away from them.

The three disciples and . . .

Agent Charlie O'Hare from the FBI being one. While others, the editor of the *New York Post*, Hamilton Fitch along with Annie Carter from the Catholic church who had carried the name, Sister Benedicta Marie for instance were much of interest for assassination. Fitch because of an historical association with O'Hare, Carter as the United Nations advisor to the Ecumenical Society of World Religions and special envoy to Pope John-Paul II,

. . . the man, and the entire dismantlement of the Catholic church for starters.

She needed Bat.

Favoring Van Dijk heading the department responsible for assassinations, ridding those names and other people's opposition to the Order with their deaths, rather than relying on so-called renegade army snipers, who thought themselves professional killers was a good move. Hess, a man with a good surname, who had made a hash of killing O'Hare, losing an important part of the hard drive containing file opening keys, being such an example.

She regretted not sending Van Dijk. She would have had displayed no such qualms that Hess had. She would have shot him in the back, the front, cut his head off offering it to her in a gravy of blood on a platter as John the Baptist's to Salome.

Van Dijk was taking a cold-water salt shower to ease the red raw weal's from the leather strap inflicted on her lower back catching the side of her breasts in the process by Elke. Turning around to bathe her breasts she saw what looked to be gunshot wounds across and below them. Not there a moment ago, for they only appeared in the seconds after she stepped into the shower. Where had she been to get those? Nowhere for she had only recently had a session with Elke. Sure she had tried to strangle her, but that was all. She hadn't shot her. She looked at her hands, for they were covered in something. Putting them to her nose she smelt them.

Chocolate cake and coffee?

Van Dijk turned and smiled at Kriemhild. She was seeing her lover for the first and last time in the uniform of an officer of the Third Reich. Her recollection of wounds to her breasts along with . . . what had been on my hands, faded as dreams on awakening.

'I have a mission for you, Bat. You all right?'

'Sorry, yes. Dreaming. O'Hare?'

'Not yet . . . Hess.'

KRIEMHILD MEETS THE ARYAN FARMERS

A DRESS OF HEAVY VELVET in deep maroon with cream embroidered shoulders of English Tudor matched the edging of the open front of the dresses and wrists. Its high Elizabethan collars edged in a crème fold material. On her head, a tiara of emeralds and diamonds. He said they were dresses for a Queen of the Universe; and as such, according to the Seamstress's of Harlots and Abomination on Perdition Street at least, would stay as fresh and crisp as the day she first wore them. They would neither stain, attract dirt, or crease. He told her, only she was authorized to wear them. One was to be kept in America, the other in Bavaria.

'Are you he? Of the seven heads and ten horns fame?'

'The obverse actually. For I am Ahriman.'

Saliva issued from the side of her mouth reflected in the mirror she was before. She wiped it with her sleeve, then replied with words she had no control over. Her compliance echoed down millennia's, returned with the speed of an email subscription, acknowledged with unconditional acceptance.

'I am your disciple to eternity.'

*

She convened the meeting at the Becland Diamond Conference Center. One she had had no part in organizing was waiting for her. On the wall, a poster to advertise, New Year's Eve Grand Nite, 1950. A room full of black suits and cigar smoke. Each in turn announcing and pledging support and allegiance to part of her person about to occupy the spirit entity of Ahriman. Aryan Farmers Association was back in the house. The black suits taking the appearance of cardboard cut outs were fading away from her. This was not her. She was confused. Her spiritual humanity was disorientating. A pain, sharp, somewhere between her brainstem and the cerebrum was running up and down causing migraine and eye confusion.

The black suits reformed their magical substance, congregated, laughing, jeering, and cheering her. She was among old friends having now returned from a past was not hers, only hers to recollect from Ahriman.

Clapping her hands calling to the Master of Ceremonies to acknowledge her, the man wearing a suit of red livery with gold braid and a black top hat, smiling, announced himself as,

Benny the Ponce at your service, ma'am.

She quietly muttered his name. She felt having been here before. Benny announced,

Ladies and Gentle . . . men . . . not all of you. [I'm sure], came as an aside, brought roars and guffaws of laughter. He held up his hand for silence. *One of the finest examples of shape-changers in the business. Ladies and gentlemen, ma'am, allow me to introduce to you the delightful and effervescent artiste. The business is proud to present what we call transvestitisms, and what the world of thaumaturgy . . .*

Oooo.

. . . describe as, the miracle of the disappearing todger with accompaniments.

[Though she could be a lady . . .],
came as another aside to the audience, the palm of his hand to the side of his mouth. There was laughter and cheering.

Not to be taken too seriously though . . . all the way from Austin . . . Little Miss Poppet Tupper, Trannie to the Stars . . .

[And who wouldn't?]

Hooting and whistling. Poppet Tupper on stage to the left of the top tables came on smiling.

Thank you. Ladies and gentlemen, you're so perverted,
he said pulling up a leopard-skin dress above his crotch to reveal a full set of bollocks to loud applause.

How's that for a luster cluster? Swallow these Benny, for you've a mouth big enough.

Woooah.

Using his fingertips, he pushed his penis and scrotum up inside of himself. There was a gasp from the audience. Removing his matching leopard skin top hat, he took a bow as a full-on looking woman.

Thank you very much, ladies and gentlemen. More later. For the moment I give to you our guest of honor, Mr. Frederik Spannocs . . .

Benny stumbled the introduction. He was looking around for Spannocs. Seeing only Kriemhild, he shrugged then vaporized along with the entire gathering of the Aryan Farmers Association.

She massaged a sting to her neck. The collar of the shirt of the uniform she was familiar was no longer there. She was wearing a heavy velvet dress. Having no recollection of dressing ostentatiously despite her liking for it. She felt behind the fan collar smoothing the pain away. She must have injured herself running around the castle trying to escape shadows she no longer had any fear. She was Direktorin Elke Kriemhild, Queen of the Universe.

She was possessed of a power from the shadow before her.

'We will take His army,' Ahriman said.

'Are you not His equal?' she asked.

His expulsion from the universe from this make-believe Creator was not His to make. He had exceeded the powers granted to Him. Those powers of glory were not of His creation, they were stolen from a true creator of the dark universe, its existence long before he was cast into oblivion by Him for the knowing of the secret. A dark universe waiting to be discovered and exploited. She was to be the one to unlock the key exposing Him as a sham.

'I have done penitence for His wronging. For there are Others who have power over Him, for I cannot take this pretender on a second time.'

The history of the Christian Order of the Most Divine Third Circle bringing to earth one of the holy trinities for the knowledge it possessed was not new to her. And there she had doubts over its ownership. Believing its possession actually belonged to those creatures at the bottom of the Atlantic Ocean returned to take back what was theirs, than God's or Ahriman's.

He had left her side. She sexually climaxed at his parting.

Clicking the inside of her mouth with her tongue, she looked at herself in her full-length vanity mirror. A demon myth, knowing women's desires from previous attempts of incarnation, before her.

Satan in Ahriman was in enraged. An error of judgment for the removal of doubt of authenticity for his ultimate aim had migrated from Giuseppi to Spannocs and in turn, to Kriemhild. She was in possession of his real motives. He remained within her. The capacity to bring on a good dose of dementia should his earthly control and obedience over her diminish. For he was the executioner to carry forward the judgement, *Wages for sin; death eternal.*

Van Dijk came to her. Expecting her to be wearing the uniform of an officer of the Third Reich she gasped. Seeing what she was wearing instead fell at her feet in glorification. Her head lowered revealed a small needle mark.

Kriemhild gently erased it away with her finger. 'Like it?' Kriemhild asked elevatoring her head.

'Like it . . . I *love* it.'

'Then you'll have to get the hang of muffing me with these, Bat.' She raised her dress, then manipulated her newly donated penis, with attached testicle, up inside of herself, in readiness for Van Dijk's tongue.

VAN DIJK COMES FOR CHARLIE

O'HARE WAS BACK IN THE BIG APPLE. Laughed, then muttered to himself,

The dream of every lad that ever threw a leg over a thoroughbred, the goal of all horsemen. There's only one Big Apple. That's New York. Yes, siree.

Laughed once more. He was inclined to silly thoughts and indulgences; hardly anyone he knew understood these idiosyncrasies of his. It didn't concern him. Understanding himself was good enough.

Despite his protestations, Ronstandt had taken Hess into custody. He shouldn't have been surprised. He was army and they were keen for his return. As for himself, well, there was chance of an arrest for faking his own death. He had to admit he had got a perverse enjoyment hearing the accolades of people at his funeral. People now know him. Was he vainly making comparisons? With the carpenter, perhaps.

Reading his obituary was weird. All his planning, his plotting with friends and relatives, had to be kept secret. Dying twice a day, two days running would take explaining. He might be called to account for his abilities of mind over God.

He thought deeply about the alien, with a sense of

humanity for the saving of life. In this instance his great-grandniece, Mary, a classic example of humanity extending into time and evolution. Suggesting humanity was hard-wired into the DNA of all creatures, from whatever region of time and space they might come. Which was difficult to understand after the killing of the marines by them. But weren't there such examples on earth by resident humanity. He supposed there must be.

Had it not been for the family mortician, Tommy Scripps, and his daughter, Daniella, the rumors surrounding his passing had been set in stone. His death, as was his tomb stone, as fake as the story of George Washington leveling a cherry tree to the ground with an axe. Speaking of which, he must remind himself to put flowers on his own grave, not for memory, more as thanks to the two people kept him alive. Seeing as his second cousin, Gerty O'Sullivan, threatened to ban him from ever setting foot in Castle Rose again, not allowing him to rest in entombed in its chapel crypt:

Charles Seamus O'Hare

An Irish New Yorker

Born 1890–Died 1997

He shall keep this stone for a truly subsequent occasion:

Charles Seamus O'Hare

An Irish New Yorker

Born 1938–Died 1997

and allow the mason to re-cut the passing date, then wonder.

Right birth, wrong date; by a stone fashioner using birth records without putting much thought into the length of time ascribed between birth and death. He needed to cease walking the streets looking a man of fifty when he was closer to a century and ten. When it came to getting work in the Big Apple . . . he had heard ageism laws were no longer a consideration . . . *but c'mon.*

He opened the gate, then shuddered. Whether it was from the cold chill of the morning or what he was here for, he couldn't think. Why was it necessary for cemetery gates to be old, rusty always in need of a fresh coat of black paint? Or had they been built and decorated in that way to create atmosphere? A planning regulation perhaps, going back eons from the district for public parks and cemeteries. He had come to oversee the removal of the grave before anyone took notice he was walking the streets as a ghost in the day. He knew his fake death was going to have to be made public, sooner than later; was all be a matter of timing and honest journalism. He looked up at the sky. The weather was bright, although on a fresh side, as he began walking along the compacted dirt path separating the graves on one side to those on the other. He wondered if there was any relevance to which side of the cemetery one was laid to rest for, they all seemed equally numbered. Graves neat and in tidy lines for this was not any old cemetery, it held important people. Not him especially, for this was Green-Wood. The last resting place in New York and District for important rascals.

He could hear a disturbance in the distance. Coming from the far end of the cemetery. Around a corner between a magnificent white angel on a plinth and a family vault the size of a small house, one time having been white, was now black and green with age and moss, a funeral was in progress. The mourners grouped around an unfinished grave in their Sunday best despite it being Thursday. A plethora of relations, the ladies at its center dressed in their obligatory black dresses with hats large enough to cover facial despair. The men in old suits dug out for the occasion. Unmatching ties attached to white shirts bought and worn for no other occasion, was all so depressingly essential.

The grave dug, earth mounded to one side, covered in artificial grass. He wondered where fashion first originated for such seamless decoration. He supposed it was to temper the harshness of a burial into open and fresh dug earth exuding odor of damp root. An abhorrent ending for people, in the normal cause of events of living kept themselves clean and tidy, and where in this simple act of laying a person into the earth went against all common hygiene. Being here was a first-time event for the patient, earth not normally mentioned in this respect, unless you were a gardener. Earth to earth, ashes to ashes, dust to dust, in the sure and certain hope etc, is not exactly true. No one ever came from earth, ash, or dust as such. And certainly not from the damp brown stuff at the bottom of a hole. Ministers overseeing such arrangements spoke of committing this dearly departed to the ground, as if it was starting point, instead of a yesterday thirteen-odd billion years since, when dust and dirt was created in a clean and sterile environment, in an explosion of a mega intensity, heat and light; and not damp, cold, dirty earth for the purpose of rotting and breaking down mortal remains. We came from the fire and violence of a universe in its creation, the destination of our mortal remains and everything else when the universe reverts back to a dot on a horizon, no longer in being. A much cleaner option. Cleaner in the interim though, he'll go for cremation.

As for talk of being risen on judgment day, he wondered if God really expected the remains of all these people to come forth for judgment on one single day. A line from here to eternity. The logistics impossible. Bodies and souls needed to be dispatched immediately, else chaos and plague would ensue.

Machinery. He looked up and into the direction of its sound. A digger had arrived and was being unloaded off its trailer. His job in hand. His burial plot was to be restored to what it once was, for the interim at least, to one of vacancy for another long-term patient. Another day.

For him at least, a day to die tomorrow.

He was asked for the official paperwork for removal which he showed them. The operator wearing a yellow mac, and a white safety helmet, cracked to one side nodded at him, set to work. A remote controller in his hand moved the heavy steel grab across to the white marble cross. The claw took hold of it, then elevatored it from the ground, swinging it away and raising it at the same time, dropped it into the back of the open lorry alongside. The suspension dropped under its weight. The grab returned. Marble bed quarter at a time, repeated until all four pieces had been dropped in alongside the cross.

He had arranged for the cross and stone bed to be reclaimed for the use of a family not having the means to provide for their loved one. The brass plaque screwed to its cross, a temporary name plate, his own name polished out for the use of another.

A cemetery worker seated at the controls of a Volvo mini scraper waited for him to finish. O'Hare nodded. With no grave hole to be filled the site was leveled in minutes. The digger was driven onto its trailer, hitched to the back of a pickup, the cemetery worker salute waved at him, got into the Toyota and drove off out of the cemetery, not bothering to question him as to why no grave had been dug.

There was warmth from the sun now. After the chill he felt when he first came, very welcome. Taking one last look at the resting place used only for the deception, he made his way to leave. Figuring out a next move against the organization nobody seemed able to shut off the steam from, or even want to.

He came back to his earlier thought of how he was to announce to the world his resurrection. Sitting on his regular barstool in Donheny & Nesbitt's, drinking a Guinness and a whiskey, was going to take some thought. The barman not bothering, he'd known him too long to go there. New York was big.

The Big Apple.

Walking on water aside, to go a-stepping the five boroughs of The Bronx, Brooklyn, Manhattan, Queens, and Staten Island the whole of your life and not bump into the same person twice. He had no real need to worry. He was looking thirty years younger than when he was supposed to have died. And if anybody he didn't personally know made a connection, say you must be mistaken old son, my name's not Charlie, it's Sin.

He smiled at the idea of calling himself after his uncle. He rather fancied himself a Sin. It had a certain, je ne sais quoi quality, taken into the jaws of hell without question as to which side of the biblical fence he was viewing, had advantages.

He was in no hurry. He was not residing in his burial plot,

yet. Not unless another Coxly Hess comes along to have another pop at him. What did the man say?

You've had a good run, Irish . . . so you have. Nothing personal, eh?

He was public enemy number one as far as the Order were concerned. Hess shooting him down persuaded no one he was dead. They needed a body. The Order, mashing with Illuminati, Freemasonry and Kriemhild's own Fourth Reich, to impose a tyrannical governing structure as if it was ordained in the Bible as fulfilment of prophecy for end time; with ambitions for a New World Order of autocracy. From an Order's aspect of turning historical events into their versions, was bollocks beyond the pale, tagged to reinforce the righteousness of their New World Order. Making deals, even with a concept of Satan, was not a deal of equals. Only personal. A fucking personal slight to the human rights of everyone on the planet. Although to them, there would be no problem they could see. Of course they couldn't.

And of course, they would not let it slip from these sucker's minds, the Alien invasion, when it comes to light, using their version of the Book of Revelations, for it being God's work. Never mind the book wasn't written by God, any more than He had subscribed to any of its pages. Despite it suiting religious fundamentalists when it came to reinforcing religious arguments. An Alien displaying human emotion for protecting a child of another alien race was unexpected, bearing in mind they had already killed forty-two marines when they first came to earth. The Alien getting inside his coffin to tear it apart to find the hard drive, to him, wasn't personal. He'd figured out they needed the hard drive and what it contained not from any senseless ideals of taking control of the universe, but for the survival of their species.

His brain thoughts crossing between Man and Alien showed a race of superhuman Time–Lords at the point of extinction being the real reason. Not to give guidance for an autocratic government to tell people what was good for them, when Alien truth was for survival.

Save me from conspiracists, 'unts, and 'uckers.

A confused experience for Dr. Hermenbergur Aloyious bringing him from the cataleptic state he was in. The Alien hitting into his brain to get at files implanted by another race. It had taken a trillionth of a billionth of a second to go through O'Hare's eighty billion neurons to find the nucleotides containing the stored analogue information for creation, only to be prevented access by a fire wall in his brain, implanted by another alien. A wake-up call to this advanced race of Alien Time–Lords? Possibly.

Satan's ambitions are not human ambitions; nor those of superhuman Time–Lords, who wouldn't distinguish them from a hamburger seller. His ambitions ran deeper than any new world order, or those of Direktorin Elke Kriemhild herself. They may not even be of evil intent for their implementation. Who knows? God, possibly not. If evil should manifest itself in his ambitions, it would be more luck over chance. Even so, He will not be amenable for our choosing. Good, bad or pug ugly all of us. To wipe out Satan, God will have to take all with him. End of day, we are no more than experimental fodder; not worthy of being given any other chance.

He looked to the sky. Rain clouds threatened.

The priest he had seen at the far end of the cemetery when he entered was not what he thought. She was a woman of the cloth. She smiled as she came upon him. Disarmed by charm, he watched as she pulled a syringe from a shoulder bag. She was about to inject him. It all happened so quickly, too late, he didn't have a chance to register what she was attempting to do. He pulled away from the scratch of it, but the needle had entered his upper arm. Syringe and needle were hanging from his arm as he pulled away from her. Whatever it contained was fast acting, he was losing consciousness. He was also aware she was preparing to stick another needle into him. This time to his neck. His physiological reaction kicked in bringing him into awareness.

He would need to remove the dangling one first. He could see the syringe was one third remaining. He took hold of it and pulled it out. Turning the needle and syringe around he stuck it in the priestesses' neck, drawing blood. He was now at her mercy as he felt himself passing out, then collapsed on the ground unconscious.

Life's depressions come by degrees. Bouts of unhappiness and hopelessness, to a greater or lesser degree, is common to all sooner or later. For himself, such bouts of melancholy easily pass. Depression at a clinical level requires medication, he knew, for though he occasionally suffered from black dog, bad as it was, it past as quickly as it came. Depression followed as a shadow. The shadow was slowly descending on him now. Of course, he was catholic. Brought up to see the world in terms of good and evil. He unashamedly applied those epithets to God and Satan both; he was not alone in thinking on those lines. Brain-washed since a child. He had fought against such entities since the twenties. Supposed human beings happy to live in servitude to Satan for what he would gift them. Usually nothing. Never a shortage there, they queue up around the block to join.

The Other? He was too God fearing to dare, for he was one of His creations and would not attempt to hazard a definitive answer as to what He had planned for his life. He was not unique. He was not the only person, currently, or in a past, occupying God's earth (he made no excuse for reinforcing his use of God's earth into his vocabulary); had not been there. For it was not His earth dumping the black dog of chaos and disorder into his soul right now, but the possibility of Satan's earth returning once again, Spannocs-like.

You must understand what My power and glory offers Mankind.

Satan paints an attractive picture for a fantasy land for those with rose tinted glasses; fortunately, he was never subscribed those. Finding himself once more in the company of Frederik Spannocs, he knew exactly what to expect. He was ready for the deceiver's tricks. He didn't have to wait long. Dismissing all the preludes, spitting from thick lips, he was laughing at him. For he was no more than a creation of the man he had known from the nineteen-twenties. A man he despised when mortal; and one he had ever had the displeasure to meet.

Lead on, Frederik Spannocs, or whatever guise you're in now. Give it your best shot.

He didn't have long to wait before he found himself traveling down through the centuries, secure in the thought this was not the end of his time, only God could draw those curtains. He knew he was destined to follow Kriemhild to the beginnings of time itself, if he was to get to Satan–Ahriman. Where accepted science separated from religious creationism: one 12 000 million years; the other 10 000 years before, where the possibility of multiverses co-existed in their own time with no knowledge of any other until an inadvertent crossover. Barred to Satan; only the Creator has access. And as before the images came. Once more he was being spared the reality of his true appearance. For this was no creator despite carrying the designed and reworked message as if God's,

> *Thou canst not see my face: for there shall no man see me, and live,*

was written in stone and copyrighted. Satan–Ahriman was using the same warning as if his own.

O'Hare looked at his watch. As before, the second hand was sweeping into the past, then back again. Time flowing from past through present to future; and not the paradox of future through present to past, he forged his original plan once more in the hope Satan had forgotten. Not necessarily a forlorn hope, for there was every chance he would have done. Old Clooty knew past, and present were real, only the future was not so. And he was not privy to such knowledge. Moving from present to past, knowing any other paradox flowing forward altered nothing. Despite which he steered himself toward the future that the paradox might open for him giving him advantage. It didn't. Following to confront hundreds of the same, passing around him in zoetrope fashion. Each identical to the one before, a dizzying line-up of doppelgängers of him en masse.

Satan seethe. His only influence was through his disciples, God settling on the fact the evil laid on man by him on earth would eventually dilute through the weariness of genes through natural selection. Then he becomes God the undisputed Creator of all. But Satan cannot be allowed to die. That was the rub. This was his central crux for survival, and boy won't he abuse the situation.

When the images ceased, he moved further back to focus and study each in turn. He'd been here before. The doppelgängers in the pack, known to him as before, would give him no advantage. Each fixed and smiling, laughing, as he moved onto the next seeking out the once mortal Spannocs, instrumental in the worst cases of child abuse, child abduction and murder, mental and physical torture, humanity has ever had to bear. An easy task? Spannocs had played this game before, but his new disciple hadn't.

O'Hare faced him as he appeared before him, close. O'Hare's hand was shaking as he tried to hold the gun placed in his hand for the second time in a millennium, steady. This millennium.

Spannocs now aware, forgetful of any previous encounter, laughed in his face, 'Say it again, slower this time.'

And here, as before, O'Hare began the recitation,

'Mrs. Puggy Wuggy has a square cut punt,

Not a punt cut square.

It's round in the stern and blunt in the front,

Mrs. Puggy Wuggy has a square cut punt,'

over and over, faster and faster, until Spannocs, bemused, began to play the game once again. Repeated the rhyme up and down the lines, through centuries, frame by frame, laughed, recited, fell over the words, tears in his eyes, until O'Hare was satisfied. He wiped the spittle issued from Spannocs' lips from his own face, then as before, simply pulled the trigger. The images of Spannocs came together as a pack of cards, then vaporized as fog.

'You mother fucker son of an Irish bog slut, you remembered,' Spannocs croaked. 'Ahriman! Why didn't you?'

As before, the bullet entered Spannocs' voice box. A small hole, the size of a dime, ringed with a black bruise, leeched blood. The back of his head, the nape of his neck, a hole big enough to put a fist in, surrounded by brain matter, bone, and blood was as before, for Satan, sans –Ahriman was not the demon in front of him now. He spun around and a gradual disappearance of his body took place leaving one last visible trace of Spannocs as a pair of lips, brought on a Queen.

Wearing a velvet maroon dress with embroidered material shoulders, a tiara of diamonds on her head, she emerged as a pupa from his lips to stand before him. In her hand a syringe. On her knees, subdued and naked, was a woman. A paramilitary uniform was lying beside of her. She looked at it, but it was not one she recognized. Her breasts back and shoulders covered with wheals from the lashings of a whip. She fell forward onto her front, a syringe stuck from her neck. The Queen turned to him. Her lips tight. She raised her head, her eyes looked straight into his, her highbrow and eye lashes giving an appearance of a woman not to be messed with. He smiled. She appeared to be from his world, but he knew she was now in another's. She faded as Alice in Wonderland's Cheshire cat. The dawning of an idea came to him. When the voice spoke, threatening menace absolute, did it occur to him, as a time before, the memory of those cards becoming reality manifested themselves. A [dream] game to be played for the ultimate stake. Satan's domination of the universe against God's experiment of hope over despair. Two players against him. A grifter with a corrupt flim-flam croupier to aid; and a woman who would be Satan's prodigy of Queen of the Universe.

O'Hare was coming round. He gingerly raised his head from the dirt. She was screaming, the syringe she tried to plunge into him was in her own neck. Her turn to go down. Lying on the path, her black cape tangled about her. She looked like a witch having crash landed on her broomstick. Her three-peaked biretta hat, crumpled, blowing across the path onto the grass stopped at a gravestone. His eyes were drawn to it. His vision tunneled from whatever had been put into his body. He got himself up and went over to the grave. A small half stone of granite was pushed over into the earth where it had been recently set, A carved icon of the Star of David at its head had been sprayed in red paint. The flag. Furled from having blown from the gravestone it had been deliberately placed. A swastika. He picked it up. A name had been screen printed in the corner. RIP Hamilton Weinberg.

A shekel for saving your life this one time, Charlie, eh.

The voice rang from inside his head. He took a breath, elevatoring the granite stone from the soft earth he hurled it against a large rock lying close by, smashing it into pieces, then collapsed once again, this time into an open grave.

*

He was glad to be out of hospital. The attack on him in the cemetery was incidental against seeing Fitch's name and his religion desecrated in the manner it had. If ever he needed a drink, this was the time. He was going to have to call him in the morning.

He had no sooner sat himself down in his office than his printer demanded attention. He put in the codes to activate it. Whirling into life. It was from Ronstandt. Taking the A4 pages out he checked the date and time. This day. 13.35.

> For the attention of FBI agent, Mr. Charlie O'Hare:
>
> A woman going under the name of Bathilda Van Dijk has slipped through Berlin's passport control using fake documents. CCTV has identified her as Stasi agent Karla Kia wanted in Europe and the USA, her destination currently unknown.

An addendum had been added. 14.04:

> The woman in question entered America as a female priest. Current location missing.

Ronstandt had tagged further information for others as well as his own departments. 14.06:

> For the Attention of:
>
> Homeland Security and Counterterrorism (Section CIA), Jean Ronstandt; National Security Advisor to the Vice President, Abisai Campbell; and Director for Counterterrorism, Isabella Buck.

He had never heard of the woman before. Bathilda Van Dijk was not a name easily forgotten. For sure, she was no Mary Poppins. Such a woman's presence in the States was not for anybody's health if her curriculum vitae was anything to go by.

He looked at his watch. She entered the country one day before he came to Green-Wood. Was his attacker in the cemetery Van Dijk? He shook his head. No, too much of a coincidence. He was being delusional.

Delusional or not, the body of the witch attacking him, was not found, alive or dead. What he did have though, was somebody's drying blood and skin under his fingernails. To his mind, his grapnels could do with the attention of a forensic laboratory before he ate his next meal.

WOODEN INDIAN COFFEECO

‘WELL. YOU SENT ME ON A RIGHT FOOLS ERRAND.’ Fitch said to O’Hare in the Wooden Indian CoffeeCo close by his offices of the *New York Post* on 32nd Street. ‘Returned for another basin of tsuris, have you?’

O’Hare shuddered.

‘Finding you at the bottom of a freshly dug grave was lucky for you, not me. It wasn’t my grave, my headstone. As for the Star of David being decorated with red paint, the artist hoping to send me into fits of despair, forget it,’ Fitch said.

‘Hatred poured on you for thousands of years is not the same directed against you family over two generations.’

‘What would you have me do with half my family being murdered by these people, hide under a stone. Stones are for the scum of this world to crawl under.’ He took a mouthful of coffee and looked up at black clouds looming overhead. ‘Rain, methinks. You shuddered.’

‘Because someone walked over my grave, not yours. Anyway . . . this tsuris of yours, what’s it taste of?’

‘What does trouble generally taste of? Shit, what else. Let’s get back to you though. Did they find out what you’d been pumped up with?’

O'Hare wished he hadn't asked the question. To say it was embarrassing was to be an understatement. 'A solution of cyanide and human semen. Fortunately, the witch putting me in hospital had not managed to get it all into me. I gave her a dose. The mix I mean, not the pox. She went off screaming. By the time the cyanide had taken effect I finished up where you found me.'

'Whose semen?'

'Animal. A donkey's by all account. Did you say they didn't find the woman?'

'Only you in a grave. You must have imagined her.'

'I didn't spend three weeks recovering from imaginary donkey sperm laced with poison, Hamilton.'

'No, of course you didn't. It's cyanide effecting your ability to separate fact from fiction.'

'Not to mention the donkey. NYPD carried out a thorough search of the cemetery. All they found was a nun's habit. After she attacked me; after I turned the tables on her, she went off screaming. A third of the syringe put me on my back close to death. She took two thirds. Ordinarily a lethal dose. She must have died where she fell. No question.'

'Her body must have been removed by those that sent her.' Fitch paused. O'Hare had feigned death, perhaps she had done the same. 'Staying in Ireland would have been a better option for you. At least until all this had blown over.'

O'Hare shrugged. 'I would have loved to have stayed among family, although, what I brought to their door hadn't made my welcome long-lasting. Who removed it . . . ? For I couldn't stay there forever. I was ordered to arrest Hess and bring him home.'

Fitch tried to conjure possible suspects being paid to keep schtum. 'Graveyard staff?'

'Not likely is it? Anyway, apart from donkey sperm swimming around me bloodstream there's other feelings in me water. . . . Frederik Spannocs swimming upstream alongside of them.'

'Another coffee?'

He looked down at the half empty cup, it had gone cold. 'Same, Americano.' Fitch looked around for the waiter. 'And a whiskey top up.'

'Surely he's dead.'

'From dust come forth Ahriman, host of Kriemhild.'

The waiter brought out a tray with two more coffees and a whiskey on a paper doily. O'Hare tipped the whiskey into the coffee, took a sip. He pulled a face.

'Not enough sugar?'

'Not enough malt. His influence is in her now. She's the granddaughter of the Nazi aristocrat, Prince Artur Kriemhild of Prussia, how much further from a tree can an apple fall. She's an ideal subject for his plans.'

'If she's been infected she'll rot on the ground,' Fitch said.

'Your faith is stronger than mine, Hamilton.'

'And why shouldn't it be, it's been around a lot longer than Catholicism.'

O'Hare left Starbucks leaving Fitch to pick up the tab for two coffees, a Danish pastry, a whiskey. He wondered how long it had taken the Honorary FBI agent to have come around to it. Detective! Took his time. Question. How was he to play out the game if what he said about Kriemhild were true. She was already controlling a vast network of disinformation in America and Europe. Who was going to listen to him? She was stirring up trouble to start a war. East on West. This was a new world order with intentions of crushing democracy in its wake. Who was to back down? Call her bluff? No President Henry Clancy Montgomery III in the chair this time, a president too ill to do the business, his vice, seemingly not noticing.

SENTINEL MOTHER RESPONDS

ATLANTIC OCEAN | 40°00'00.0"N 50°00'00.0"W.

SENTINEL MASTER–EVT sought direction from Sentinel Mother as to how they found a way round the force field of water containing them. The automated artificial reply returned.

TIME LAPSED INFERIOR HUMAN RACE OCCUPYING EARTH CONSIDERED EXPENDABLE | CREATION BLUEPRINT TIME–VERSE NO LONGER VALID | TIME–PORTALS GENERATED HELD IN PLACE AT STRATEGIC POINTS ON EARTH FOR FULL INVASION | OCCUPATION IMMINENT | CREATION BLUEPRINT PROGRAM INVALID BEYOND GENESIS | –EVT CHRIIKUN EXPENDABLE.

SENTINEL MASTER questioned SENTINEL MOTHER whether Creation Blueprint was any longer required. The alternative for earth invasion, its occupation and ultimate destruction of the human race in this place made no ethical sense to it. The biological DNA consistence of their make-up was one per cent homo sapiens accounting for this ethic. There was also the consideration of transferring their entire race of three billion ExtraVerseTerrestrials out of one Time–Verse into another. One had never been tested. The virus program once installed and activated, if SENTINEL MASTER–EVT was up to date with the laws of Time and Physics their entire race was about to implode, one after the other, unable to stop themselves following the one before them.

If those laws were wrong, and they were to survive, there was another consideration. Engaging the human race as they came through their Time–Portals; coming under an attack from a race preferring death over slavery was a confrontation too far. For evidence was showing earth humans were not as inferior as they first thought. They had technology to destroy our Time–Portals.

SENTINEL MASTER–EVT bypassed SENTINEL MOTHER informing SENTINEL–MASTER COMMANDER SYSTEM an alien myth had infiltrated SENTINEL MOTHER data with an automated artificial code and was to be deleted.

FITCH GETS A WARNING

THE ENVELOPE BROWN AND DUSTY was delivered by hand. Finding its way into his regular mail bundle he tore it open and began reading,

> Hamilton (Weinberg) Fitch the Jew. Sarah Gold the Jew
> wife of Frank Weinberg the Jew. Yes we know all your
> histories. You can hide but we shall find and kill you all.
> Soon the name of Weinberg will be as dust on the land.
> Grandmother and grandson to go. Love to the children.
> Onemo.

He'd had threats before, critics of his editorial articles in the main, with the occasional bile as to Israel's occupation of the Left Bank. He was not an Israeli, none of which seemed to matter to his critics. Despite his views as to what was going on in those lands, he didn't necessarily subscribe to his chosen people. He was an American following Judaism when he had time, that's it. In all other aspects he considered himself a regular guy seeing pedophilia as an abhorrence to both man and God, the subject of editorials, as and when such cases presented themselves, as national news. The letter hit him where it hurt.

Qnemo. He'd heard of their reputation for ballot box threats during American elections. Threats to electoral officers and those casting votes was not new. America was after all vast. States a long way from Washington, having their share of insularity and parochialism from certain quarters in small towns, directed at races and creeds outside of their understanding, was the expected norm. Different this time. The mention of his family, the history of his grandfather and grandmother with a passing reference to children, added to one thing. They had either always had information to hand or, the reference to children in the same content as his family suggested, they had been infiltrated by the Order. Easily confirmed. Charlie O'Hare and Annie Carter had similar threats. Despite them being two-third Catholic, all three of them were instrumental in bringing down Frederik Spannocs and the Order first time around, preventing world war three.

He looked down the open plan office at the numerous desks of sub editors. Some working on hard paper editions of the *Post*, others, the paper's beta testing online edition; no doubt at the same time prophesizing the future for newspapers and journalism. Of course, there had been a whole heap of new faces since Max Stenna was promoted to CEO of Media Group Newspapers. A good move for both of them as it turned out. He was appointed the editor-in-chief as consolation prize, as he saw it.

He had a team of hardened people the likes of Mike Crawford, Johnny Bingham, Heinz Oakley (he finally gave up smoking), and Dave Davidson. All people he had known and worked with for years still with him.

He put his head in his hands throwing the letter down,

looked towards the acoustic proof ceiling of the *Post*'s open plan offices. He needed to contact the police, Charlie . . . then Annie Carter.

Mike Crawford watched him throw a letter down on his desk. He saw the expression on his face. One brought on after reading its unpalatable content meant one of two reasons. A close family member had died, or Stenna had sacked him. The latter being extremely unlikely, could only mean the other. Or something else. He got up from his desk, came across to his office and knocked on the glass partition.

'What is it?'

There had been no need for Fitch to give a verbal invitation, for a tap on the glass was sufficient for any of them to speak with him without the formality of waiting. As it was, he was the other side of his desk when he asked the question.

'Bad news, Ham?' Crawford said as his phone rang. Fitch passed him the note he had already taken on board. Annoyed with the interruption of an unwelcome ring call he angrily elevatored the phone.

'What? . . . Synagogue. . . . A fire-bomb? Of course I know where it is— Who is this?'

Without warning, Fitch got up from his desk sending his chair wheeling backwards into a filing cabinet. He grabbed his jacket off the floor and went out of the door into the corridor toward the elevators.

Crawford stood with his mouth open. His boss was clearly upset by what had been said to him on the phone. He opted to go after him. He was too late. He got to the elevator, but Fitch was gone. The indicator board was displaying one on its way down. He pressed the button and waited. It needed to get to the first floor and let him out before coming back up. He began reading the note, quickly scanning it until he reached the signature at the bottom. The two of them had been through this before, as had Davidson, Bingham . . . and Oakley.

Dé·jà *fucking* vu, or what? He hammered at the call button until it pinged the floor. Recalling Fitch's reference to knowing where it was, Crawford likely guessed the subject of the conversation was the David Ben-Gurion Free Synagogue, no more than half a mile away from the *Post*'s offices. The synagogue he took his grandmother on the Sabbath. Taking her in her wheelchair from the care home close by. Although today was not Saturday. Made no difference. Fitch finding himself in a life-threatening encounter without thinking of his own good health would go for it. Typical of the man. He ran. Fitch had a two-minute start on him. He ran faster. With any kind of luck he would catch up with him before he did anything stupid. Seeing the synagogue was as far as he got before it was swallowed in a mist. An explosion from inside the building had taken the door out and onto the street in a cloud of smoke and dust. He watched as Fitch went through the gap where the door had been; the glass windows above were cascading down over him.

'HAM!' Crawford shouted out his name into the building. He couldn't see him. Smoke and dust was everywhere. 'HAM! Get out of there. There's another rigged—'

The warning no sooner out of his mouth than the building shook. What was left of the windows became rectangles of brickwork, plain and simple. Fitch staggered toward him clutched his neck and shoulders. Blood poured from his head down his face into his eyes, misted where he was going for any attempt for rescue of anyone still alive.

'Fuck-a-rubber-duck.'

'Never mind rubber ducks, Ham. See that wiring, its running to another bomb that hasn't gone off, yet.'

'Gotta go in. There's people still alive.' He pulled himself away from Crawford's attempts to restrain and help him then re-entered the building.

Crawford went in. Whether it was to get him out, or to help out, he couldn't be sure of his motives. Whatever it was, he didn't have time to argue or think about his actions. He followed him in.

Fitch was in the temple now. What he saw was utter devastation. Furniture in the prayer room was splintered and blown against the wall. The Ark, along with the Torah scrolls and the Menorah, tangled together, were spread across the floor. By a miracle the synagogue's Ner Tamid was still hanging in place from the ceiling, though no longer shining its light. Fitch hurried along the remains of seats looking for bodies. Fortunately it wasn't the Sabbath. Except. He heard moans of anguish between bouts of coughing. He'd know that cough anywhere. He went through a curtain of dust, Rabbi Isaac Jehiel, was lying under one of the seats struggling to get up from under a pile of plaster no longer iced to the ceiling. The Rabbi was blast-burned and covered in blood. Fitch pulled the long bench seat partially trapping him away.

'Who did this, Yimakh shemo?' the Rabbi asked, then seeing him said, 'Hamilton Weinberg. In the flesh. Listen. I've a great story for your evening edition, son.'

Crawford helped him get the Rabbi out onto the street.

Wailing of sirens and screeching from emergency vehicles came into the area. The Rabbi dazed, muttered all manner of obscenities he would not have expected from a holy man. A second bomb still wired up, had mercifully not gone up.

'It's not *his* name needed to be erased, Isaac. It's *theirs*. This is the work of the Order of the Most Divine Third Circle. They came for me, and you're collateral damage.'

KRIEMHILD CONTESTS AHRIMAN

How you are fallen from
heaven, O day-star, son of the
morning! how you are cut
down to the ground, did lay low
the nations
ISAIAH 14:12.

'BE CAREFUL WHAT YOU WISH FOR, QUEENNIE, for this is no highway to Damascus. Your Nazi bloodline may qualify you, but you are not yet close enough for my designs. Four Quarters are my deception road, with no return ticket for failure. Your dreams. Faded on the journey, never to be replaced on awakening. All die.'

She shrugged the notion away.

'So death is not your fear. Let me tell you this then. Death comes in two forms.'

Her lips shaped arrogance.

'No, I wasn't expecting you to understand the concept. The hope is you won't have to. Having said, you will be in scarce company. The company of loners, a totality of darkness and sound. Alone. A lonesomeness of a billion years. Each one a division of a thousand, leading to the heat death of the universe. Unseen advancements of creation's equation will turn man to superman. Only one will go into the dark arena to reemerge with a new set of rules. An equation only One knows. All remaining perish. You seem unprepared for what I am offering.'

'What was the second form?'

'You've just had it.'

The penny dropped. She was having imaginary conversational threats with herself. Dark loneliness devoid of sound? Death? Ja, genau. Neither were his game. As for the power to carry them forward, this myth, suffering delusions of adequacy were matched only by his poor judgement in thinking auto suggestion would work on her. She had breeding. A Nazi bloodline, one he was quick to point out, anyone could have researched and discovered about her. As for smoke-mirroring a medieval costume, any second-rate stage magician, with a flourish and a round of applause, was capable.

'And your bollocks, did those come in a cloud of smoke, too?'

Ahriman was no longer in a mood for mortal fun or feeble ambition. If she couldn't take it, there were plenty more arseholes to choose from. For Ahriman demanded souls plucked clean of any saving graces they possessed for their wishes. His bidding came without question or mercy. For God's blueprint for creation was all that mattered to him. The meddling of human beings allowing Spannocs, whose time on earth was well past its sell-by-date when he became dust, needed him to begin again where he had failed. An ending satisfying both him and a God wearied from man's thousand-year interpretive incarceration of his alter ego, Satan-Ahriman. For why else had He released him if not for a final solution? God was in His corner now. On a rack of His own making.

Kriemhild ran through corridors knocking into her people in the course of their business. Passing air conditioning units, only stopping when she stepped into the organization's World Operations Center. She gathered her breath. This was insane. She was running from a shadow. An incorporeal abstract. She tried to come to terms with her body having been taken over by an invasive entity. Losing control of her being, she had not expected it to be this way.

An engineer approached her. He was wearing the Order's designer blue coveralls, the logo of the Order machined in colored gold threads over the breast pocket. The name of his department above it told her he was Program Development. Chinese. She didn't know his name. It was not important.

Her hands flat up against one of the castle's whitewashed walls, she was trying to compose herself. He asked if he could help. She ignored him and ran to the steel door in the next section. The large room on the other side carried the Order's ears into the United States and Europe on one side, computer systems programed for face recognition on the other. Automatic scamming computers humming, the heat coming off them was of hot rubber and dust. This was where the hacking into the United States driving license offices were kept and for the time, were the end of the road for her, for work was being carried out at the far end blocking access through. She needed to go back if she was to escape the shadow.

She reasoned. Wasn't she, Nazi queen of a Fourth Reich? She elevatored her chin. An air of arrogant superiority washed over her. She turned and calmly returned the way she had come. The shadow of whatever was following, now lost in a world of a thousand pulsing lights from network servers continually changing colors. She felt safe as she re-entered the section she had come. The Program Development engineer was still there. He had switched the lights down to enable him to identify faults. On his knees, his head inside a server cabinet he had open for routine maintenance.

The shadow was upon her once more.

She pulled her luger from her belt, shot him. The Program Development engineer fell backward from the server access compartment dead. The shadow gone now; she replaced the pistol in its holster. Crossing to a telephone on the wall she picked it up. A security voice answered. She called for the body to be removed from section W12. A second call for assistance. A change of mind. Not made. The darkness of the shadow returning. She pulled the pistol from its holster and run in the direction of her office. Slamming shut a riveted steel door behind her, through into the entrance to another section, finding it unfamiliar. She pulled the heavy bolts operating its locking system down. Five bolts locked in. She looked around. A dim half-light was glowing in the distance. Coming through a solid iron door, the shadow was once more with her. She turned and voluntarily walked into the dark with no further fear.

The light came. A blinder, stronger than the sun. She was in a world of myth and legend once more. Hell. For if she thought differently than where she was, having all will and manual dexterity taken from her body, where she was now, if not in that place. Were these images and shadows the consequence of electrical discharges, microwaves, from the equipment surrounding her?

Creatures banned from the eyes of humans. Distorted, mangled and half-finished detritus of forms short of natural development, in a swirling mass of dark matter from a billion years in the past told to her. An alien world of creatures preparing to occupy space the earth and universe offered only to fail. Life and spirits forming becoming armies of screaming souls occupied the dimension. The sounds of misery, conflict survival, evolution of non-human mutations becoming extinct before their time, leaving only flesh of man to become the supreme primage of His creation. The beginnings of bio configuration enabling natural brain development of the human race, eventually leading through evolution to the widening of a female primate's pelvis to allow her offspring with its enlarged brain to pass through.

A lower degree of development of the brain at birth to be followed by a longer period of extra-uterine maturation never occurring again in nature, eventually leading man to his own extinction screwing up his first- and only-time opportunity for life. A one-shot chance for the human race never to be replicated.

The sound from their voices with no other evidence they had been there to diminish to the end of time and the universe, there to engage with the choir of all those gone before then left . . . what four, three, two. A God no longer with His plan, and Satan to create his version of a universe. And she . . . no longer human . . . the recipient of the gift of corporealism. A curse of immortality.

The shadow was enlightenment. Not of salvation, though.

She succumbed to her situation sooner than Ahriman had predicted. The shit stayed within her, as did her nausea, finding herself in the company of demons with class. Ancestral aspirations flowed through her. She was to be the queen of a domain she had been witness; one promising life everlasting. Her bloodline, an assurance she was the right side of evolution. Her Nazi ancestors not despised, as they had been in the world of flesh. An obsequiousness surrounding them, never envisaged in a world where man, tempered by false myth of what was right; what was wrong, left confused.

She felt a power and a glory thrust upon her. One no crown on earth matched any of the Divine's servants. Satan's alone.

Do not put the Lord God to the test in my company,
all remained before her anointment. One of human faith to Him. Her mind took the counter argument, had she been in the company of a magician, a liar, a master deceiver even. She had him where she wanted. The power within merely reinforced itself. She tested. How she would test!

Van Dijk plunged the syringe into the stranger's neck.

Standing over her. A face, a man, different. She was aware he was floating in the air looking down on her. There was another. A girl. Stupid. She gave the impression of being an angel. A tall woman, with vast wings powerfully connected to broad smooth shoulders, never realized before they were those she subliminally fantasized over. The angel wept. One of her wings severed was hanging awkwardly from her shoulder. The blood from the rent of her wing ran down her arm leaving a stain on the ground quickly evaporated. At first thinking it was her own taken from her bare back by Van Dijk, screaming for the whip to be laid harder in her masochistic ecstasy. All she had, apart from her sexual climax, were weal's from the strapping. A quiet voice whispered in her head,

You're in the company of princes. You have chosen wisely. Your lover's resurrection proof of my powers.

She opened her eyes. The shadow was no longer there. All remaining, a mythical number in her head. A worm living within her for an eternity; took with her into a bottomless pit for a thousand years before releasing an accepted realization. A wormhole in Space–Time forced to enter. A respite for the unforgiven going before, one relishing human suffering for its own sake, enriching without any understanding, enhancing an evil of his choosing. For he was spirit made from dust of the universe. His survival depended for flesh; while He was fast losing ground for as long as His blueprint for creation remained on earth for others to duplicate; lost by the Divine Spirit while He was about other business, no longer in reach.

She asked who he was?

Ahriman.

He asked who she was?

Your soul, within the body of Elke Kriemhild, Queen of the Universe.

She asked of Another? A tortured reply returned,

He is of no consequence.

*

Her established teachings in the subject came to her as being one-sided. If God created Satan with good will and good desires, it is unclear where his evil impulse to sin arose, she reasoned on more than one occasion. The sin within Satan, took root in God's failure to rein him in. In which case God, and not Satan was to blame for his evil. A consequence of oversight? One, Satan was not responsible.

She had God's failings coursing through her veins. They would reinforce his hold over her.

She tested the theory to its ultimate destruction. For she was indoctrinated into a realm, taken back all remaining holy lose change clinking around in her soul, putting it into her penny jar. Tickets available for small change. The price for admission.

Scanning recommended automatically without SENTINEL MOTHER authorization. SENTINEL–MASTER SYSTEM picked up a signal downloaded it to –EVT CHRIIKUN. Labeled earth. The screen showed a file picture program of a MYTH with the earth name, ELK KRIEM in possession of the blueprint. An alien, morphed into a strange MYTH status. The MYTH's location given in the known physics of Space–Time using one temporal and three spatial coordinates giving two events was clear. The four-dimensional coordinated system readout gave locations above them, specifically Eduard Kerschbaumer und Bier in Queens in another place. –EVT CHRIIKUN went into stand-by mode ready to be released from the Sphere of water holding them suspended.

VAN DIJK ATTEMPTS TO KILL HESS

HESS WAS SITTING IN FAT FRANK'S EATERY on Desbrosses Street, close by Suicide Curve, a section of Manhattan's elevated train system located at West 110th Street. A terrifying amusement ride earning its name not so much from the number of trains coming off its rails falling onto the street below, more the number of people who leapt to their deaths from it. The café waitress, a woman in her fifties, with short curly blonde hair wearing a white shirt with a black waistcoat over topped off with a red bowtie, served coffee to him. He nodded by way of thanks. She didn't smile. Her pay wouldn't have been enough, he thought. He emptied four paper rolls of Muscovado sugar into his carton cup of coffee stirring them in. He thought about those paychecks plopping into his bank on a monthly basis being looked into by O'Hare and Ronstandt. They came through an intermediary company called Ignis, which, amazingly, no one seemed to have heard of. His regular donations since being seconded out of the army from killing duties, before taking up other killing duties elsewhere, were technically nothing to do with anyone but himself and those paymasters overseeing them. And he wasn't going to tell them. The shadowy department of the CIA retaining him for duties as and when, he guessed without knowing for sure, was the same excuse for a fiddle-fuckin' law agency O'Hare belonged, held him on their books. East is East, West is West; never the twain shall meet. Except we do, without knowing any allegiance.

Assuming they didn't decide he'd been paid without their realizing, wanting the money returned, he reckoned on keeping his mouth well and truly closed. Act dumb. For he'd earned his thirty pieces of silver the hard way, no point putting one's head over the parapet. Of course he'd've done a lot better had he been paid the fifty thousand dollars fulfilling Kriemhild's contract. Paid twice for the same goods, kiss goodbye to both for now, at least. He had no intention for seeking compensation expenses for failure from her. He was good as a professional killer, not so talking himself out of a situation surrounded by her heavies. She and the Order were bad news for all concerned. Of course him being alive wasn't going to stop those same dogs out looking for him. He would also have to bear being scapegoat for the death of her niece, Roisin. Family would not have gone down well in that quarter. Or was she her daughter? He laughed. Convincing her the other Kriemhild had been torn to shreds by an alien, her death having nothing to do with him, would spare him nothing.

Hmm. An alien. Reported in the news as being a Sci-Fi film. A Stay-Puft Marshmallow Man of sorts, stunted at a German embassy. *Hmm.* So they said. Another one for Charlie with his FBI honorarium. Wonder what he had to say about it.

'Get you another?'

He looked up at the waitress and nodded. He had drunk the first cup in record time without thinking, her standing over him, reckoned his sitting at the table was passed customer availability slot, where he should've ordered another, or to put it into plainer vernacular, time you fucked off, sir. We've got people waiting for a table.

'And one of your apple turnovers,' he shouted over to her as she walked away.

'Yes. Sir.'

An acknowledgement to grind stone if you like. When his second cup arrived, along with the apple pastry, she smiled at him,

'Enjoy.'

He smiled back as genuinely as he was able. She was returning to the inside of the café as he was about to take his first bite when a hand clamped around his wrist twisting it sideways causing him to drop dripping apple onto the plate.

'I wouldn't eat that if I was you, Coxly old son.'

'O'Hare!'

He turned away from him at the sound of an engine revving up. A big one. A throaty sounder. His service waitress was getting onto the back of a motor bike. A curly wig thrown to the ground revealed true blonde flaxen hair under. She was not the woman in her fifties he had first taken her for. He quickly stood up to see rider and pillion turning left away from Suicide Curve. 'What in fuck's name . . . ? O'Hare?'

O'Hare took his plate throwing the apple pastry on it out onto the sidewalk. A pigeon swooped in to take it up. 'Watch'. Lift-off. The bird dropped from the air back onto the sidewalk dead from an ingredient not included from the pastry chef's recipe.

Hess instinctively went to his shoulder holster before

realizing Ronstandt had relieved him of it at Fort Hamilton. He'd forgotten to collect another from the armory when he was picked up. He opened both hands palm up to him in surrender.

'How many times do I have to save your life before you give up trying to kill me off? Come on. You don't want to eat here, too much fat, bad for your health. Now you do owe me my life.'

'Charlie O'Hare,' Hess said. 'As I live and breathe, who's the broad you brought along?'

'Err . . . Err. The Wicked Witch of the West from Salem? Can I get you a date?'

SPIRITS ARE NOT ABOVE WORRYING

THE MORTALITY of any remaining in her was partial. For her mental processes were being pulled by more than Ahriman here. She looked at herself in the full-length mirror somewhere, praying she could return to full humanity once more. Ahriman was no longer needed by her. He was a sham. She needed to concentrate her mind if she was to return to human reality. He had ignored her basic human need despite his promises. Was this her price to pay. Alone in the robes of coronation. Tears of misgivings about what she had allowed to happen to her rolled down her cheeks red, marking them before repairing as they went. He had cautioned her from the very beginning of the path she was to tread, her overriding ambitions for a thousand-year Reich had driven her to him. And now, it looked as though she might just have found a road back. For those forces ever as powerful as Ahriman's were enveloping her. Where they emanated she had no idea; nor would she concern herself, for she could see a way to turn the tables on him.

Ahriman rancored with this 'Queen of the Universe', an

apparent consequence of his previous pretender, an upstart, 'Prince of Darkness' attempting reincarnation, a come-back kid, had to be him. Creating nuisance for the destruction of His self-created universe for the promises he had made her and her followers, and what she called herself,

Tausendjähriges Reich.

Well think again Queenie, his was to last considerably longer than those of any predecessors' war-like thousand years, whether Holy Roman Empire or a Third Reich ambition. His were an eternity. A new universe sans God. Set in stone. For the coded data for creation, only deliverable from human form to spirit, was slipping from him due to this copycat 'Prince of Darkness'.

The man known on earth as Frederik Spannocs', meddlesomeness with his Queen would interfere with plans to deny the existence of God and His truth. His architectural stones crushed, the matrix for another's creation abolishing His for all of time. He would return to the desert and give the pretender a good kicking with a permeance he will remember. Forever and Ever. Ɐɯǝu.

Kriemhild had been betrayed in the worst of all possible ways. For standing alongside of her was the reflected image of her lover Bathilda as a dark shadow, one she was not permitted to see clearly. Words not spoken,

You are deceived. You are not the first of His creations to take him into your body. Death will follow you to eternity for what you have allowed.

Ahriman countered,

You are of my same creation.

As if to underline his deception, the dark shadow replied,

The 1 000-year Reich he promised, an anathema to you and all who follow; not his to deliver.

Ahriman replied, as a voice, laughing,

Your God Creator is no longer here to alter my agenda.

Ahriman's assured mirth went through Kriemhild as a bad joke.

He is always with you, as He is all others of His creation.

The thought transference of the dark shadow to underline God's authority.

I am Satan, Ahriman, Brahm-Kaal, Shaitan. I am all. I am alone on earth. From going to and fro and from walking up and down in it, I have the Creator's permission.

The dark shadow considered this lie, then spoke audibly for Kriemhild to hear,

He possesses none of those titles. She returned to Kriemhild. *You are of His same creation; He is both our Creator.* She looked to him. *You are none of those names, for they are, as the name, Lucifer, sprung forth from fable tellers.*

Ahriman considered the dark shadow's estimation of him.

Scribes and tellers? Not yours? Lies and deceptions from your Creator, implanted in the brains of primates since dawn of time of His so-called almighty works. You cannot have it both ways, shadow. And now, you stand alone . . .

Ahriman was in the promised land of Moses. The shadow of Mount Nemo over him,

You know I have His consent for being among men. I am tired of repeating myself, for He is gone. His data, obsolete.

She stood before him at the Land of Canaan. He knew the document he had faked was for God to witness.

Tire yourself to eternity then. If He has departed, it is of no consequence, for the sufferance of the wrath of His Divine Trinity will always remain to destroy followers of your magik. Not His.

Satan felt the depth of the angel's words echo through the darkness of eternity through Ahriman. The closeness of threats was not unknown from past encounters. He had never spoken truth, only recognizing it when it was voiced by others. She had slew him once before, not permanently for permission had not been given then, neither sought by the angel now. Without Him being a part of the universe it would implode. The balance between good and evil was essentially maintained between His world and Man's.

The Divine Spirit he feared most. For he worked within different parameters. And like him, a fallen maverick. While his own universe of influence was limited to man's world, when it came to Divine Spirit, he was untouchable. For the Divine Trinity was within Him, as Ahriman was part of him. The conflicting trinities of Father, Son and Divine Spirit; juxtaposed equally with Satan, Antichrist, and the False Prophet part of the same program. For his part, called on as false prophet as and when needed to challenge faith. *Hah!* Was implanted faith in man any better than his world of deception when it came to job description? He considered not.

As Spannocs before her, Kriemhild one in a line of His current challenges. Her ability to obtain the data for creation from the original organization of the Order of the Most Divine Third Circle considered themselves having biblical connections with God Himself was paramount in the faith game. Founded on the visit to earth of the Divine Spirit seen at

Christ's Crucifixion. *Hah!* Another of His challenges into the world of faith he was forced to take part. Where creation for a new universe came naturally for the taking from Him, pushed boundaries, chancing man's disbelief in Him to the very limit. Hah! An Achillies heel if you like. A crack for him to gain permeance. A chink in His armor pushing their relationship boundary over the edge with him for good and all of time. God's intention for temptations of man using him as the conduit will not be guaranteed forever. His final decision; the experiment run its course will bring closure for all, man and spirit, when He makes a final coming, one breaking His promise,

No man shall look upon my face, and live,
a condition for man's eternal life blown away, the shadows of all angels fading as a world war, currently held in abeyance, brings on closure of one universe, heralding on another for his program.

If you are all spoken out, Ahriman; with all your powers you profess to have, then restore to me the ability to fuck another human being once again, before it's too late.

Direktorin Elke Kriemhild saw herself, earth Queen of the Universe, the New World Order and the advancement of the Reichsbürger Movement. Her resolve to obtain the data for creation unquenched. Creative in her ambitions. Her betrayers came to her as they hadn't to any predecessors' before. She had it in her power to go after the man preventing the Order's re-possession of the blueprint for creation. Those working for the Order and the US Government exposed. Their names highlighted to her from a marquee scroller down a computer screen. People she had trusted. Those close colleagues working out of Malaka's Corner; occasionally Drogstadt Castle. People her predecessor did not realize were working against the Order right under their noses. Nathaniel Johnson. Tom Dorcas: a $1000 suited, clean cut, clean shaven, smelling as the inside of a prostitute's handbag the little shit was. Then she saw Corrine Diaz's name appear. She looked closer. Real name Madeleine Tubman, CIA Intelligence Analyst. Even Kerstin Hartmann. She called security telling them to work on Johnson first, reveal names from him of everyone working within the Order at Malaka's Corner.

She was close to their ambitions. She had countries willing. With the wealth the Order accumulated, pariah states not holding a tenth, enlisting oppressed people to their deaths for an outcome favoring their leaders.

Ahriman believes he's getting access to what's on those hard drives. A ghost! A myth thinking, he's Satan, has yet to cotton on to the fact he cannot work in the world of living entities. The files for creation came from the spirit world; and the material world is not symbiotic to it. For we and man's creations are Promethean. Ahriman has overlooked fact. He will reach out to take it, only finding it running as sand from a clenched hand. She had deceived him. For she had both Ahriman's power and glory now. And . . . she could fuck once more.

FREEING JOHNSON AND TUBMAN

NATHANIEL JOHNSON WAS OVERCOME in the basement office he had occupied for the better part of half a century. He had fought Kriemhild's security thugs poorly, for they were younger and more powerful than him. Twenty years ago, a different story. He shrugged at his memories. It would have been them pleading for mercy. Kriemhild was in Bavaria. He guessed they had been given their orders on how to deal with the man betraying her while she was out of the country. Stripped naked and tied to a chair with wet ropes he instinctively knew his time was up. He couldn't be sure of any true outcome, for he was an immortal as O'Hare. Possessed of an immortality unable to naturally die. What was concerning him was the manner of his killing. Unlike Frederik Spannocs the Goat, the previous incumbent in charge of the zoo, her cruelty was legendary. As were the records Kriemhild held on him. . . .

> Curriculum vitae: Clown, First Congener, Operational
> Mastermind within the Order of the Most Divine Third
> Circle; Head of Special Surveillance Operations under J.
> Edgar Hoover, Director of the Bureau of Investigation; also
> known as Wharfmaster, Nathaniel Claypole; an all-round

. . . Pleas for mercy on the grounds he didn't mean any harm, contributed to her physical inability to hear what he had to say in mitigation not wanting to listen, about right.

He hadn't seen her too many times at Malaka's. On the one rare occasion he had he was outside smoking his curled pipe. She smiled. He knew it wasn't the practice of his habit she was smiling at but what she knew about him. He had been an FBI government informer with the Order in one form or other for over eighty years. Despite his appearance. Looked more fifty than a hundred. He was an immortal. He knew his employment with the Order, as his time on earth, was at termination point under Direktorin Elke Kriemhild.

He had been an informer since the 1920s when he was first employed as a long-deep mole with one of the government's Special Secret department's as it were known, for he never knew if it was FBI, CIA or a department from Mission Impossible. Although, when he had first applied, it was to the Department of Justice. He was a lawyer then. Still was, actually. They asked him if he would consider a position within the government's new legal team within the D of J. Working undercover while being a lawyer appealed to him and he accepted. Before he knew what was happening he found himself within the Bureau of Investigation through to a Special Branch of something or other, one of a circumlocution-pleonasm, or other mysterious outfit he could never be sure of. Being paid a decent salary he never asked for fear of his position being looked into before 'powers that be' deciding he should not be getting what he was, before demoting him out from whoever he was working for. When you're young, successfully remunerated for whatever you're there for, who questions?

What he did know was that he had worked for some damned unsavory people over the years while being undercover, Frederik Spannocs being not the least of them. He had had to turn the other way when it came to the organization's activities. Child exploitation bottom of the barrel. Frederik Spannocs started life as Marco Giuseppi. Of Italian stock. An immigrant from Sicily, useful with his fists, he had fought his way to taking over the union in one of New York's dockyards at the start of the first world war. The management were more concerned with keeping its union members working for them in check and order. Here he used intimidation and violence. Which was all well and good for there was a lot of it about them days, still is, becoming involved with what he had called the dark side of man. A crossing over. Not so much seeing the light, more the darkness, for he went on to encourage the corruption of others into child abuses and slavery. The money offered not only spoke but screamed. Blindness to this corruption went to the top of government. But for other reasons.

He had come across the name Charlie O'Hare then. A beat cop with the NYPD. O'Hare along with his boss, a lieutenant (his name escaped him), were determined to bust Giuseppi and his followers after the abduction of an infant girl from a mother of north-American origin and a Russian father from Alaska. For his part he was both obliged and ordered not to get involved despite his being a lawman. His job was to watch. Indeed, while being temporarily employed in the dockyard. His job was Wharfmaster, his undercover name, Nathaniel Claypole. He had a partner, Daniel Sullivan, Deputy Director of Special Surveillance. The darker side of their jobs was their early involvement with Marco Giuseppe and the Order itself, where he was known as the Clown; Sullivan: the Bloodhound. He shuddered over their other activities involving murder in the name of law.

Promoted Head of Special Surveillance, still keeping his undercover activities, he became mastermind and First Congener of the Order of the Most Divine Third Circle itself. Both he and Sullivan were partly responsible for the assassination by the shooting down of O'Hare's boss. Sullivan was to later get decapitated by a spring box put on his head, twisted his head from his body. A just end, for he was actually a double agent for the Order within the FBI.

His thumb burned like hell from the contraption that held it. The phalange seriously injured from the screw penetrating. He was to be left overnight with a promise they would be back the following morning to check it was still tight enough should it have come loose, his tormentors' parting shot. Through tears running from his eyes he said it really wouldn't be necessary. They shrugged their shoulders, as a thug of a man, staggered in carrying an acetylene bottle and torch over his shoulders dumping it down in the corner of his office, laughing. He guessed they had come over from Drogstadt with Kriemhild, for he didn't recognize any of them. Was the space going to be redesignated an auto repair shop he wondered? His thought was answered. 'For the morning, in the unlikely event you're still withholding information as to who's kosher and who's not working for our queen.'

Informers. They left. Trussed up like the fourth Thursday in November, Thanksgiving turkey, his thumb, ever unlikely to tamp tobacco down in the bowl of his pipe again, this was not looking good. It wasn't so much the thumb screw, painfully bad as it was, but the acetylene bottles they were going to use on him the following morning, the excruciating pain from the gas flames it would deliver to skin would be too much for him. Too much for anybody, really. He took the decision. Game over. For though he couldn't die, he could be killed. And an oxygen plus acetylene flame would be a ticket to hell. A suicide tablet in his desk drawer had to be the answer. The trick was to get himself over to the drawer it was in, take it from the matchbox, pop it in his mouth, then goodnight cruel world. Problem. Useless thumb and finger to get at it.

Half-conscious he was aware he was being taken out into the open air. Air wet from a rain storm he didn't have any clothes on. The rain hitting against his skin, was for the most part a blessed relief from the pain that should have left him by now. He was conscious a rope was being tied around his ankles. Then he was upside down, hanging from something. Swinging. A light from a concrete standard faded away. Thank God. Something good works around here. He then fell into an unconscious final stage before death.

Johnson failed to answer his phone that morning. Dorcas thought unusual. He called Diaz. Apparently there had been an emergency overnight after Kriemhild turned up at Malaka's Corner to process a member of her staff. A turn around in her plans. A terrorist attack in Europe she had in the planning, needing immediate attention back at Drogstadt Castle, being the reason. A helicopter arrived to collect her, and her professional team of thugs, to take them back overnight.

Hartmann sent her and Dorcas to Johnson's basement office to find the reason he wasn't answering his phone. Finding the door open, she went in followed by Dorcas. Johnson's desk drawer was smashed open on the floor, pipe, tobacco and matches were scattered all around as if he had wanted a quick smoke before leaving. Hurriedly. A no-time to pack a bag one. She would go outside, through the foyer entrance, past where Hazzan, not already arrived for duty yet jealously guarded a desk coffee machine. She suggested Dorcas stay where he was in case Johnson turned up unexpectedly.

He was more than willing to keep out of trouble for as long as possible. In a previous life, when he had tried to take over the Order himself, the memory still lingered of seeing one of his security people being subjected to a crown cap beer bottle being shoved up his caboose as an example to others with similar ambitions. The notion something more painful could be used to open a bottle, hard to imagine. Word was the man suffered sepsis after it severed a cluster of his hemorrhoids being forcibly extracted.

In morning half-light, she saw a body hanging upside down from one of the car park's light poles. Its energy-saving high intensity halide bulb beginning to dim as daylight luminosity increased. She had no doubt as to who it was.

Confirmed when she approached. Oh, my God. What've they done to you? Hanging, his wrists cable-tied together, a metal tube on each thumb with a wingnuts attached. Medieval, or what? She was going to have to get him down and for that she would need Dorcas's help.

Between herself and a reluctant Dorcas, they untied ropes and lowered him down, carried him back to his office. Laying him out on the floor among match sticks and his calabash pipe, she listened for signs of life, first at his mouth and then his chest. She wasn't sure. He was soaking wet, the color of his skin showed signs of exposure from being out in the night air, naked. She wrapped him in an old overcoat of his hanging from a nail on the back of his toilet door, if for no other reason, more to keep him warm than preserving dignity. She removed the contraptions split into the bones of both thumbs. Dark brown-bluish, red with dried blood from bruising, all remained after the wingnuts were released. All the time, Dorcas looked on with fear, a need to rid himself of this place and the Order showed in his face. She was in the same frame of mind. She wrinkled her nose. A smell. A faint whiff of almonds was in the air around him. Cyanide? She needed to let Hartmann know they had found him, dead.

Hartmann figured Johnson, informer or not, found dead on the premises would compromise Kriemhild's operation. She had to call Kriemhild. If it later turned-out Johnson was an informer, she would have to explain to her why she didn't know. Kriemhild was a shoot first ask after interrogator. Even so, she wouldn't want police looking into the death of one of her staff. Especially one the Order suspected of being an informer; likely bringing the roof down on their operation at Malaka's Corner for a second time. Hartmann asked Dorcas to get somebody in to see to it.

Dorcas let herself into the Order's armory with a key she had copied in the event of an emergency. Her imagination didn't have to wander too far into the future after they discovered she was an informer as well. Taking down two Glock automatics, one for her and one for Dorcas, she returned to Johnson's office. 'Here take this.'

Dorcas was shaking, crapping his pants. Suffering psychogenic pain from witnessing a bottle, crown metal cap attached, being inserted where the sun doesn't shine, was playing out in his mind. He took the Glock handed to him by Diaz, his brain temporarily too confused to argue, wondered how to use it and would they shoot back at him.

She would call a mortician. He was probably dead and if he wasn't then it wouldn't be long before he was. But first. She would risk calling up O'Hare, if she could remember how to operate the system. She went to the secret mail server. Well, not exactly secret, so much as concealed in plain sight. Inside an old Baby Daisy vacuum cleaner casing actually. She took the lid off, pulled out the manual keyboard attached, typed a message and waited. She didn't know where the other end went, prayed he was somewhere close to acting when he got it. As in yesterday, please. Five minutes' later, a whirr of clock wheels, springs and cogs along with a reply typed along a length of paper ascii tape. She read it. Picked up one of Johnson's red matches from the floor and scratched it down the wall. Set it alight. Held onto it until it was about to burn her hand dropped the charred remains onto the floor, scuffed it around with her shoe until it became one with the rest of the dust in this place.

He had sent a hearse. Probably as well for Johnson was clearly dead from his treatment. A black Mercedes van with matched colored tinted windows, its entry previously authorized by Hartmann came to the security cabin window at the entrance to Malaka's Corner. Stopped. A finger pointed directing the driver to where Nathaniel Johnson's basement office was. The Merc drove in parked outside where they were. The driver and his assistant got out. An older man with a young woman. They were wearing black suits, white shirts and black ties.

They came in. Dorcas panicked. Shaking, pointed the Glock occasionally between the man, the woman, herself and Johnson.

'Put the gun down, sonny, before you have an accident with it. I'm Tommy Scripps. This my daughter, Ella. And you are?'

'Corrine Diaz, and this is—'

The body of Nathaniel Johnson laid out on the floor, covered in an old overcoat, looked for all the world out of it, then stirred. His chest expanded as a much-needed breath of air went in. It was about to explode, then it expired and deflated with a cough; the other end of his body with a fart.

'I don't think so.' He smiled. 'You're Madeleine Tubman, assistant to CIA for Homeland Security and Counterterrorism; and you're out of here.' He turned to his daughter. 'See to Mr. Johnson, will you, Ella?'

TOMMY 'TRICKY' SCRIPPS AND DAUGHTER

'CYANIDE, FATHER. HIS BEING ALIVE IS AWKWARD. He needs hospital. Private mortuary ambulance, erring on the side of problem getting him out with those gorillas on the gate.'

'Getting him out . . . in that case—'

'Gladstone.'

Daniella had already sussed her father's intention. A man still alive. One the Order had apparently gone to a deal of trouble to murder, breathing, would be a giveaway. They were undertakers called in for purpose; not paramedics.

'Gladstone. You know where it is, Ella? While you're about it . . .'

'Pall bearers?'

Diaz was confused. What are they up to? Were they going to murder Johnson to get him out? What about me and Dorcas, were they intending to do the same to us? 'What's so special about Gladstone and pall bearers?'

'Haloperidol.'

'Haloperidol? Heard the name. Are you intending to finish what the Order started by murdering Johnson yourselves instead.'

Tommy Scripps had been down this road before, explaining the effect of this poison and how dangerous it was on the human body. Administering it to O'Hare was with consent of the man himself. In the case of Johnson no such consent could be given soberly. Or in any other way, to all intents and purposes he was out of this world. He was mindful Madeleine Tubman, an employee of the State Department, well aware of what her roles and responsibilities were when it comes to law. An explanation of what he was going to do could go one of two ways. If anything was to happen to Johnson the result of his actions would she prosecute on the grounds of human rights? And support from Charlie O'Hare couldn't be assumed. It would compromise the man's own beliefs for the sanctity of life if Johnson didn't respond. 'Intentionally? No, not if I can help it. Let me explain. It will leave him with a rigid body and limbs, loss of muscle control, a breathing rate close to zero, and no concept of what is going on around him. To the layman, he will be dead. An induced catalepsy. He won't suffer; he won't know a thing.'

'Oh, sure. The man tries to take himself out with a cyanide tablet; and you want to put him in a cataleptic state, possibly killing him in the process. You do know how old he is, don't you?'

'I know exactly how old he is. Not as old as Adam, granted. But ever so much as Charlie O'Hare, and he survived.'

'You gave it to him?'

'For his own survival. And I'll administer it to Johnson for his, if I'm to get him out of this hell hole. Dead, later resurrected.'

'I'm not sure about this.' He nodded understandably. 'Out

of curiosity, will he recover? How do you bring someone out of a . . . co—?'

'Catalepsy. It's not coma. Rapamycin. An eminent doctor specialist in its use, Hermenbergur Aloyious, will bring him back, as he did Charlie.'

Daniella took the poison and a syringe from her father's Gladstone. She inserted the needle into the phial, drew off a quantity of the poison, tapped the end to remove any residue of air, and took his arm injected him. A slight flick from his body at the scratch, and there was no more. She immediately packed the Gladstone, took it back outside to the ambulance.

Dorcas passed out.

'Fuck sake Tom,' Tubman said getting him to his feet before he hit the floor. 'Pull yourself together, man. We're moving from torture, death, day-to-day stress working for a psychopath, to getting out of here in one piece and all you want to do is relax on the floor.'

Tommy Scripps was relieved for what she said to Dorcas, importantly, making no mention of the introduction of a dangerous poison into Johnson's body; knowing she would be guilty by association for not preventing what they had done.

Daniella came in from the ambulance. Two suit carriers over one arm. 'Here, put these on. When they open the back doors, all anyone's going to see, will be a body bag, and two pall bearers.'

Tom Dorcas, previous CEO of the Order of the Most Divine Third Circle, received a brown envelope from Internal Revenue. He had unpaid tax owing on $5 billion previously rested in his account. Where had it gone?

He jumped from the Golden Gate Bridge. Coast Guard found a body in Marin County. Forensic report stated the man died from shattered and broken internal organs, consequence of hitting San Francisco Bay and the Pacific Ocean water at eighty mile an hour.

Madeleine Tubman received a brown envelope from the US Office of Personnel Management asking for a statement of income while employed by Graf & Mayer as Deputy Director of Operations for Star Birth (USA).

The Company Pension Contributions' statement not requested.

She handed it to her boss, Jean Ronstandt with the words:

'You know where you can shove this, don't you?'

ATTACK ON VATICAN IMMINENT

AN ATTACK ON THE VATICAN WAS IMMINENT. Information received from an unknown source landed on his desk. Ronstandt was concerned as to who the source was now Tubman and, for want of who he really was, the man known as Nathaniel Johnson had been removed from Malaka's Corner. He called O'Hare.

Of course he knew Johnson, O'Hare had been in communication with him for years, no secret, he'd told Ronstandt that himself. He knew. So where in hell had the communication come from if not from Johnson? For its source mailer showed Malaka's Corner, narrowed down to both men's old outdated electronic mail serving system.

He called up Tubman, asked if she knew of any other persons having access to it; anybody else she knew would be an informer, working alongside Johnson in the building? She didn't know.

'How did the message come in? Was it a conventional email, only the one they used was ascii tape, capable of being read from either recipient or sender.' Tubman went on. 'Far as I know, Charlie's machine was a Fairchild Teletypesetter he salvaged from Reuters news agency years back. A perforated tape ran a golf-ball head typewriter printing the message out. Johnson's wasn't as sophisticated as that, his was an electronic mailer server from the Department of Defense that Charlie's secretary had adapted for his use. Still ascii tape though. I used that one to contact O'Hare to organize our escape.'

'So you're familiar with its use?'

'Familiar, yes. As to who might have used it after we got out, no. But you still haven't answered me as to what form the message took?'

'You mentioned Department of Defense?'

'Yes, the old system adapted for Johnson by OHare installed at Malaka's Corner. Coincidentally hidden in a Daisy vacuum cleaner casing.'

Ronstandt laughed. Thought he was getting too old for all of this. No, he was too old. 'That was where the message came to us. Through a defense radar screen.'

'A what?'

'Gobbledygook to you or me. A fruit salad to our IT people who managed to break some of the code down into language. They replied to the obscure email address showing at the beginning, asking for them to verify their device and protocols. So far there has been no reply.'

'So how did you find out an attack on the Vatican was imminent?'

'Our people kept scanning down through the coding, picking up odd bits and pieces, until we had enough to make up a sentence: "attack on vatican imminent". Took over an hour.'

DIAZ BECOMES TUBMAN ONCE AGAIN

DESPITE HIS PROTESTATIONS, MADELEINE TUBMAN insisted to Ronstandt she was best man for the job. Hadn't she said more times than enough, she being, *au fait* with the current layout and security arrangements at Malaka's Corner, knowing Kriemhild's cat's-arse machinery for her operation, from the inside out put her there. Hadn't she already risked life and limb being Deputy Director of Operations for Star Birth (USA) for over a year? Who else had credentials coming anywhere near close to hers?

Ronstandt was not being obtuse, he was concerned for her safety that's all. To his way of thinking she had done more than her duty doing what she had done. Putting her among a team of FBI Assault officers, with guns popping off randomly in all directions, he was worried. For all that, he reluctantly gave way.

A public asset. Still leased by Pension and Welfare Benefits Administration, an arrangement she guessed was known by more people than were ever going to let on, administrative (annex ii-38) section gov.pen was a suspicious and peculiar entity. If it had secrets beyond the obvious, then

O'Hare and Johnson were persons knowing them. From the policy Office of Science and Technology, Henry Ford to Janet Watson-Forbes, Director of National Intelligence through to her own department of Jean Ronstandt, assistant to the President for Homeland Security and Counterterrorism (CIA) himself, US Government men and women to the core, she was sure, would collectively know less than what Johnson and O'Hare kept under their hats. Unlikely to question any existing peculiarities from the days of Frederik Spannocs? Betcha life they won't.

But. Even to her way of thinking, there was a Wonderful Wizard of Oz turning wheels somewhere, operating machinery, projecting ghostly images for the possession of data containing, God knows what (the Wizard knew what), given out tokens to maintain *God knows what* is for the eventual good use of mankind. But. She doubted it.

There was something she did not feel able to tell Ronstandt for joining the assault headed by O'Hare. A simple qualification; and given the circumstances of O'Hare's request, sensitive, though why it should be; just the way things were.

She nodded and smiled. He understood her not asking, nothing to do with her being a woman, but an important part of the operation. As far as O'Hare was concerned the matter was to be between the two of them, no one else involved; not for the moment anyway; not until he had got the evidence he needed. How would it look to Ronstandt, O'Hare needing the woman's dress, along with her undergarments? And Charlie, being Charlie, was once again playing a deep game.

Of course she was not going to ask if he had some kind of

perversive reason for what he wanted. Not her business. She hoped not, but who knows what's in the head of an old man when it comes to him wanting women's outer clothing with under accompaniments. There's a lot of it about. In this case it was to be Kriemhild's wardrobe, or whatever there was of it in her office-cum-accommodation suite while she was in the country.

He must have had read her mind. For the expression on her face begged the reason why.

'We need her DNA.'

She smiled at him. 'From any particular part of her vitals? Ummh.'

Those particular vitals necessitated calling in America's federal law enforcement agency to join the CIA. A section of the United States Secret Service team of their experts were to later carry out a forensic examination of those clothes. They could not risk a compromise of the clothing by any other agencies handling them.

'Soon as we're clear of the building. All those remaining of Kriemhild's people taken into custody, all shooting has ceased, office furniture and office clearance gone in, then you go. Not before. Got it?'

She put two thumbs up to him in mock cynicism, that she really didn't need to be told how to deal with an assault. He ignored her.

Codename Daemon Once and For All Time. Threatening world peace for too long with their various criminal CEOs, President Ryder 'Black Dick' Howe gave an executive order for complete removal of the Order of the Most Divine Circle from American soil. A joint assault team of Central Intelligence Agency and the National Security Agency were ordered the disbandment.

Paramilitary uniforms, carrying heavy automatic weapons, with Tubman following, the operation began. A forensic team followed her for she had her own agenda, well, Charlie's really. Not surprisingly, Kriemhild's armed security, manning the front gate, gave up without so much as a squeak. She knew no one was going to put up any resistance. She led officers to the second floor, a call center, out into her old Star Birth office where Kerstin Hartmann was standing.

'What the . . . !'

'You're under arrest, Hartmann.' She smiled. 'How you doing, Kerstin? Don't let her touch or remove anything from the building.'

Hartmann took out the pack from her handbag. Labeled, Hartmann's Gersundheits-Binden fur Damen in her hand. 'Pure coincidence, Corrine.'

Tubman took the pack from her. A forensic officer handed her an open plastic bag for its safekeeping. She put it in.

'Go with these people, Kerstin.'

Staff were getting to their feet at this intrusion by paramilitary officers. Surrounded on all side she shouted for calm. Paramilitaries' with automatic rifles, shouting, created panic. A semblance of order followed as she made her way to Kriemhild's private quarters.

She felt ill at ease opening the door fearing the woman returning. For at times she seemed to have a knack of appearing and disappearing without anyone seeing her coming or going. Some called her the Lady of the Green Kirtle for her ability.

She had been to her office herself on numerous occasions. In fact she had signed her contract with Heinrich Stein of Graf & Mayer Recruitment Consultants when she was taken on as deputy director of operations for Star Birth (USA) in there. Where she had not been before, were Kriemhild's private apartment attached to the office. She knocked on the door with the dangerous end of her automatic rifle pointed forward to be on the safe side. An electronic lock required, she guessed needed an imprint of Kriemhild's finger to gain entry, was installed on a wall next to the door. A problem? Not to the assault officer standing alongside of her it wasn't. Pulling goggles down over his eyes he pushed her to one side. He was about to blast the lock off the wall with his weapon when he was stopped from what he was about to do.

'Can't do that, Agent. Government property. Has to be kept intact.'

A young fellow with a lap-top in his hand. He pulled an assortment of high-tech gear he had in a shoulder bag and placed them on the floor. Putting a sensor to its detector pad he pulled ear pads on and listened. Puzzled he removed his ear pods replaced them with a stethoscope. He opened the settings icon on the laptop opened up its screen. Scrolled down until he found an icon showing FINGERPRINTS put his own on the sensor. Removed it. Read some instructions then put his finger against the keypad sensor. Nothing. The lock was going nowhere. He repeated the process and tried once more. Negative. He turned to her.

'Whoever lives here is short on whorls, loops, and arches.'

The Agent officer stepped forward, pushed the both of them safely out of harm's way, fired off as short burst at it. The door fell open. She nodded and walked in. Alone.

She looked in on this inner sanctum of depravity with reservation, she was no prude. She knew Kriemhild was evil bordering on the sadistic when it came to torture and humiliation. Although to be fair none of what presented itself in this room was any surprise to her any more than the Stasi uniform hanging next to a gray business suit belonging to her lover were. On a hook tucked in behind the Nazi uniform a photograph, Kriemhild wearing a velvet and maroon dress; and there it was, the real thing. Hanging pristine, crease free. This was better than she had hoped for. Charlie had mentioned a dress and here one was. She had two identical apparently. One in Bavaria, the other at Malaka's Corner. How he would have known, she had no idea?

She carefully removed it from its hangar. A waft of warm perfume came away from it. For this was a boudoir of depravity. A miscellany of BDSM apparel were spread haphazardly about the room. She stood back not wanting to compromise the area more than she had to, for forensics were coming later. She laid the dress out over the mirror of her dressing table, then began going through her drawers, removed the woman's underwear and other paraphernalia, possibly for later interest. None of this was going to be of use for DNA, she needed the dirty stuff. She looked into a shower room closet. In a basket, in the corner. Women are no different from each other no matter who they are. Frillies of lace, a blooded Basque, with whips that had caused the staining turned her previous thoughts around. She gathered up the dress, the basket of dirties, whips and all, departed the lady's boudoir.

'Bag them will you. Everything together. For there's another person of interest here.' The forensic agent from National Security nodded.

Early afternoon, the US Government offices, formerly known as administrative (annex ii-38) section gov.pen were cleared of staff working for the Order. Removal trucks were already waiting on the perimeter as CIA assault teams moved out, leaving forensic teams going through computers, and those secrets of the bed chamber interests. She got in her car and drove off.

Driving away from Washington DC towards New York, on Highway & 3rd Street Northeast, a vicious sting caught across her back. It came on so suddenly she had to make an emergency stop. Her body went into shock and pain as further assaults followed. She stepped out of the car and was close to tears. Whatever she did she couldn't stop the pain increasing with ferocity. Her mind went back to Kriemhild's room. Those whips hanging. Was she doing this to herself by auto suggestion?

She tried to rationalize the situation she found herself. She couldn't. All she knew was she had been driving. All thoughts following washed away. Her breathing had become fast and shallow. Perhaps stinging nettles had lodged between her clothes and her skin. Afterall, the grounds were overgrown on its perimeter. An allergic reaction? A reason both ridiculous and impossible, one she immediately disregarded. She ripped her top off from her body. She was soaked wet from blood.

Hers. She went into shock. Nauseum and sweating became too much for her. She collapsed unconscious to the ground in front of the Highway Patrol car, stopped to see why she was parked where she shouldn't have been.

THEY FIND MADELEINE TUBMAN

RONSTANDT WAS SPEAKING ON THE PHONE. 'She was found at the side of the highway by a patrol car!'

'Alive? O'Hare questioned anxiously. For she was an old colleague; one of few he trusted within the law enforcement agency they both belonged.

'She is. In a right mess though. She was returning to New York after the Star Birth debacle when something unexplained happened. You want to see her back. Looks like she's been keel-hauled.'

'I take it you've got her in hospital?'

'At Sibley General.'

'Okay I'll get over there. Just one thing Jean. I asked her to bring some clothes for forensics and DNA testing. Did she have them with her when she was found?'

'Suitcase of them. Being processed by Secret Service as we speak.'

'Soon as I've seen her I'll get over there and collect them later. Anything else?'

'As you asked, yes, Charlie. Bit delicate really. I haven't known Tubman as long as you. Of course, since she's been working for me with Homeland I know her well enough. . . .

But then, do we really know anybody?'

O'Hare listened for continuation of conversation. Had he collapsed on the floor? Had the line gone dead? 'Do we what Jean, spit it out?'

'Secrets of the bed chamber— What people get up to there, well, that's their business—'

'Ask the question Jean. Before one of us dies.'

'Was Madeleine into sadomasochism?'

The word struck old fears into him. Of child abuse and slavery caried out by Frederik Spannocs and his cohorts back in the day. Was Kriemhild a reincarnation of him? Had Madeleine Tubman been abused by this woman, and in this way, while she was carrying out the operation. Had Kriemhild ordered a hit on Tubman finding out she had been working undercover with the CIA all the while being employed as an executive of Star Birth? Why Jean asked her if she had such tendencies annoyed him. Sadism? Madeleine? No. Not possible. Why did the man from Homeland Security have such thoughts about an assistant he'd personally known for a couple of years anyway? Hadn't his own security found out everything they needed to know about her before employing her?

'What are you talking about? Not a chance. I'm surprised you have to ask such questions of a woman that's been on your team for years. Found injured by the side of the road. Where does sadomasochism come into any of it?'

'It probably doesn't. But among those items of clothing she had with her in the car were whips used by sadomasochists. Fresh blood. As if it'd come from Madeleine's back.'

*

O'Hare read the forensic report. Two samples of body fluid from different people of unknown sex didn't surprise him. A separate sample of DNA tested taken from Kriemhild's wardrobe showed as coming from another person however did. A female. He pulled out a previous forensic report, his own. The Witch of the West attack in Green-Wood cemetery. Blood taken from under his fingernails, after scratching her, matched one of those from Kriemhild's room at Malaka's Corner. As then, there was still no DNA match on record of who that attacker had been. He, however, had his own ideas on that one. Ex-Stasi agent Karla Kia. Kriemhild's lover. Is firmly established in the house America.

Tubman was livid over thoughts Ronstandt made about her, however subtle and well-meaning. Thinking she had had any kind of sexual encounter with Kriemhild at Malaka's Corner. Could he have really believed that of her. She being Kriemhild's lover? Of course, he apologized profusely, saying he had been in this business too long, and other such platitudes.

Problem was, the blood sample taken from her matched those found on the whip, which in normal circumstances would damn anyone, except her, she felt, assuming you knew her without knowing them. There was still the problem samples taken from the discarded nickers found in the used laundry basket, she herself had removed, passed to forensics, showed another person as being the owner, left her blood on a whip without an explanation. She couldn't give one. How could she?

O'HARE QUESTIONS JOHNSON

———————————

THE MAN WITH MORE ALIASES THAN ENOUGH was recovering from a fracture to the base of the thumb metacarpal along with all other manner of injuries inflicted upon him. He had been told he had been diagnosed with early-stage dementia by the doctor at the facility. None of which came as a surprise to him after what he had gone through.

'She never spoke to me, you know. Kriemhild.'

O'Hare studied the man lying on the bed, his onetime nemesis. The man likely responsible for the murder of Lieutenant Frank Weinberg his partner, as well as Hamilton Fitch's grandfather in 1925; with another man. Daniel Sullivan. Both men worked undercover for a Special Surveillance Organisation group then, that much he did know; one he was still trying to get to the bottom of. It was his involvement with Marco Giuseppe, as Spannocs was known then, with a child abduction ring of New York's great and good, ready to barter for, and the Government he didn't. A bull market organized in the basement of Algonquins Grave, his house in midtown Manhattan. Johnson, a prospective agent for the purchasing of immigrant children for sexual exploitation by many of America's social elite. And how did he disguise himself? He remembered now. A clown mask. And of course we mustn't forget, Sullivan. Another buyer of the precious commodity. How did he hide his identity? He also remembered. A bloodhound. What with Giuseppe sporting the head of a goat; a roomful of people wearing various other disguises, such a collective fucking madhouse of deranged humanity, you wouldn't want to meet in your dreams . . .

Until divine intervention came along spoiling things.

Question he had always asked himself? Were this pair of reprobates on the side of law and order? For if they were, then they were good, for the crimes they committed in its name. Keeping themselves hidden, confusing all about when it came to the law. Protected. So much for security service teamwork and cooperation.

'Smiled once.'

'They tell me you're suffering dementia.'

'Only when it comes to me memory.' He laughed. 'Got immortality as well. But then you know that, don't you.'

He did indeed, mores the pity. As he himself, facing a divine intervention of sorts in the likeness of an angel. Supposedly to take on Satan. A poor substitute for Him to fulfil the promise made between Him and His creation. The battle of Armageddon. Good and evil, where His triumph, short-lived never began, His absence from the fray, a pomposity never to be questioned in religious circles. Why not, I continually ask of Him?

'I'll come straight to the point, Nathaniel. With your condition deteriorating, as it will, 'bout time you told me, who the hell is running the show you've been dancing to?'

Johnson smiled. Painfully striking the match he'd been

fumbling with. 'Reach across me pipe, tamp it down for me will you? Having trouble with the old thumb.'

The pipe in question had been with the man ever since he had first clapped eyes on him in the dockyard in the 20's shortly after the first world war. He was designated government Wharfmaster in the naval dockyard under an alias of Claypole. Claypipes and Claypole. He remembered the confusion bumping into him in the same drugstore they both bought their tobacco. O'Hare came out smoking a Lordhamercy. He happened to mention claypipes to him as they passed. Nathaneil Claypole, as was, thinking he was addressing him by his name, asking for a job in the dockyard. He surely would have known he was a beat cop with the NYPD.

He reached across him and took up his pipe, pressed the tobacco, then passed it back. Johnson nodded, struck up a match, put it to the bowl, drawing breath until the burning tobacco became ember, then coughed gently. O'Hare caught a whiff from the smoke. His senses came flooding in. Sutliff Ries Three Star Blue, seven cents an ounce. Those were days.

'Got you and Frank into something, didn't we?'

'Did you do us any favors though? Murdered a good officer. Tried to murder me.' Johnson shrugged, puffed contentedly. 'Who got you into your favors? Did you have a mind to ask?'

'Didn't have to. We were, me and Daniel Sullivan, Special Surveillance. "For the protection of American interests and developments". Originally conceived a Government designated UFO tracking operation, general paranormal activity, as and when it occurred.'

'As in the Order of the Most Divine Third Circle. What of

them? How did the promotion of child abuse and exploitation come under that radar? Didn't give you any sleepless nights?'

'Does any abuse toward humanity by governments or politicians give people in general sleepless nights? Of course it don't. Any more than pariah states the governments of the world are supposedly so keen on bringing down do. Truth is Charlie, nobody gives a damn as long they're keeping their pariahs in check. Kriemhild is but another in a long line of unsavory people foisted on us from time-to-time.' He laughed, quietly muttered. 'Nose 'oles, ear 'oles, with an emphasis on, arse 'oles. Legal, bureaucratic authority; traditional authority; or charismatic potentate, take your pick. Kim Il-Sung, Pol Pot, Joseph Stalin, Mao Zedong, Leopold II, Idi Amin, Mengistu Haile Mariam. All excuses for being in one of those three categories, all claiming legitimate authority, all suffering, larger than the average man's penis, syndrome. Do I need to go on? We mustn't forget the ones closest to the present incumbent. Adolf Hitler, along with, *next patient, please*, the good, Dr. Josef Mengele. Her current Nazi stock holding possession. A Fourth Reich. Granted power to take on the universe as her masters. Make of it what you will, I cannot help you. Clue. Nothing's changed. Choose your poison, Charlie.'

Johnson was not wrong in this, his resume. As much a scholar of evil and power by corruption as anyone. 'And you've been involved with an organisations seeking to take over the world for the better part of your life. Are you proud, Nathaniel?'

'As they say, old man. Parr for the course. As Agatha Christie writ, *It's a rotten job, somebody's gotta do it.*' O'Hare nodded, turned to leave. 'By the way. I knew you were wearing body armor; people were watching me. We *still* have your back.'

O'Hare was no more forward in his investigations into who was running all of this than the day he started. What he did know was whoever was running things had lost sight of why it all started in the first place, simply following the orders and directives of the man in charge at the particular time. For his part, all he had was Jean Ronstandt calling current day shots, as opposed to FBI Director Franklin Lomax, his old boss from the 1920s. The surveillance passing between Johnson, Ronstandt and himself, up until now, with none of the three of them knowing, over the years, using an outdated electronic mailing system, with improvements by his IT queen, out of Malaka's Corner had been . . . useful of a sort.

KRIEMHILD MEETS FELLOW ROYALS

DROGSTADT CASTLE LANDING AND SAFETY CREW strapped the airplane down before its blades had even stopped turning. Standing on the top step its passenger waited impatiently for assistance in seeing her down. Above, Mount Drogstadt and clear blue sky. In the valley below the mountain, Weinberghöhe town, its people woken. The roof above rolled slowly to close. The whirring from its hydraulics and rail system echoed inside the dome, progressively deafening until the world outside was concealed. A single slam sound, then silence, then acclimatic air conditioning kicked in, its fans smoothly oscillated. Droplets of evaporated water trickled down onto her. An umbrella provided by a stewardess hastily covered. Kriemhild's security staff stepped forward to assist her down the few remaining steps. Her own security immediately intervened ushered them to one side. These people not worthy. For they acted for the supreme leader. A demi-god. From a country bordered with iron. Two of her bodyguards, automatic weapons pointed forward, nodded to Drogstadt Castle security to step away from their country's supreme highness. Looking first to one side of them, then the other, her own protection service confirmed it was safe for her to move forward.

Bojang Kija was leader of a totalitarian state of twenty-nine million repressed men, women and children. Even though she had an army of a million, an arsenal of intercontinental nuclear ballistic missiles at her disposal, in this place, she was out of her comfort zone. Sanctions against her and her country meant traveling anywhere in the world put her at risk of being arrested for crimes against humanity, corruption and genocide. In this region of Germany however, she was partially at ease, for she had been educated close by in Switzerland. A country secretly holding her assets in trust, unlikely ever to be unraveled by any expert in economics for a hundred years, wealth considered safe. She liked what she'd heard of Direktorin Elke Kriemhild and her Order. A rumor Kriemhild was granddaughter of an SS Nazi commander prepared to carry out what Adolf Hitler had failed within the new Reichsbürger movement added to her liking. His one people, One Reich, One Ruler with her ambition to put right her family's past added to her impression of her.

For she was Supreme Leader, one of few remaining from the bloodline stock of the Goguryeo. There was not a man or woman coming close to her genealogy. Not even Kriemhild. For the granddaughter of Prince Ernst II of the Saxe-Altenburg was no match for the greatness of her ancestry.

Kriemhild had reservations for this Mongolian ruler. Taking leadership of her country after poisoning her brother with Novichok would bring, paus off dich, to a new level. Her definition for world domination using a sheriff system of autocracy was not her idea for a working relationship. A leader whose ideas for world domination using puppet administrators to rule was not governable. Totalitarianism was eternal, unlike ideas from an upstart they had already been to war with.

Ahriman reminded her she was his, Queen of the Universe. Assuring her of no other, he would, *Watch her back.*

Over the course of the day more helicopters arrived each choreographed into the underground hangar, space enough for eight Sikorsky size airplanes. One bore the emblem of a Red Cross and Red Crescent over a faded out red hammer and sickle; another, a red star in front of a red band.

Others' suffering sanctions and travel bans from the rest of the world arrived. Not content with enjoying wealth stolen from their people, they wanted more. Kriemhild promised a world playground for them, the like of which they could only dream. Such greed would bring a following to the Order quicker than enough.

Benny the Ponce, minister of Propaganda and Public Enlightenment, formally brought proceedings underway by introducing Direktorin Elke Kriemhild.

One of Ahriman's disciples. A rat-catcher. A conqueror of souls. Not of this world; nor of any time, for he was there for Frederik Spannocs as he was for her. Dressed in his familiar red livery of suit with gold braiding, and black top hat shining as a 12-inch LP record, was in the wrong place.

'Ladies and gentlemen . . .' unaware he was not addressing the Aryan Farmers, Texas branch, began his introduction. 'One of the finest examples of shape-changers in the business, allow me to introduce to you one of the most delightful and effervescent artistes in the business of what we call transvestic, and what the world of thaumaturgy . . .' he paused for an expected Oooo! from his sesquipedalian quip. The conference was became agitated. 'Describe as the miracle of the disappearing todger with accompaniments [*though she could be a woman*]' he said as an aside . . . paused for laughter and cheering, not coming, fast becoming angry shouts, continued. 'Not to be taken too seriously though . . . all the way from Austin . . . Little Miss Poppet Tupper, Direktorin Elke Kriemhild . . . and who wouldn't—?'

Dressed in her finery, Kriemhild stepped out onto the auditorium to boos and shouts of, *Treating us as fools? Bringing a clown out for an introduction?* Her face scarlet below her immaculate face make up. Her lips quivered at the shambolic introduction given her. Was Ahriman beginning to make a fool of her? Had he realised she was going to turn tables on this demi-god?

'Supreme leaders, ladies and gentlemen. Profuse apologies. I cannot understand how that happened. I assure you; my ambitions are yours. Ambitions we can work together to bring about. With your patience, please let me explain.

'Where past leaders with similar ambitions used their own people and armies to bring a breakdown in world order none subscribed to, we have other ideas. We have already tilted the world in our favor. A world of different religions and faiths are at each other's throats, inflamed and organized through social media by the Order, bringing war and terrorism we have already brought about. The Order has already locked in war lords and drug barons in places to add into the mix, but now the Order which I hope you will belong, need you for that to continue. Your kind of leadership. Having been ostracized, to keep western capitalism in their hands, constraining your own, has to stop. None of which can be achieved by democracy, as you've all amply shown.

'Further. Versions of illegality, with talk of human rights, law and order, being put on you by them, using words of criminality to keep you in check. You are not criminals simply because of beliefs you don't subscribe to for this agenda of goodness they hold as their own. How many of you have been told you cannot have certain weapons to defend yourselves, when they have all they need to counter yours?'

The once hostile audience were beginning to warm to her, except one, Bojang Kija.

'Well its backfired on them now. All international laws, conventions, treaties, your predecessors were once signatory to are to be thrown in the trashcan, for there is nothing they can do to prevent that happening. Many of you have weapons, the Order will see to it that those not having them will be supplied. We have manufacturers of armaments ready to sell to you.

'And if any of you are in doubt, my predecessor in the Order came close to bringing about a third world war—'

'And what prevented it? The Order was to control everything then, but the free world was having none of it. They would rather die than be subjected to the yoke.'

He did. Come close. She had asked Ahriman. It was not so much he didn't have an answer as to why Frederik Spannocs had failed, for if he did, no reasons as to why came to her. It was not so much he had been dismissive of her; a mist had descended on the matter. Question unanswered. A philosophical conundrum as: Who was the true architect for creation? God or Satan? What was Ahriman's future in all of this? For he was one of many spirits, given appearance as human by Satan. Her understanding of who he was had only come to her in dreams and magic: mirrors and light.

She was sure Ahriman was concealing an agenda of his own. Was hast du denn davon gehalten? Her thoughts and understanding lost; she continued without answer from Ahriman of what he was going to get out of all of this?

'There are those thwarting us. People known to the Order. Monitored and watched over by the US Government itself since, well before the 1920s—'

'America is our number enemy, the nation; its people—' The reaction from those she looked to for a world domination under the Order was fast losing interest. A bombshell. One she did not want to confide in them for her own ends. Where the keys of the hard-drive, floated directly over them, from information cyber hacked by her people into the US Government's Thule Air Base in Greenland. 'There are alien starships in the Atlantic Ocean? [*the audience muttered to each other*] The US Government is keeping it shtum—'

'Ridiculous!' A man shouted at the top of his voice.

The call-out lost. A shadow crossed before her. She focussed. A girl slowly come into focus. Long black hair. She looked American Indian. A war-band around her forehead. She was moving toward her. A belt with a sheath around her waist. A hunting knife? Hadn't she got everyone to hand their weapons over as soon as they arrived? Guns. Had she not mentioned knives to her security people?

She felt something familiar going on, but for the life of her she couldn't put a finger on what it was. She also felt something happening to herself. Her part personality slowly, bit at a time, thoughts, mindset, were dissolving into another place. Had her soul departed? For another seemed to waiting in the wings for its replacement. She concentrated hard to maintain her identity, for if this was Ahriman doing this to her, she was having none of him. It was just that it was all . . . coming on so fast she was unable to block these influences effecting her. She was incarnating, somewhere between a dead soul arising and one falling backward into hell.

Grey eminence worked the incomplete impoverished and deconstructed universe of His making in an attempt to override and deprive Ahriman of his powers. This sequential potentiality afforded Satan in the beginning without meaning, not thought out by Him, was never intended to pass through alter egos, ad infinitum, he was sure. For Ahriman's investment of those part powers into human-demi-spirit, counter to His plans, would eventually bring a collapse of the physical properties of mass-energy contained within the universe. For the ascendancy of this misplaced authority would eventually deny Him of His universal creation, putting it in the hands of the other for a finite-model re-creation, in his image.

The Algonquian girl faced Spannocs down. A twelve-inch bladed knife, with its narwhal carved tusk handle, grasped in her hand; glistened from the light bouncing from all directions down onto it. Her voice deep, echoed as a boom of thunder:

I'm still your nemesis. I see through your disguise, Ahriman. You cannot hide from us.

You! . . . You haven't changed since last we met. You are still a freak from a cave. Daughter of all Harlots. Your powers are useless and feeble here.

Spannocs and Ahriman, with a confusion of mind and human form, with the addition of Kriemhild, were unable to escape the portion of time they were part. With neither able to react within the verse frame, the angel's knife came down. Unable to spiritualize his present form, Spannocs's flesh took the cut. The leached fluid from him, black and thick; burned into the floor gave off an odor of acridity.

Ahriman turned aside. He had no need to confront her. Time-Verse would see to that. The download to shift between them was still his. He could step in and out, cross verse, and as before, leave her in this place. Still tired and earth-bound creature she was. Aged and fading as a mortal she had spent too much time among men. He laughed the laugh of an audience as he once more witnessed six dozen clowns in marching circle, kicking the one in front up the arse; blaming the one behind for infuriating the already swollen blood vessels inside their rectums.

No! It is you who are powerless . . .

Her voice resonated from the rock interior of Mount Drogstadt. A shining blade in her hand hanging in front of Ahriman's face brought doubt that his powers were not what he once thought they were. From His blessed data; for the creation of universes, came the thought, the ever-changing end code from the equation for creation he sought for completion, was his current salvation.

I am spirit of Wormwood: His assassinator! Beware Ahriman.

Powerless. For my destruction is forbidden you, and all those sending you here.

A knife flashed through earth's fifth element of aether, took part soul from the shell of the closest, and no more. She was gone now, left Ahriman and Kriemhild exposed, but unharmed.

Kriemhild dried. Had Ahriman taken a day's leave? She had to take control of this audience on her own. She held her hand up for patience, took up a glass of water, and sipped. Her feelings turning to anger. She now knew why. Fortunately her Nazi ancestry for superiority of race was coming to the fore, without Ahriman's magic. He told her he had inflicted Heir Hitler with his presence persuading him to kill himself for salvation with him. Was he doing this now? Was Heir Hitler her replacement? Either way Ahriman hadn't deserted her for his magic was taking a different twist. Her offices. The tingling in her fingers had progressed to her hands. Her whip hand. The muttering of the audience were dying away. They were cardboard cutouts.

For she was about to experience the full force of her magic four thousand miles away. The whip she and Bathilda played with back in Malaka's Corner was live. She began laying lashes across the back of the woman who betrayed her. At the same time a sexual feeling bordering on climax was releasing itself in her. Her flow of speech combined with other body flows, fell away into undecipherable words. Her face red from sweat, she swallowed and tried to continue her spiel.

'Lords of the New World Order. Meet your Queen of the Universe. *O-h-h-h.* Es tut mir leid. Apologies,' she said caressing the cause of her pause, a combination of fanny and new-found penis. The cry of sexual excitement she thought unheard, however, clearly audible to all, for what it was. For the looks of laughter, nudges and astonished faces from her masturbatory experience were all around the conference now. *O-h-h-h* felt so good, she didn't give a scheiße what anyone thought. She continued not knowing or listening to what she was saying.

'Fact. Yes, ladies and gentlemen. A concerted effort is being put into discrediting them before we take them out. One in particular. The FBI agent known as Charlie O'Hare has been involved with all our destruction since the 1920s; and apart from one or two before him, he has managed to survive all our efforts to assassinate him. He has powerful friends in the FBI and the CIA. What is more troubling is he his close alliance with Russia.' She looked down at the self-anointed, Supreme upstart leader sitting in front of her. 'No need to look nervous, Kija, I am speaking of ex-President Sergei Bezukladnikov of the old Soviet Union; not the present bald-arsed incumbent sitting close by you now. Nevertheless—'

Kija spit bile. 'I think we've heard enough. For myself I will work toward our own agenda for world domination. Not your, "Queen of the Universe" pantomime for one. You call us self-proclaimed. My ancestry gives me more claim to self-proclamation, than yours ever did.' She stood and turned her attention on other potential followers. 'Putting your reliance on a woman dressed as a low-class whore; looking as if she comes from a House of Tudor England. A woman who cannot control flicking her bean in front of others, is not a way forward for world domination where we come from.'

Kriemhild laughed at her and looked across at the Chinese leader who nodded his approval, for the take down of his country's traditional ally, never being able to trust her after the murder of her brother, showed pleasure Kriemhild ignored her rant.

'Anyone else?' Kriemhild asked.

The leaders of two other countries, one in Africa, the other from a military junta occupying a portion of south-east Asia made the point, 'If the Supreme Leader of a country could be treated in such manner, what chance respect for them?'

'Open up your dome . . . Your Majesty. No euphemism implied,' Kija called out to her. 'We are leaving.'

Any of the countries here had the capacity to launch an attack on Drogstadt Castle after they left. They had the co-ordinates now. Only Kija had ultimate weaponry and force; and she being in a volatile leadership position, unlikely to survive an assassination attempt from one of her own family in a not-too-distant future, their country bend to her Order then, she would allow her to leave unmolested. Most of any remaining, after being treated to sumptuous dinner, would not be allowed to.

Her paramilitary spoke to her on the phone. She nodded to open the dome and allow Kija and her people to leave. All others were to be annihilated.

With Kija gone it was left to Drogstadt Castle's landing and safety crews to hangar out helicopters belonging to the de facto leaders of the African, and south-east Asian military into position before withdrawing leaving pilots, crew and the two countries entourages alone. Warlords and overblown generals were too volatile to cement any constructive relationships. Then Ahriman can deal the cards. See how they like the suits of his hands, instead of my own.

ScorpiX the chaos-monster infected with the skin and blood of Satan's claw. Ahriman, Satan's alter ego, the permitted leash holder. For the creature initially created by God, inferior and abandoned. The detritus of parts half-in half-out of a world struggling for natural life, this creature created from biological life forms ordinarily not registered on creation's scale, brought mist from the dark material of the universe's ancient past He had no control over. As dogs of war, Satan could not control the ScorpiX personally. For the termination of Satan as an evil opposing the love force was beyond even Him. By default the physics of creation of a universe was of opposing forces, even the Engineer had to accept if it were to successfully work.

The spawn of ScorpiX: DavaXz and EavaXz. The descriptive word loose in its meaning for any explanation of a natural creation before its possession by Satan. Bereft of legs, or the burnings on their bodies, for any resemblance, apart from the desire of human mortal flesh, between them and a *mad*-dog being purely coincidental, *mad*ness in this context being no attachment to any psychological disorder.

DavaXz and EavaXz came out from the burning particles of brimstone. Any anticipation from the screaming as their victims were being consumed; assistance for succour was ignored. Governance by Him to prevent the inevitability of human outcome and suffering of man's descent into hell with this singular forgiveness was permanent. For ScorpiX was a sledgehammer to crack a nut too far: not all sin forgivable, bypassing forgiveness opportunity without His awareness.

One man seeing the screaming horror of what he was in the midst of took the chance for survival by leaping into the mountain chasm below the castle.

The castle cleaners were sent out with no explanation as to what had occurred under the dome inside the mountain. Their job, remove the mashed and mixed bodies of dissenters off the hangar platform. Using gas-powered forklifts fitted with bull shovels, body parts along with their owners' planes were unceremoniously dumped into the chasm below. A cargo of plastic barrels of gasoline and acetylene bottles swiftly followed, ensured everyone had a decent cremation.

Tanks of foam and water issued from pipes in the cupola high above the landing area washed clean all evidence of human remains. Those leaving later in their own planes unaware of what went on, for the odour in the air of burnt beef made some wonder why they hadn't been offered burgers to eat instead of the seasoned hard-boiled eggs, onion salad, spinach & chicken ravioli of German cuisine on the buffet tables.

Well, that went okay, Queenie!

A US reconnaissance spy satellite passed overhead as the roof, open to allow body fumes to escape, slowly slid across, closed.

O'HARE CALLS CARTER

THE ORDER'S MEDIA PLATFORM went into overdrive putting out political and religious war propaganda. Orchestrated and bounced around the world it quickly spread into a hundred of the regular social media platforms across the world and into a thousand on the dark web. Dark netting through an Onion Routing path, had for years protected the identity of individual people with self-interest. It was open season. The Order's message for a new world order was an accurate description for quality; encouraging religious fundamentalists' an unrestricted liberty to carry out mayhem and terror anywhere in the world. According to O'Hare, coming out into the open and speaking with the Post's world affairs correspondent,

History had the habit of moving people mentally from rough to calm seas. The Order was doing the opposite.

O'Hare was driving while on his cell phone. He was calling Annie Carter in Rome. A Gregorian chant was playing while he waited. Calming to the ear and soul; answering personally better. She told him if he ever needed to contact her and she was working, the call number redirected to the Vatican. Apparently there were operator nuns with a knowledge of foreign languages (including Irish), working twenty-four hours a day in six-hour shifts. He called direct. Before he had time to put his hands back on the steering wheel while switching his cell phone to hands free an automated voice began reciting instructions. He released his knees he used to secure the steering wheel.

If your call is about the Pope's recent visit to Ireland, please press 1.

If you have concerns about contraception or abortion, please press 2.

If you would like to speak with a Cardinal, please press 3.

If you are enquiring about a particular department, please press 4.

For all other enquiries, please press 5.

He pressed 5. There was a brief interval of chant before a human answered.

He asked for her by name. All they wanted from him was his name and her extension. Have neither of those, he thought. Gave an alias, saying he didn't have an extension.

'Did you say, Sin?'

'Yes. I am a Sin from the bishop of Rome's side of righteousness.'

'I'm sure you are, Mr. Sin. Please hold the line, I'll find her for you.'

He patiently waited listening to more Gregorian chant.

'Mr. Sin. . . .'

'You're through caller,' an overriding voice announced.

'How have you been?'

'Fine, all things considered—'

'Sounds ominous.'

They were being eavesdropped by the CIA. Catholic Intelligence Agency or Holy Alliance, the Vatican equivalent of the FBI and the CIA all rolled into one with the Secret Service thrown in for measure. A formidable organisation to be the wrong side of. The world had come some way since formation of the Holy Roman Church. For good reason. They had bitter experience when it came to intrigues, conspiracy, counter and otherwise down the centuries. A fact not on any student of religious history's curriculum. He considered the call.

'Call me back, Annie. I'm about to be pulled over by a traffic cop?'

She had returned his call within two minutes.

'That was quick. News. Hamilton.' On the hoof, with his foot on the gas pedal, he was trying to put together a story not being construed as a coded message. 'He's been given the Freedom of the City of New York . . . for . . . jour-na-lism . . . yes, journalism. You know, highlighting crimes of abuse against children in New York and district.'

'Great news. You must be proud. As if he was you own son,' she answered sneeringly.

'Yes, I'll have a whiskey and cigar to celebrate. Perhaps you'll join me for a Marlboro later?'

The reference to Marlboro triggered a single thought in her of the seriousness of what was happening. The clue being the time she was a Carmelite carrying out research. Of how she had tried to save the life of Father Joseph Donne from an attack by two men purporting to be Teutonic Knights. They tortured and murdered him, putting her in hospital in the process. He was head archivist then. It concerned . . . that *damned* scroll. That piece of written and fake libel from the past, falling into the hands of Frederik Spannocs, its sacred words subtly falsified to read Jesus was a pedophile. It had been found on the floor at a gala ball in Becland before being forensically examined. Fortuitously. For all Christians, as other religions following him as either Son of God or prophet this had been proved otherwise. It was a close call.

The foretold Messianic belief from the Book of Isaiah, Jesus of Nazareth ascribed as the anointed King was never going to be acceptable to the High Priests 2 000 years-ago, anymore, she supposed, than they were to Christians and non-Christians followers today. The accepted implication was the man known by thousands for his miracles and good works was the Messiah damning the Son of God, along with all other comers, with this enlightenment; its falsification by man forever condemning him, whether messiah or prophet. Carbon dating of the ink used showed the falsification had occurred 200 years before his birth. Tested. Tested, and tested again. For all the detailed examining the mystery remained. Father Joseph Donne did not live long enough to know the truth before those . . . *cursed* brothers of Christ came and stole it.

They were wearing white suits with small red brooch crosses on their right lapels, you know, was how she described them at the time. One indelibly imprinted on her mind, for she had stabbed one in the eye with Charlie's aforementioned cigarette while it was glowing ember red. Gunned down for her trouble she might have died for half an inch of miracle. A déjà vu moment was to unfold.

O'Hare gave caution to the wind.

'You will need to put your authority on notice, Annie.'

THE WOMAN ONCE KNOWN AS SISTER BENEDICTA MARIE

THE VATICAN APOSTOLIC ARCHIVE had undergone a revamp since 1997 when she first came to work there. It was known as the Vatican Secret Archive. A segregated female apostolic medieval entrance door was down a dark and damp lane having no identification of what was beyond a secure door with the words, PRIVATE. NO ENTRANCE TO THE PUBLIC emblazoned to discourage curiosity. There was no signs, no security, no doorman, an open invitation to anyone, Teutonic Knights in particular, to enter and carry out a vicious murder of a holy father to get what they wanted. She had suffered terrible injuries in a failed attempt to save his life.

With renovations to the building carried out in 2002 along with a widening of the lane to a road it had become a less inhospitable place of work. Security, and cctv had been beefed up in an attempt to prevent any repeat performance involving death and injury. Swiss Guards were put on a twenty-four-hour rotation of shifts keeping the building safe and secure. Or so she had been assured.

She had been granted dispensation from her vows from the Carmelite order to become full-time head researcher for the library on the recommendation of Pope John Gregory at the time. After the death of Father Joseph. It seemed to her the world had become a more complicated and insecure place since then. The introduction of social media and the internet brought anonymous threats as opposed to letters, voices, or demonstrations against the Catholic church. Then argument to a lesser or greater degree, depending on your version of truth, was confronted head on. The word for truth corrupted to the word conspiracy. Conspiracies eagerly sought and indoctrinated into people's minds and psyches by those far cleverer than their followers. A death threat against a person in the public's eye, for whatever reason, guaranteeing someone, somewhere, sometime, carrying it forward keeping the author's hands stain free of any blood.

Apostolic archivist Dr. Agata Fellowes was perusing a bookcase in the Vatican Secret Library when she was approached by a man wearing a white suit. A man with a left eye white skinned over. Not recognising, or having seen him around the library before, she took him to be an academic.

'Can I be of assistance, sir?'

The man smiled. 'Sister Benedicta, please.'

'Annie Carter. She's no longer archivist or sister here. Can I help? But I need written authority of who you are?'

'You can.'

Wearing surgical gloves, he removed a cloth from a Vatican City coat-of-arms tote bag. She had not seen or was aware of someone else behind her. She was restrained with strong arms around her chest, while the man, she took as an academic, wiped around her mouth and nose with a cream.

*

The first assault came by way of the River Tiber. Posing as revelers aboard a tourist pleasure boat, they came ashore singing and dancing, before pulling out weapons and opening fire on all and everyone they came across including the police. Ten officers, with over two hundred members of the public were gunned down. Fifty dying from their injuries.

It was summer, the tourist season, Vatican Square was teeming with visitors queuing to go into the Sistine Chapel, its museums, and St. Peter's Basilica in particular. Men, women and children, from all nations of the world, were then added to that list. Gunned down mercilessly before any security had time to act. In the context of terrorism, they were suicide terrorists, not halting their killing until they had either wiped out or were wiped out themselves in acts of genocide against followers of the Roman rites. Seventeen hundred died, and eighty-nine injured. The Square, wet with blood from lives lost, wept.

The noise and shooting from automatic weapons echoing around Vatican Square told her she was too late confirming what he had told her. A holy war by any other name by followers of the Order of the Most Divine Third Circle under Direktorin Elke Kriemhild had already started.

She had returned the call to Charlie too late. Not so for her to act, because information he had received had come to him, too late. He had told her he was not in the position to pass the information further down the line personally.

She immediately rang the Carabinieri, then the Swiss Guard. A pointless exercise, for gunfire, had already alerted them to act. Ordinarily the first point of contact for a situation involving the Vatican were the Swiss Guard. Depending on its seriousness they referred it on to the Vatican Gendarmerie Corps. In this case events were far out of hand for them to get an order to act from the Papal authorities quick enough. With time not being on their side, seeing events unfolding in the Square, they swung into a counteroffensive.

All armed officers from all security services were having difficulty separating terrorist from tourist. Innocent lives were lost in their endeavour to repel the terrorists from the Square.

The Great Synagogue in the Jewish Quarter was the front for a second terrorist assault. Showing the flag of the Sunni Islamist Resistance Movement, the terrorists assaulted the building, randomly firing on worshippers and visitors inside with abandon, placing bombs detonating them as they went. The scene outside, as Vatican Square, was of utter carnage. No one inside the synagogue survived. All remained was anger and a need for revenge against each of the three monotheistic religions of Judaism, Christianity and Islam from each of the three in turn from those not directly involved around the world, had exported these violent acts of terrorism. Media platforms running with the internet went into melt down from the volume of hate traffic crossing the world before providers recognised what was going on closed them off. The closure triggered the Order's own servers to come online switching over to 4.7 Zettabytes of internet traffic.

Totalitarian, corrupted and failed states they were installed were technically untouchable from the western world. Nuclear armed states standing-by to counter launch attacks into the west, were armed and ready, forewarned this was a clear coded signal a third world war was in the offing, until further intelligence told them otherwise. Stood down.

Over the coming weeks groups from all three blamed each other for the deaths, began arming themselves and attacking churches, mosques, and synagogues around the world before moving on to other targets authority linked.

The security door to this area Carter worked was accessible to the Swiss Guard. It was instrumental to their job. In the few days following the terrorist attack, she took the phrase, faith internecine, for there were other smaller ones to follow. Every bit as effective as the first major assaults. For they were not planned. Random. Wolf. Typical of others wishing to follow the affray generated by the Order's social media conspiracy copywriters. The Swiss Guard were to work closely with the Vatican Gendarmerie Corps and the Italian army securing Rome from any further attacks.

She knew it was only a matter of time before they got around to asking questions as to what she knew. Shortly before those attacks. Her call. Her reply. All conversation recorded on the Vatican switchboard. She would be the known recipient for any caller. And FBI agent, Charlie O'Hare, would not have gone amiss.

STEINER AND COHEN

A HAUPTMANN IN THE SERVICE OF THE SWISS GUARD, Einrich Steiner was mindful there were infiltrators in the Vatican's security service. As any organization, the odds against there not being any, nil. Fortunately he had powers when it came to any investigation he decided on without pontifical obstruction. The Guard's gathering of information about dangerous organizations threatening the stability of the seven Churches of Rome, along with societies they represented around the world was, for their information and records, not the Church. For Steiner was more Sword than Cross. Anyone who thought cassocked priests along with strangely dressed soldiers from the Swiss Guard were for show were sadly mistaken. He carried a SIG Sauer P220 semi-automatic pistol as a matter of course and duty. All his people were trained by the Swiss Army of which he had once been an officer. He was supposed to have retired. The attempted murder of a Vatican apostolic using a nerve agent, followed by an assault by terrorists on innocent people, put thoughts of any such abdication on hold. He knew the reason why, who, and how to exact punishment on those responsible.

The need to protect the Holy See and the Pontificia was

first priority. He was a trained assassin and a cross-work agent with L'Entità. With this affrontery to his Church of Rome he concentrated his efforts working in their shadow. Of course there were other networks within the Church he could call on. His skills coming to the attention of Russicum being one. Political embarrassment for the Vatican and the Holy See whenever misdemeanours occurred within the Church, then they would be called on. As a rule, unsavory; often put on the back burner, in this case not relevant. He had too much experience of things going wrong. When it came to dark arts, L'Entità was his calling card, for they had a vast network of spies across the world to enable justice and revenge for those who tried to bring Canon law of the Catholic church into the dirt. There were enough arseholes in the world seeking justification for Catholicism as there were for Judaism, Christianity, and Islamism.

All three linked one to the other. Christianity from Judaism, Islam from the other two. For these investigations to work he needed to strip one from the other. When it came to the occurrence of these two events involving his and Cohen's religious faith, he considered him a brother-in-arms. And in consequence of these atrocious attacks; in the matter of other faiths, he had an ally.

He telephoned the Embassy of Israel in Rome asking to speak with Mossad's deputy director Rohen Cohen. Not unexpectedly the man was already heavily involved asking questions with what had gone on at the Great Synagogue. For an attack on the synagogue in Rome, although threatened from time to time, was no more than the usual antisemitic language doing the rounds on social media. Recent heavy activity on the internet had not warranted Internal Security to provide additional protection from that already in place. He buried a seed in the desert asking him to make some inquiries through his sources.

The Institute for Intelligence and Special Operations had offices around the world. Cohen had been field officer, operating in various theaters from Russia to Africa to the Middle East, and as other Mossad agents, relied on intelligence coming from informers. In the matter of this attack on the Great Synagogue, although via another source, was nonetheless kosher. He had personally dealt with the man over the years, for sensitive information of interest to the Jewish State in Israel. Coincidentally the name mentioned by Steiner, was worth more than a preliminary investigation. He hadn't gone too far into the ether before he came up with two other names linked with the man. Worrying.

When reality turns to the fantastic normal people turn away. But with both him and Steiner having strong religious beliefs; apart from protecting their own interests with cross and gun, he . . . Cohen of course, could only speak for himself, but he was sure Steiner wouldn't be too far and away from the world of the fantastical as himself. Which is what they had here. Cohen had dug deep. And if it was too far removed from what Steiner had already, then he would eat his kippah.

Going through records at Mossad's headquarters, he came across some interesting documents. Of course, a deal of cross-reference had been required, but he eventually got there. And of course, he was going to have to report to Steiner information he acquired on Vatican secret documents. How far he would have to go when speaking with him when it came to his divulging some or all, well, see what Steiner had on Mossad, eh? Of course, the near apocalypse of the world a few years back, both men were aware. So was the rest of the world come to that. An explosion, so vast it shook the planet, actually taking time off the clock, or so it was said. Becland in the USA its epicenter. The US Department of State issued a press statement at the time first saying it was caused by the lid blowing off the reactor at the Chernobyl nuclear power plant, in the Ukraine. Later an asteroid. Neither of those facts particularly important on their own, but why the change of reason?

Three names in the frame, up to their necks, in that, reason for change; all with close contact to the US Government, in one form or other. All acquaintances, like, as in, close. More. One involved with the Russian premier at the time. Purpose? The two men prevented a third world war. And who was the major contributor in the conversation for a Russian climbdown? An FBI agent, name of Charlie O'Hare. The Russian premier at the time, Sergei Bezukladnikov. O'Hare's trump card to the man: Malmstrom, Montana, Minot, North Dakota, Wyoming; all America's ICBM sites stacked up, counting down, ready to go. Um. A brief outlook record showed all three of them were at a party together in Becland shortly before the explosion. Coincidence?

So as it stands, looks as if Fitch and Carter were being held together by that FBI agent . . . what, reputed to be one-hundred-eight-years of age. Someone's not done their homework properly putting this file together. And where does Satan come into any of this, he thought?

Steiner asked for the reliability of his information. For the moment he was reluctant to say. For information held in Mossad's files, with him not sure of their accuracy, resorted to another source. As both men were on the phone, not able to look the other in the eye for sincerity, he reinforced an affirmatory of his source by answering:

'. . . As good as your Mary, mother of Jesus, whispering such intelligence in your ear.'

Steiner picked up on a slight hesitation in Cohen's speech. Whether it was an unlikely source he had since thought about before dismissing it, he couldn't be sure, for the deputy director went on to say, it came from the editor of a newspaper in the USA who had been keeping him abreast of Jewish rumor and unprintable news around New York for a couple of years now . . . 'Hamilton Fitch, of the *New York Post*, actually.'

'And where did this Fitch, where'd he get his information?'

The more he thought about the intelligence Mossad had, the more he was inclined to tell Steiner everything on that single statement of his asking. For there seemed to be more going on here than he first thought. Carter and her links with two others to mention just a few. Cohen could see this was going to put a strain on the professional relationships the two men had with each other when it came to security of both their houses and decided to fill him in completely with what he had. Afterall, too many people had been murdered by this terrorist attack; holy wars usually had an underlying element to them. Time to reveal what each other knew about all they had.

Steiner was to conduct an interrogation of Annie Carter at the Vatican. He asked Cohen if he'd like to attend.

'She nearly died from Novichok nerve agent,' Steiner said before the interview. 'And what's annoying. Under our noses. The same building. Five years ago, to the day. The only difference being the current archivist wasn't there this time. The whole building had to be closed for decontamination. Experts will take months to clean all traces of the substance from the building, making forensic examination difficult for our people.'

'Who was the victim?'

'Dr. Agata Fellowes. She happened to be in the same library as the archivist, Father Joseph Donne was murdered. It was Sister Benedicta Marie who was working alongside Father Joseph at the time. Both shot, the Father died from his injuries. She recovered after surgery. She has since left the Carmelite order reverting back to her civilian name of Annie Carter,' Steiner said.

'Was Fellowes the intended victim this time?'

'Not likely. Before she died, she said they were after the archivist, Carter. I looked at the previous report on the incident. It involved a scroll. Jewish. Stolen. We don't know what was written in it causing the murder of two archivists and the near fatal injury of another.

'You said five years ago, what, 1997?'

'Yeh. The latest is captured on CCTV. I've put out an all ports and airport search with the Italian police. We are looking for two men, one has an injury to his left eye. The other bore witness to his receiving the injury. And I've a feeling in me water we're not going to find them.'

'How'd you work that out?'

'Forced entry into the Vatican was hard enough. To get

inside its Secret Library, well . . . I was going to say—. Those dogs were professional. The only way in is with the help of an insider.'

Cohen thought about what Steiner said, and he was right. Security being what it was of late, lax, they had been asking for trouble. 'I'll look into the scroll business, see if I can find anything more. What did you say it was called?'

Cohen was introduced to Annie Carter. An elegant woman. He was told she was supposed to be sixty. She looked closer to thirty. A onetime Carmelite nun, and if his sources were trustworthy, an advisor to the FBI. He was impressed by her standing within the Catholic church. She had been Special Envoy to Pope John-Paul II, and presently UN advisor to the Ecumenical Society of World Religions. All impeccable credentials. Except for the FBI. Did Steiner have thoughts on her having the capacity for an advisor with the FBI, he wondered?

'A second attempt at murder to have happened in your place of work in five years is suspicious, Miss Carter. As to the terrorists assault on the Vatican and the Great Synagogue, you called the Carabinieri within minutes of the attack taking place before calling us and the Vatican Gendarmerie Corps. Were you aware these people were attacking the Great Synagogue at the same time?' Steiner asked.

'No. Of course not.' She looked at Cohen before returning her attention to Steiner. 'I was miles away.'

'Tell me. Was calling the Carabinieri your first thought? Were you having a change of heart seeing all those people being mown down, realising the same was occurring elsewhere in Rome knowing the best chance to call a halt to it was calling them instead of our people?' Steiner asked.

She studied both men before turning her attention to Cohen.

'Whatever faith, all are sacrosanct to me. As to the attack, I had nothing to do with it or those carrying it out. The fact I called the Carabinieri first was for their expediency in handling such matters. Had there been any delay in getting the Gendarmerie or the Guard out, more lives could have been taken.'

'You did have a call shortly before the incident. A man, name of Sin. Tell me Miss Carter, if you were not involved in all of this, was the man calling you responsible? Enemy or foe?' Steiner asked.

'An ecumenical matter.'

'Well, covers a multitude when it comes to a reply,' Steiner said.

'Let me get this right, Miss Carter. A Mr. Sin, who has never called you before, or to put it another way, has never used the name before, speaks to you in a familiar way about a person by the name of Hamilton. A journalist . . .' Steiner said.

'An editor actually.'

'An attempted murder within the Vatican museum, coinciding with the attack in Rome of the Catholic Church and the Great Synagogue. If you were sitting where I am, questioning you, wouldn't you be suspicious?'

'It's your job to be suspicious, not mine Hauptmann Steiner.'

'Let me ask you about the attempted murder you were an unfortunate victim before coming onto who this Mr. Sin is.

Five years to the day. When you and Father Joseph were attacked over a scroll. Was Dr. Fellowes in possession of it when she was attacked?'

'She was not.'

'You sure?'

'Well it's no longer in the possession of the church.'

'Can you tell me the content of the scroll?'

She looked at Cohen. 'All I will say is it belonged to the Israelis. A Jewish relic found balancing on part of a wall among the remains of an ancient tabernacle hit by a missile during the Yom Kippur War. We were asked to keep it safe, that's all.'

Cohen interrupted Steiner. 'We did look into the scroll, as you asked, Einrich. The people I contacted were not aware of the existence of any such scroll being handed over to the Catholic church for its safekeeping.'

'If your people are denying its existence there's nothing more to be said. However, I assure you it did exist,' Carter said.

'Do you think the recent attempted murder of Dr. Fellowes and the attempt on your own life are related, to do with any scroll?' Steiner asked.

'Only in as much as one of the men murdered Dr. Fellowes had one eye. If I looked into his face at a line-up, I'm sure, if there was any expression of guilt in his eyes then I'd see it. For the one shooting me before murdering Father Joseph came in with two good eyes; . . . left with one. Concealing such a facial deformity, should I see him again, would not be lost on me.

She related to both men for the existence of the scroll. She imagined the cell window at the time, open to the streets of Rome. She spoke of the Vatican's archivist, her mentor at the time, Father Joseph Donne.

'He was tortured then murdered by those two men, saying they were Knights of the Teutonic Order. They were after the code to unlock the ark the scroll was sealed in. Father Joseph denied them possession.'

'Do you reckon it's still in their possession. These Knights?' Cohen asked.

'Far as I know, the authorities in America have it. Hidden.'

'A Jewish antiquity in . . . ?' Cohen remarked.

'An important, possibly damning historical scroll, removed for what it might reveal is all I can say.'

'Nothing to do with the, Jesus Does Not Exist, conspiracy theory, then?'

'I'm afraid you're going to have to take that up with your own people at, Israeli Civil Administration, if you want further details, Deputy Director Cohen. And good luck with that one.'

O'HARE SEEKS A SEAMSTRESS

'RIGHT! I'VE SENT THE PHOTOGRAPH. Note. I am not asking why you want a picture of Kriemhild, I'm having enough trouble of my own. What you do in your own time is your business. Just saying, the government wants its return for their records when you're done.'

O'Hare laughed at Tubman's implication of any personal proclivities he had. He was not to wear it. Nor had he any desires to. An actress was to carry out the mission. He was not going into details with Ronstandt. If it goes wrong, it's down to him.

O'Hare called the Secret Service telling them of his plan. With the consideration of his standing within the US Government, presidents past and present, it should have been a piece of piss. Well to him, it should have been. But it wasn't. Facts were, there were people to be considered, they said. A bank of men and women willing to risk life and limb for their country, knowing the risk of losing either, going unnamed, unknown in this service was not the point. Their bravery was not to be in question. They told him they would be in touch as soon as possible, cautioning him of those facts, as did Joe

McClusky, O'Hare was in a hurry, and it was his only plan.

When the Secret Service got back to him he hesitated at first. For it was not only him being put at risk of, *Seeing God's face*, there were others too. Events took hold. It was impossible now to go back to his plan. They had a woman fluent in German, a dead ringer if the photograph was to go by, a seamstress and one-time costumier for Disney: The Lion, the Witch and the Wardrobe, which was fitting. He was engaged in this plan, hook line and sinker, while McClusky was knocking on his door wanting to know what he was doing. He had told him nothing, only to trust him further and be patient.

What was happening was no more than O'Hare expected. The incident in Rome was particularly bloody. Put simply the Order had ratchetted up to a fourth gear; one he had hoped was a sixth and final, but he knew it wouldn't be.

Businesses and organisations in the USA and the western world were coming under a sustained barrage of cyberattacks from ransomware and computer file information thieves, affecting telecoms, education, finance, manufacturing, retail, and health care in more countries in the western world than enough. Those attacks were extending into Europe. The United Kingdom's National Crime Agency and Europol, in close cooperation with the FBI, were managing to keep ahead of them, for the moment at least, for how much longer, the hackers were operating out of North Korea, Russia, Bavaria and eastern European countries using their own internet servers, it was becoming increasingly difficult to close them down. Despite government cross media briefings to the contrary, news of world war three being about to break out was beginning to cause panic among a public easily manipulated by social media hyper-news. The snowflake of fake news becoming a snowball was rolling downhill getting bigger all the time. He hoped the lady designated didn't get run down in her mission.

OLD FRIENDS. A LAST MEETING

'AND WHAT HAVE YOU GOT?' Stonercrop asked O'Hare. 'Come on. All this time. All your efforts.' O'Hare looked at the man lying before him. He was waiting for an answer. 'I'll tell you shall I? Absolutely nothing. A hard drive with two medieval files unable to be opened, contained in a gift pack for creation, with the logo, God on the outside. File icons, created to fool.'

'You seem to know all about them. Are you still on their subscriber list?'

'Do me a favor, Charlie. They've turned proper science into a joke. What we were trying to achieve was for the benefit of all mankind.'

'Try telling all the children murdered and abused it was for mankind's benefit,' O'Hare said.

'That's where proper science became farce. Child exploitation came when Spannocs got hold of the reins. When the government had its best chance to step in to prevent those crimes, what did they do? And you could have done more.'

'So you tell me, what was the name of the government department keeping Spannocs from prosecution?'

Stonercrop laughed. 'I was not one of them. I was a scientist, not a politician.'

'So there was one. What were their plans for the data?'

'Well it had nothing to do with current thinking. Creating another universe was not on our agenda. Exchanging one big bang for another would give no advantage to anyone. We were seeking science of the future. A science we might eventually arrive at without the natural progression of seeking it into the future. None of which involved the creation of other worlds currently being bandied about by the Order's latest incumbent.'

'The government department, Sax?'

'As I said, Charlie, I'm a scientist not a politician. Top-secret government departments, though known to me, are not available to me? Now you be honest. If anyone knows, it was goin' be you. So you tell me.'

'So this creation nonsense, is it all bull?'

'Let me give you a history lesson, Charlie. There's a country in East Asia with a leader preparing for war. Ordinarily a cause for humor, saber rattling from someone believing she can win a war against the west. A leader stupid enough to fall for the belief being offered to her for the creation of another world, another universe even, putting her in the league for becoming a goddess, as opposed to the self-appointed, self-believer she currently is. A country with the worst human rights record on the planet. A one-party totalitarian dictatorship systematically imprisoning what in any civilized parlance would be regarded as people with an opposition to their corrupted ideas, designating them criminals. Treated as slaves. Worked to death. They have been building what will become the largest energy particle collider on the planet. A creation nonsense? Well, she doesn't think so.'

'Let me get this right. What you are saying is anything other than what the original Order wanted from the data, assuming those files were opened, the consequences for the data to be downloaded; its data correctly applied by physicists to manipulate an atom, colliding it with another, similar, would achieve such a scenario?'

Of course, O'Hare was well aware such data existed. Aliens from another Time–Verse did not come to earth seeking it for a day out. The ability to perform magic to a level we can only presuppose will put them well beyond our understanding. The creation of another universe being science final and finite would be counterproductive to any aliens incapable of shifting in Time-Verse to avoid a catastrophe.

'Of course, there will be no gods, manmade or otherwise influencing the minds of the people on earth. Putting herself as a goddess a complete waste of time and energy for no one is going to worship her. Which is where this woman has it all wrong. She as many others before her will have been deceived by the greatest of all deceivers.'

He knew everything. Problem was, did Direktorin Elke Kriemhild know of the destruction any more than Frederik Spannocs did. Perhaps, how she thought of it. Destruction as opposed to complete wipe-out of everything. Back to before the big bang and the Pyrotechnician who set it all in motion.

Still he was no closer to getting the information he had been seeking for more decades than enough. A government department had encouraged the Order of the Most Divine Spirit, Frederik Spannocs and his child exploitations creating the wealth for Direktorin Elke Kriemhild's icing on the cake. Someone knew something. How can such a department surround itself in so much mystery for so long without anyone blowing the whistle on it? His best bet had always been Stonercrop, and the man was denying it all.

Stonercrop waved him closer better to listen. A supposed immortal with all the appearance of a man in his fifties; real time probably closer to a hundred, was dying. Either O'Hare had got those witnessing events at White Bear wrong or Stonercrop had been poisoned. For unlike himself and his own long age, Stonercrop's breathing was labored, a sign to him at least, the man was on his way out. His pallid expression give the appearance of someone being deliberately drugged, deprived even for keeping him alive, to hurry along the inevitable.

'Forget data for the creation of the universe. The creature we first brought to earth for the purpose of downloading what was in its brain, set a divine ball in motion threatening us all. God will step in if this persists.'

'And if God is no longer with us?'

He smiled. 'There is a myth doing the rounds, man is in the image of God. A similar myth abounds, man is also in Satan's image. Truth is we are not. It's all bullshit. You're an intelligent man Charlie, you must believe yourself.' He nodded. 'This kingdom of angels, ghosts, spirits, all coming from a black leather-bound book with a gold cross on its cover is no more than vivid interpretation and hope, held together with blind belief and faith. Bring faith into a world of reality and what have you got? A Creator open to interrogation. Our reward for the knowing will be the ultimate destruction of the universe who seeing Him, hold out their hands in a gesture of . . . so what! Who cares? His being, diluted to the point of the lowest common denominator species on earth, will mean nothing to them. We would learn no more; everything would be for nothing from then on. As you and I watch on awaiting death with bated breath, watch those believers, for they will be swallowed up. Under such revelations it couldn't come quick enough. The truth is creation came from an ultra-intelligence made up of complex particles of protons, neutrons and electrons looking to secure their own survival. And we're threatening their survival. And you know it, don't deny it, Charlie.'

He couldn't. For both men were present at the United States Air Force base White Bear in Alaska when the Order downloaded the data. The consequence of rubbing shoulders with the divine had opened a whole can of worms for all of them.

'You have immortality, Sax.'

'Immortality! You're deluding yourself. An intelligent man as yourself believing God's going to gift life everlasting to the like of us, come on. He'd have more regard for man's sanity. It might be fun to begin with, as quickly turn sour in normal twilight years. God wouldn't inflict it on his worst enemy, Satan might though, if he had the power. Let's thank the Lord he doesn't have. Huh. We're old men, Charlie. Get over it. Immortality! Not in our lifetime.'

'What you witnessed at White Bear . . .'

'I witnessed nothing at White Bear. That part of the Holy Grail promising immortality made no such appearance. Not for you, nor me. We were subjected to hallucinatory gases being developed for warfare. That's it.'

O'Hare listened to his tutor from a world past when he

had taken a degree in religious studies. brought mirth to Franklin Lomax, his boss in the FBI at the time. Stonercrop was in denial for what they witnessed at White Bear. Why a man of science was unable to accept and record what was in front of his eyes he was unable to fathom.

'Look in the mirror, Sax. You're older than me by what . . . ten years? Two people performing a magic trick in two places at one time, there's a scientific enigma for you, if you like. You're immortal. You know it. Get over it.'

There was silence.

He watched the man with a once great brain. Still did have; one having researched a possible theory of a four-stranded quadruple helix in the DNA of human cells, struggling with his health. Erasing his involvement with those engaged in crimes against children from his memory. He had been close to a spirit that did not take prisoners, as he was. Were they subjected to a hallucinatory gas was being developed? Absolutely not.

O'Hare left Heavens Flower's Care and Residential Home. He considered, perhaps Stonercrop was right, and that he wasn't long for this world after all. He was top scientist working with the Order at White Bear, the US Air Force base in Alaska. Then on lease to Ocean International from the Defense Department. There were those involved at the beginning still working, researching the damnable, AG-MX-960 being held by the government. All unable or wanting to recollect what they witnessed. All of them in their forties and fifties, depleted of knowledge for what they were working on with the Order. A few of them had worked for Fermilab, the United States national physics accelerator program laboratory under, Professor Kurtz Konig . . . God. Am I losing it here, or what? Konig. The particle physicist. Didn't he recently holiday in South Korea?

He felt alone. Skeptical of Stonercrop's interpretation of God and Satan being no more than ultra-intelligences composed of complex particles of protons, neutrons and electrons, still preferred his own catholic faith interpretation of the good word, for no other reason than preferring mental wellbeing comfort gained from a God in human form than an atom. He felt he was last man standing for God against Satan on earth. Not a particularly happy disposition.

He returned to New York making his way to Doheny & Nesbitt's bar on 42nd Street. He sat on his regular bar stool, and gave thanks to the Father, the Son, and an overly emphasized large whiskey Spirit, warmed reverently in his hand, for the purpose of reinforcing his faith. Stonercrop was wrong in his belief. He was immortal. Their witnessing of a creature, he took, and certainly the Order took, as being Divine and seen at White Bear by many; inadvertently brought from the heavens an immortality God had not sanctioned, reinforcing the belief to many, God no longer existed.

A week later Dr. Sax Stonercrop passed away after a brief illness. O'Hare asked the nature of the illness from the matron of the care home he was in.

'Alzheimer's of course. What else?'

ANOTHER REPOSSESSION. ANOTHER DOLLAR

WEBB AND COLEMAN HAD TAKEN TIME OUT from their moonlighting repossession business to assist the Federal Agency of the United States Secret Service. They were to secure a computer hard drive from an important lady. If that was all it was, then it wouldn't be a bad day's work, but it wasn't.

Along with the other agency, they were press-ganged by the FBI for further work. The Critical Incident Response agency, involved, needed a helicopter, not any old helicopter, s special one, from a certain place.

'No problem Spider, up our street.'

Part of the penalty for being minor criminals, was being allowed to continue in their work, only this work didn't pay.

'Government pilot rates only this time, I'm afraid, Zac.'

'Who's in charge?'

'Guess?'

'Oh, fuck! O'Hare?' A rhetorical question he wasn't expecting an answer. Webb just smiled.

'He's not coming. He's sending his assistant, Kaleigh Daly and an actress.'

Coleman, a look of incredulity in his expression.

'And a couple of armed agency people from the CIR for good measure.'

Webb and Coleman were once more employed in one of O'Hare's half-brained exercises in pushing death ever closer to the edge of life. Both seconded to an operation, pushing their mettle to the ultimate. They were to introduce a Direktorin Elke Kriemhild lookalike into Drogstadt Castle.

O'Hare asked Jean Ronstandt if he had any informers within the castle. He asked the same from Janet Watson-Forbes, Director of National Intelligence. A double-edged sword inquiry, some departments like to keep some of their secrets safe from others.

Of course, he had to be careful when any name came up from his past for their trustworthiness. Any involvement with an organisation such as the Order; or the people inducted by Ahriman needing an escape clause when it came to criminality, or treason against America was a person in the no camp.

'I would have told you before now if we did have.' Ronstandt's reply.

Watson-Forbes's reply came with more positivity.

'Not my field of operation really. However, I'll put the word out. Can I ask why you need such sensitive information, Charlie?'

'We're trying to identify and infiltrate a drugs cartel operating in Germany close to the Bavarian border. By coincidence it happens to be near to Castle Drogstadt. An undercover agent, working within, with a working knowledge of what's going on around Weinberghöhe is required.'

Watson-Forbes tone changed at the reason. She

immediately identified someone who could point his team in the right direction.

'And it's nothing to do with Castle Drogstadt?'

'Certainly not, Janet. As I said, local knowledge, nothing to do with castles or historical buildings, is all I need.'

'Tarney. Marshal Tarney. Agented in Weinberghöhe. I'll give you his contact details. A word to the wise, Charlie. He's thoroughly professional. If he thought his cover was about to be blown, he'd kill you without batting an eyelid. He'd kill me if it was to save his skin . . . and I'm his handler.'

'Aren't we all, Janet.'

'No. Not this one. Don't underestimate Tarney. Just keep away from the castle. Understand?'

'All the way, Janet. I won't go anywhere near the castle.'

Now there's a name to conjure, he thought. Nicknamed 'Ear of the White House'. Tarney had been one time head of vetting for the Secret Service. If anyone had the expertise to find the hard drive, then Tarney was the man. Fortunately he wasn't going on this mission. So he hadn't lied to Watson-Forbes about him going anywhere near it. Nevertheless, a warning had to be given out to those that were, without exposing the man. And if they did, they would need to shoot first.

Webb and Coleman arrived at Wiesbaden Air Base, Erbenheim. A US military flight took them from there to Ingolstadt and the Fliegerhorst airfield where Kriemhild's helicopter was hangered. Webb handed over a copy of German Law on the Restriction of Arrest of Aircraft to the airport authority. They studied it, permitted the plane's removal.

The Bell 430 was slowly wheeled from its hangar. Pre-checks carried out and readied. On board, four CIR officers, a Secret Service agent, Kayleigh Daly, and . . . Direktorin Elke Kriemhild.

Secret Service agent Margaret Unholster, a dead-ringer for the woman she was to impersonate in looks, as well as language, commented to the crew assisting her on, Passt auf das Kleid auf, Jungs. Ich bin bereit, England zu regieren.

Wearing Seamstress Aggie Huggett's special creation, she straightened the dress, said once more, this time to Coleman, 'Watch the dress, boys. I'm ready to rule England.'

Coleman navigated their course. Baxter was to fly the Bell to the town of Weinberghöhe town and Mount Drogstadt.

In half-an-hour they were over the great dome of Drogstadt Castle. Webb slowly circled waited on the castle's traffic controllers to ask for their authorization code. They didn't have one to hand. Daly worked furiously to lock into one while they hovered. One wasn't asked for. The Bell was obviously exempt. A hole in the top of the mountain got bigger as the door went across exposing a landing deck below.

'We're going down,' Webb said. 'You okay, Kriemhild?' She nodded that she was.

Baxter went through dropping the Bell onto the Castle's landing pad. Immediately a team of security leapt into position to tie the plane down. The door slowly closed shut above them. Baxter switched the Bell's engines down, first to a slow turn of the blades, then a complete stop. One of the Secret Service men opened the door and lowered the steps for Kriemhild to step down.

Margaret Unholster stepped out with the air of a queen.

Speaking in German while at the same time giving the impression she was annoyed at being here, her security not wishing to upset the woman, stepped aside. She looked across at Tarney.

'Here take this. My office, please.' She handed him Daly's metal case of electronic tricks and an envelope. Unholster and Daly followed, going to an entrance door, then into the mountain.

'Shall we fuel up while we're here?' Coleman asked Webb looking at a fuel pump with the sign, Avtur. Jet fuel painted on it. 'Won't have to pay for it.'

'No, you're all right. Best leave it.'

Within ten minutes Unholster emerged out onto the landing platform with Daly and Tarney. Daly held a leather case in her hand. They made their way across to the Bell, were about to reboard when a woman called out from across the landing platform.

'Elke! What are you doing here, thought you were in New York for a dinner date?'

Unholster swore quietly to herself. She ushered Kaleigh to get on the plane while she dealt with the situation. She didn't know the name of the woman calling across to her. Tarney stepped in and whispered.

'That's Bathilda Van Dijk her lover. Didn't anybody tell you she was here?'

Unholster shook her head no.

'She hasn't the time, Bathilda. They have to get back.' Tarney called to Van Dijk as she approached.

'Not even for me, Elke?' Van Dijk asked as she came close to her for an intimate greeting or a farewell. She turned to him.

An anger in her face, 'She is capable of speaking for herself, Tarney.' She hesitated. Staring closer at the woman. The lover she knew minute details of complexion and perfume of said, 'You're not, Elke. Who the fuck are you?' She looked closer at her, turned to one of the security officers. 'Take the bitch down. The woman's an imposter.'

Security were already unlashing the plane from its anchorages when clicking of safety catches from their weapons, brought the first of the Critical Incident Response officers from the doorway of the Bell. One was shot down before he had the chance to let fire his weapon. With the sound of the gunfire, a second, third and fourth agent was out of the Bell rattling off rounds from their semis. Castle Drogstad's security were unexpectedly overwhelmed. The display of firepower was not what they expected with a visit from their boss, some still thought the woman to be, confused them. They went down on their knees, more out of safety for Kriemhild than their own lives for they were not wholly convinced by Van Dijk saying the woman was not Kriemhild.

Van Dijk ran back inside the castle. She needed a weapon to stop the Bell from taking off. A rocket-propelled grenade was going to do that. Even though her luxurious mode of travel, Elke would not thank her for allowing it to fly out of here with her enemies intact. She unlocked the cage containing the weaponry, took one down.

CRI officers disarmed what remained of security, had them kneeling, hands locked behind their heads. Not the best of restraints, but it was going to have to do. Unholster boarded with all bar one of the FBI officers. He remained to stand guard over them, while the plane was readied.

He turned his weapon on Tarney, ordered him to open the roof. The man was not about to argue. He went to a control panel on the wall putting in the codes required. The roof slowly opened, then stopped quarter way.

Webb started the Bell's engine, though how he was going to get them out of here with all this blowing up he had little idea. He was going to have to go for it in spite.

The FBI agent held the fort with his automatic to the people on their knees, while Webb set about starting the Bell's Rolls-Royce 250-C40 engine. Time was not on his side for what he had to do next if they were to safely lift-off. He switched the battery on, hurriedly went through prechecks. Checked fuel boosts and engine relay. The gauges showed green. He run up the motor starter to fifteen percent then looked at the dashboard. Transmission and oil pressures all okay, engaged the starter and brought up the throttle. The four blades began to turn on the sixty per cent, he removed his finger off the starter button. He was supposed to wait a minute. But what the heck, he didn't have one. Turning and smiling to Coleman, already looking on the anxious side, he switched the generator on, followed up with the avionics. He brought the throttle to seventy per cent, this time he had to wait the other minute which, as previous, became half a minute a throw. I'm done. Shouted out to all to strap in. Throttle up to hundred, he rocked the plane up and down, waited for his passengers.

Kaleigh Daly came in. Her laptop open, software going through its million permutations to find the six-digit code to fully open the dome door.

Coleman grabbed the wrist of the CRI officer carrying out watch duties get in. Half in, half out of the plane he lost his grip of the officer's wrist. The plane, half a yard off the deck: Webb had no choice than to drop it back down. Then he saw the woman come running toward them, an RPG-7 loaded with its grenade, slung across her chest. Fook.

Van Dijk stood to one-side of the CRI agent, between him and her stood Tarney. She smiled at him, and he knew she was about to blow them all to kingdom come before Webb lifted another inch. Idea born of desperation. Risky? Was it ever, but chances were his game; his passengers, unfortunately part of his team in that game. But then knew what they signed up for when they joined their individual agencies. Career professional to a man; and woman. In the front line when it came to defending the US from enemies of their nation; willing to die for what they believed. O'Hare had tipped him the wink, Tarney was one of their own, even so, not to give him a chance. The world of such people is full of misinformation. Infiltrators implanted into an illegal or criminal organisation, keen to resume their work were often called on to spill their own people's blood to continue in that work. He was with O'Hare on that one, you can't trust an informer to keep you safe for their own agenda. His only immediate worry, what Tarney was preparing to do to protect them in getting out of here with that, bitch of a woman with that rocket-propelled thingy across her shoulder. Would he tackle her to the ground? He looked to Coleman. A partner who could often be relied upon to come up with a solution to any problem, eventually. Yes.

'We could duck.'

'Not the solution I was seeking, Zac.'

If the sharpy-end of the rocket was just threatening, no problem. Fact was, the woman had a determined look, not seeking any excuse to fire off and let rip that pointy end straight at us. He momentarily questioned whether she realized it wasn't Kriemhild's luxury pie in the sky, holding fire. No, she wasn't bothered either way.

'Hang on to your vitals everybody.'

Webb opened the throttle fully. The Bell, already primed and shaking to take off, come away off the platform like a coiled spring. He was going to take a flyer with this woman. Quite literally. With the Bell swinging sideways across the hangar, he went straight towards her and Tarney, stopped, then hovered. Tarney separated himself from the woman and run towards the roof door, open and close panel. Van Dijk, seeing what he was about to do, pulled a pistol from an arse holster and shot him down. If he was one of ours, then she had rumbled him. The CRI agent took advantage of the diversion and dived into the swinging door of the Bell, it closed from the vibrations of its engine. His timing was perfect. Webb ran the wheels of the Bell towards Van Dijk as she was replacing her pistol. She needed two hands for the RPG. Now she had them. She was a professional from an old school. Her alma mater, according to a records agency from East Germany received by O'Hare, Stasi. She would have been indoctrinated with not so much as a shred of indecisiveness when it came to taking a plane down, killing everyone aboard in a shower of exploding and burning debris.

He gritted his teeth, flew across the hangar and dropped the Bell hard across her shoulder with its port wheel. She reeled from the force of the impact. Even so, holding the RPG readied and pointed at them, any advantage he was out for achieving, was no better than seconds before. So close now if she let go with the grenade they were finished for sure. Of course she was about to die with the rest of them from the fuel in the Bell. There were also tanks of aviation fuel alongside the platform to be added into the mix. The damage from the explosion and the ensuing fire would put Castle Drogstadt and their operation here out of business for the foreseeable future. A risk too far for her life and the Order's facilities? If the fuse had been shortened, the explosive force and shrapnel would be triggered while the grenade was attached to its rocket on its upward trajectory, widening the spread. Blowing up a helicopter along with its passengers, taking her own life in the process. He headed to the open dome. Not yet fully open, Daly feverishly working, the computer's software, scanning pass key numbers, shrugged at him. Would Van Dijk dare?

Fook! She just did.

The trace of the RPG-7's grenade went across the front screen, missed the Bell altogether. He waited for the inevitable blast.

It didn't come. The rocket grenade carried on its trajectory straight on out through the roof span, exploded down into the mountain ravine. Was this intentional? Had she missed? None of those likely; more, the RPG-7 was primed with a long fuse. Error confirmed when she saw below, her smiling at him. She was reloading a second rocket into its launcher. He dropped the plane back down, then slowly maneuvered the Bell in time to her shoulder movement.

His thoughts went back to the time of the Daemon Crush mission. Another of O'Hare's jollies. Another helicopter ride. Another flight from an ignoble death.

A band of idiots trying to bring him and his passengers

down from the skies. And they were Americans, not supposed to be enemies.

On that occasion a guy jumped up to catch hold of one of the wheel stanchions of the helicopter, then began swinging on it. He had tried to shake the idiot off, and would have done, until another like-minded mug launched a Laws missile at them jamming his main driving rotor gear. The helicopter lurched violently to one side leaving Annie Carter leaning heavily against the side clinging to him; with nothing better to do, began screaming. He had fought with the controls as the plane moved first one way then the other before hitting a tree. The rotors' trying to defoliate it lost first one blade, followed in rotation by the other. He had tried to keep the plane horizontal knowing he had little chance for recovery before the plane tipped sideways and hit the ground. The electrics shorted out, hissed, glowed red, ignited the fuel spewing under pressure from its tanks. There was a short delay, silence. Those savvy enough, smelling aviation fuel, knowing what comes next, run, leaving the brave, and the pure stupid, liberally sprinkled and primed with accelerant to burn alive in the fire ball that followed. What come next was too much out of this world for explanation; not for O'Hare, Carter, or Fitch though. Passengers who had been into the world of supernatural with angels as guides, apparently. He hadn't believed them. He should have had more faith. For all were saved from a terrifying ordeal by fire, with him no more coming up with an explanation or reason for salvation than the helping hand from Iris, the goddess of the sky.

She was to come again.

*

They looked on in horror, waited, for the inevitable solution to man's problems. Bathilda Van Dijk, finger pressing the trigger of an effective weapon against soft and hard targets. Lover of Direktorin Elke Kriemhild. Ex-Stasi. A living and alternative evil version of Lara Croft, turned her head, then turned it further, a turn of the screw too far, her head fell from her shoulders onto the ground in a pool of blood. So much blood, he would have liked to have said he had never seen before, only he had, as witness to the remains of marines slaughtered at Becland by aliens, documented.

Peculiar occurrence, according to Margaret Unholster coming shortly before, in which she saw an alien being pointing a finger at her, as if to say you're next, was the horror of the scene played out before Van Dijk's demise.

One small procedural taskette before finally leaving. Castle's Drogstad's security team no longer interested after what they had seen. Take a blood sample from Lara Croft.

A repossession too far? Whatever.

'Okay. Got it. Lift off,' Coleman said. 'Give us one of your fags Spider.'

'Your hands, please. Here antibacterial wipes,' Unholster said passing the Arachnid logoed pack across to him from Webb. 'By God, she was one piece of fanny though. Understand why Kriemhild fancied her. Would have given her one myself under other circumstances.' She turned to Daly. 'And did you see that bit of gold bling hanging round her waist; didn't come from any Christmas cracker. Wonder what pleasure she gave to acquire that.'

LAYING OFF A DEMON?

'WHERE WAS MY SECURITY? What were the Bavarian authorities doing allowing American secret service into my castle?' She was confused. A loss of memory. A shift in something. *What's happening, Ahriman?* The flow of thought from her once self into the other for the answer to this perplexing question. For she had changed from her dress of state, into a blue serge business suit, for a job interview.

'My castle, Kriemhild. My castle.' The inquisitor looked sideways at the person next to him, gently laughed. 'Our castle, Direktorin Elke Kriemhild. Our cavern in the mountains. For we are the people responsible. We. Own. Castle Drogstadt. Not you, your Reichsbürger, or the Order. Which, we have more than an active interest, as we do the Reichsbürger movement you are so fond, for some ancestral family ties with the Third Reich. In fact, Direktorin Elke Kriemhild, we own and run you. Your personal raid on Castle Drogstadt; using your plane to gain access, using the excuse it was the secret service carrying out the operation, "Nothing to do with me", pathetic. It had everything to do with you, as was the murder of an important member of its staff, you had intimate relations.'

'Who are you? What murder?'

'Bathilda Van Dijk. And our agent, Karla Kia. You went there for the express purpose of removing data belonging to us. When Kia tried to stop you. You also murdered a number of staff, working in the castle. You've run your course, Direktorin Elke Kriemhild.'

'You haven't answered me, who are you, that you speak to me in this way?'

She looked across the large board room table. A surface, polished mahogany. A room, in semi-darkness. Silhouettes of three hooded people opposite. She thought they wanted her for a debrief of Malaka's Corner, she was ordered to abandon.

'Oh, you're the Graf & Mayer idiots, let a US Government agent informer into the business.' Sidelong glances, the only replay she was to get. 'No doubt, cocked up with your employment procedures, decided to cover it, closing the operation down.'

She stood. Not by her own hand. She was being restrained, led away into a darker arena. Wrists restrained with rope. Daylight now. She was in a gymnasium. Two US army officers in front of her. To one side, a rough wooden box she supposed was to be her coffin, a prison chaplain. One a sergeant, the other a military policeman. She was over a trapdoor on a scaffold. A rope put round her neck with no consideration of the knot being under her left ear ensuring an instant break to her neck. Instead she was to strangle to death, hanging half in and half out of the trapdoor. She screamed innocence, then whispered to the Lutheran chaplain as the hood was placed over her head:

'I'll see you again.'

She dropped through the trapdoor, scrapped her sides,

drew blood, as she went through, swinged, choked, then hit the ground, unconsciously dead? Or waited resurrection dead, she couldn't say.

Don't try and cross me again, Queenie!

DESIRES OF A DEMON?

O'HARE NEED NOT HAVE WORRIED. Although, he did at the time. Coming out of the blue, a letter with the postmark, midtown Manhattan addressed to his home in New York. The writing, in faded dark brown ink on a printed letterhead. He sensed hollow laughter, while slicing the letter open. Not for the first time a chill went through him. The company heading at the top of the letterhead, Oceans Galactica, with the business address location, Floor 24, Ocean Mansions, Staten Island, NY. An address no longer existing, except in the mind of the sender. A finite backward shift in time of 10^{-15} of a second ensured the building's continuum. Of course the company had Frederik Spannocs as its CEO then, no longer with us in current time, nevertheless. . . .

Oceans Galactica, razed to the ground on the orders of the president, Henry Clancy Montgomery III then, for the reestablishment of world order, being held in jeopardy by Spannocs and his affiliations with the Order of the Most Divine Third Circle. O'Hare had the ability to forever recognize Satan whatever guise he chose to make further appearances on earth. If he was right, believing Satan begat Ahriman, along with Kriemhild, his latest incarnation, were there to be others playing out this numbers game getting to where he wants to be? Delayed for the time. For Kriemhild had misappropriated half a program he desperately needed. And if she was in any doubts as to his powers, the death of her beloved Bathilda Van Dijk would have reinforced his power over her, taking her killing, as by his hand. Power of life and death is not his to manage, overlooked by her. Another pup she had been fed, along with all others in the litter.

She invited him to dine with her. Problem. Was he to accept an invitation, walk into a nest of snakes, as he had in the past, or give her a rain check. For although he had nested there before, on such occasion defeating him, doing a second time . . . well, lap of the god's. Satan took on experiences from past encounters, and unless he came up with another solution outside the box, only then would the triumph be his. Then the world, once more on the brink of an apocalypse, the human race believing such events impossible, would simply slip away, unnoticed, along with the universe. Damnation out of our hands and into those of another. Human race salvation stretched to its limit, with complacency all to blame. Forget judgment day. There wouldn't be time or desire for verdict when the clash came. We'd all be thrown into the lake of fire, splash and swim around with the bastard. No time to pick and choose the good from the bad. Throw the whole lot in and start again being His only option. Would He make such a decision with a spin of a coin or with considered judgment?

He considered the best option for God's survival of the human race would be the spin of a coin; not considered judgment, which to his way of thinking, doom the world to a vast and decisive conflict. A prophesized confrontation between good and evil entitled, End Time.

A final Har Magedon, coinciding with Satan's time of little season, when the world under his leadership of anti-Christian government, anti-Christian religion; dragon, beast, and other such false prophets gathered around the world; His human race awoken from evil oppression from all sides, seek too late; for a longer stay, say a couple of millennium, please, before bringing on Your prophesized apocalypse.

He spent the evening into the early morning drafting his final will and testament. Not out of any sense of it being read, more out of habit in case he had got all of this wrong, with people remaining to read it. Not one containing a distribution of his wealth, for he had pledged those to children's charities long since, for what he was about to reveal to the United States Government in event. His death at the hands of Satan should he lose, was one he would face for others and not his own salvation. He would face terror and dread alone not because he was brave, stupid even, for he had both of those in equal measure; but because Satan used methods of violation against both mind and body, while He . . . well, would wash his hands, ignoring interference in matters concerning mortals, and only mortals.

He wondered how English noblemen fallen from favor with their king faced being hanged, drawn and quartered, while at the same time being aware of what was happening to them. Satan had tools to bring that on. After which he had no further jurisdiction, not until the fires of hell, quenched by water, took the innocent away from his perdition on the road to purgatory. The operative word being innocent. For sure, he wasn't in any league when it came to the saints, a sinning monk seeking end of day absolution, perhaps?

Sweet Mary mother of Jesus. He wondered if there wasn't a better religion for all this suffering on earth and what was to come than the one he had. For this was his religious doctrine speaking to him, hoping it was all complete bollocks. Perhaps New Age esotericism have the answer to one. It'll do for me. Trees and dancing naked had more going for it than fires of hell. Even to prove Ahriman and his cohorts were nothing more than aliens from another time, universe, verse, or whatever. Now, there's a thought. For all he would be unable to move away from the occult and mysticism going along with the philosophies of Frederik Spannocs and the Order craving the creation's data for a new universe and other recruits.

He sent the letter to a company dealing with fakes and questionable documents for analysis. In twenty-four hours they came back telling him the printed heading was about ten years old; the ink however was in an altogether different ballpark. They were uncertain, it needed to be investigated further. They found nothing untoward with the scroll or paper, its ancient writing used a formulation of ink, this one however was written on a modern company letterhead, with ink older than 200 BCE. He thanked them. Asked for its return.

Ahriman is with you.

He did not deliver Carter or Fitch his final testament personally, he posted it. He wasn't going to take the chance on their helping him in this quest. For quest, read third world war in the making. He would accept Kriemhild's dinner date, and hoped she pressed for nothing more from him, on this, their first and last encounter than a whiskey. The hard drive, non-negotiable.

Dining at Eduard Kerschbaumer und Bier in Queens. Well, when it's a potential last meal with a Bavarian megalomaniac, where else would one choose to dine? Her entrance was dramatic. His, a mere melo- la entrée. Tuxedos were two a dime in this theater for trenchermen. She brought the roof down, or might have done before she planned to, if lusting by her audience were to be the trigger point. Men with their wives stood as they entered as subjects to a queen, the spouses remained seated, unimpressed with this falling over; an actress of a tart, chastising them for their libidinousness. Direktorin Elke Kriemhild, looked and sashayed, all the time oozed sex, subconsciously pimped him. Although personally, a rabid dog a better preference over this woman. For he knew what was below her skin. Infected by Ahriman, a rotted corpse in waiting.

Of course husbands and lovers, not having these insights, slyly making conversation with their dining partners, while at the same time wondering to themselves what was the top bid to entice her into bed, as quickly withdrawing them when finding out it was to be their final payment on earth. Whether Kriemhild had been taken over completely, he had no way of knowing; only conversation and time would do that. She, the hostess, while he, thinking the meeting between Count Dracula and Jonathan Harker began amiably enough, disappeared quicker than the house he was supposed to be selling him. Unlike the Count though, she dressed in the style of the 15th century Hungarian serial killer, Countess Elizabeth Báthory de Ecsed. Torturing and killed hundreds of girls and women, she could be next in line for one of Dracula's Brides. Read again. Satan.

Did she still have a touch of Spannocs in her, he would wonder? Time in his, or her company, determine. Or not.

For the moment, she had no inkling of his thoughts, for in her present guise of being the self-professed Queen of the Universe, thought only of herself as controller of her own destiny. Eventually, she'd awake, remember, and understand too late. Hopefully before he had got inside her head, without her knowing. He smiled at her, while at the same time feeling the eyes and thoughts of those male diners around him, in their envy, someone his age was close to pulling this woman. He humored her as they were shown to their table.

'Bread?' He selected a roll from the center of the table with tongs, waited for her to nod. She did. He placed it on her side plate then took one for himself. Subconsciously he looked around the restaurant, more for the comings and goings of its staff than the leering faces. Seeing him, seeing them, he realized the cat was out of the bag. If she had control of her destiny when she came in, well, she'd demonstrate it now.

She laughed. Picked a Bratwurst sausage from the plate of a customer, as a waiter was passing through, and put it to her lips displaying it to the table opposite. An elderly couple bearing all the signs of respectability, were in the process of enjoying a dinner of hunter pork chops. A stockbroker. A good woman, that might or might not have been his wife. He gave her the benefit. Brought up their children (no doubt assisted by a Mexican au pair); tried their best to ignore this exhibition of depravity, were to fail miserably. Kriemhild was having none of it. Not used to being made unwelcome, reached across and grabbed the stockbroker by the arm. Then, in full sight of other diners, worked the sausage in and out of her mouth in an act of phallic depravity.

Ahriman is . . . back in her house.

She hadn't finished with these two yet. Removing it through pursed lips with a suck sound, she reached across their table, dipped the end of it into his wife's sliced mushroom and cream sauce, dressing the chops. Sucked it back in.

Oh well. Any doubts he had with the woman taking control of herself, gone the way of the devil.

Now Frederic Spannocs has joined her.

The husband began to remonstrate. While other diners, men with wives, secretaries, bits on the side, having lusted this woman when she and O'Hare first entered the restaurant, fancying the woman instead of the person they were with, began moving their attentions back to them. Better the devil you know, as they say. For the price of fancying the arse off this piece of hoochie was a cost too high in terms of reputation, marital security, along with the humiliation of a woman not giving a second thought to giving a Bratwurst a blow job in one of New York's top restaurants at the drop of a hat, or any other dining establishment for that matter.

It was now clear, if she still held previous ideas for taking him on she would be, as others, sadly disappointed. Her exhibition of dining manner aside, Kriemhild has lost her humanity, identity, plot, and her social standing among the

Reichsbürger movement, become one with her host. If she was under any allusions for deceiving Satan the Magnificent; running the world her way, she'd already learned that lesson.

Where he was to go now, he had little idea.

She had called the meeting, suggested the restaurant, make a deal with him. He was powerful in his own way, and she knew it. Knew she had failed to assassinate him, twice. Whether she also knew he was an immortal capable of being murdered, unless one of the multicast active within her had told her as much, then she wouldn't. Reason. Satan liked playing games with him. Like them even further if he could corrupt him, bringing him along with him. For to bring a soul into his domain with what he carried would be the easiest solution of all for the dissolution of the universe and its re-creation with him at the helm. Did he believe he was going to give it to him. Ha! Not a chance. Oh, yes. I know his game, and he knows it.

For a nubbin of time he saw, or thought he saw, his face. Impossible? For words, chaptered in Exodus in the Christian bible, attributed to God,

Thou canst not see my face: for there shall no man see me, and live,

are as applicable to Satan as Himself. Difference being, Satan doesn't seek faith for any existence for eternal life. He takes them in souls from those of accepted beliefs, there is nothing to follow.

'The meal not enough to make you into a bigger boy, Charlie? For what I need,' she announced to the rest of the diners no doubt listening, in a voice no one misinterpreted its meaning. 'A big boy, a large dildo or a big bang, as the one on your coming horizon.' She looked around herself. 'Along with this gathering of rubbernecks and hypocrites.'

A whispered, not her voice followed. 'She's good, isn't she. Your call, Charlie boy.'

A pressured finger on the trigger was in the making. 'Sorry, my Queen.' He used her name subconsciously. Another trick. 'Need the little boys' room.' He stood up, wiped his mouth with a serviette, and made his way into the restaurant's kitchen. Other diners seemed to take the opportunity of his exit by getting up to leave themselves. Just as well, for whatever was coming, their wellbeing was about to take a downturn.

The sous chef looked up at this unannounced entrance into his work area, about to challenge him.

'Fire alarm.'

'Over there, on the wall. Hey. What are you doing?'

He hit the button, then the commotion began, from both the alarm and the remaining diners not taken umbrage from Kriemhild's displays of vulgarity. Pandemonium continued. He pushed open the FIRE EXIT door, shouted at the chef and his entourage of sous, commis, and kitchen staff:

'Get the hell out. There's a bomb about to go off.'

Ahriman was to bring the house down, taking him with it. He was Kriemhild's date for the evening, and was not about to leave her side, if for no other reason than the protection she afforded. Not out of any gentlemanly misbehavior on his part, for past dinner dates with ladies, were always conducted with decorum by him. Although decorum, too strong a word for any explanation of interpretation she might have, for who would conduct themselves among such fellow diners, tongues hanging out, if she was any other than a vessel for some, high capital prince of darkness and his peers? A second and final confrontation on his part, a final for her, not for Satan, whose ambitions were more than taking from God, Man and his universe, and what he held himself. A default position for Satan and his new universe without man or God ever more being part. The Spannocs's, the Kriemhild's and all other demi humans playing with his magic supposing they will be Kings . . . in her case, Queen of the Universe, were to be deceived. For deception is the name of his game: has been since the creation of time with His decision for having Black against His White. For the game was one He had formulated rules for its playing out. For any He did have, had been working against Him since He had created the dawn of time.

Whether a bomb or not, the effect would be the same. Utter destruction of the restaurant, with him buried under its rubble. A blessing if it had been, for he only found out later the extent. For the moment, he was in a darkness, one not of this world. If that was not bad enough, he found himself immobile. A body lying across him. The thought it was Kriemhild sent a chill through him. He was on his back, that much he was sure of. Was she raping him, though? Her sexual activity toward a man, him in particular, surely had ulterior motive if she were aware, which he doubted. She had never hidden her preference for women over men when it came to sex. According to Tubman, at least. Her lover, Bathilda Van Dijk, being the cited example. What gain, if she was sexually exploiting him? His semen squeezed into her ovaries, procreating a copy of himself? None of which would make any sense to the lady in question, to use a loose phrase, Elke Kriemhild. The deed for any outcome, not in her interest. Ahriman, though. His an entirely different ballpark, the demon's sexual proclivity gain, if not to copy, then data in its entirety, from his brain, removed through his soul. Assuming such was possible. And who can argue with unknown physics yet to be discovered? Not him, he knew better.

A darkness descended from the incendiary of violence. A device powerful enough to bring the fifteen-story building down, dumping its rubble into a canyon deep enough to level the site to the ground. Those inside, and everywhere about for a radius of five miles; unable to escape the outward blast, with the consequent rush of air returning to fill the void, wetted dark red and blackened bodies and limbs, scattered to the four winds and back, would leave an odor of actual flesh, combined with the smell of death in the air for weeks to follow from its fallout.

Queens County in New York State was a monumental disaster zone.

When he had pushed the fire alarm, he sensed loud laughter, as if she expected his reaction. But why was laughter continuing in the manner it was now? He had made a few enemies over the years. Some going as far as attempting to murder him in cold blood. Avoidance had been the name of his game then. Sidestepping had brought him lucky counter punches, but not now. Satan and his cohorts of demi demons, spectral diabolists moping and mowing, using others for the fight, was about the dark angels mark. Excuses for evil, death, and destruction passed to man, who in turn carried blame to God. Ahriman's host, Direktorin Elke Kriemhild, was chosen for good reason, for Frederic Spannocs had turned out *fucking* useless.

He sensed Spannocs, hearing his analysis of him and those he had fallen in with, cry out for a comeback and vengeance from him.

Let's hope, if what he thought had happened to himself, with regard to being penetrated, she hadn't fully realized she was Spannocs, for she wouldn't then have had either ovaries or womb to go the distance.

Short on spunk. That's you, Spannocs.

Emergency services excavated their way through what remained of Eduard Kerschbaumer und Bier in Queens. He was breathing dust. His savior, not Kriemhild, laying on top of him, as he first thought. Yet. The manifestation standing in the ruins of what remained of Queens, sword in both hands, ready to strike out for signs of any further attack on him, had deserted her post. She was spirit; against flesh, unable to assist. She'd cocked up. Left the door open. The hard drive containing keys for medieval files to be opened, not only accessible to Aliens in the Atlantic, but also, Kriemhild. For she had a ship standing by for its recovery? His soul with the other half, downloaded and copied from him by Ahriman.

KRIEMHILD IN RESTAURANT ATLANTIC

KRIEMHILD INSTINCTIVELY KNEW where the second part of the hard drive was. The key to opening those medieval files eluded her for so long, were below the waves. O'Hare was dead, the data now with her. His Guardian Angel deserting her post to save his life, in vain. The powers given her by Ahriman, far superior to his guardian angel. Finding herself having to attend him in a charcuterie and German bratwurst sausage restaurant, now a basement. Preoccupied with saving the life of an obscure Irish policeman, at the same time attempting to recover a hard drive above an alien ship, had proved beyond her.

'Have I embarrassed you, Charlie? Can I use your first name, for we have been acquaintances for so long, it's as if we're family?' She had smiled at him.

'You can, but you may not. For I'm no family of yours or any of your kind. Family implies humanity. You have long since been expelled from His humanity. You are context subdivision, where evil spirit meet human species, whose only work ethic is the corruption of souls. We once knew each other, that's true. A long time since. A different you. A different world. One you will soon begin to comprehend. In line with his, the same with its common misconception . . .'

She painfully cringed with its connotation.

'One that will plague you. For by the time he's finished flattening those tits of yours, with an iron from the furnace, pulled your bowels out, formed them into a tail to stick contemporarily from your arse, tore your lying tongue from your mouth with pliers, broken all bones in your body until you're as bent as the demon that brought you to this point, you'll be ready to join all the other transgressors down below.

'And lest ye forget, madam Direktorin, Satan did not evolve hell. God did. Cast Satan into it. Nor will it be Ahriman exacting punishments on you. For he will wash his hands of you. It will be the Divine Spirit. So choke it up, Queen of the Universe . . . and . . . *Have you been a good girl today, Elke? Have you?*'

Her expression changed.

She had laughed at his hurry. Disappeared from his meal to have a so-called piss. She noticed GUYS, DAMES, and SERVERY names on the doors as he went. Her displays had emptied the restaurant now. She laughed as a leiter, hurried through with a tray, meals tipped on the floor, after hearing a fire bell going off, with a following ruction coming from its kitchen servery. Arsch über den kopf, striking it as the door swung back then lay on the floor. He would not have a headache for much longer, she thought, continued laughing.

O'Hare didn't have to be pulled from the rubble, for it was as mist. He had mysteriously come to the surface. He turned himself over, took his weight on his hands and arms, stood up. He ran his hands through a piece of concrete. They passed right through unhindered.

'Right. Last time I eat here.'

The past began its journey of reliving before the building came down on him. He was arriving in a taxi, watching the building collapse on itself. His recollection, scant in time. An explosion, then a grandfather clock, an ExtraVersialTerrestrial invader dematerializing from the scene, he had been buried. A certain and final resting place.

Naked as the day he was born, neither a stitch on, nor a scratch to show for his ordeal he found himself among American Rescue Workers. A splinter group of the Salvation Army. He was immediately covered in a blanket, rushed away from the scene of this apparent earthquake on a gurney, and asked what he had been eating, and who with.

'A woman, perhaps? Is she still down there?'

'At my age! Chance'd be a fine thing!'

The Order's Ultra-Deep submersible vessel, RV *von Reuter* settled on the Atlantic ocean floor beside three enormous Alien ships locked inside a Sphere.

The woman next to Kapitänleutnant Karl Schulz, wearing the regalia of an Allgemeine SS officer, obviously cut for a woman of luxuriant proportions; hair groomed in some traditional braided crown, with makeup of an artificial natural cosmetic, considered over the top, overdressed; not his place to comment, watched proceedings below on the cctv. 'They're on the move.'

'Not captured in that sphere they won't be. Trust me.'

Schulz ignored her. The ship's hydrophones picking up soundings gave him a different definition of trust, for whatever was holding them in place was slipping away. He knew of these Alien ships but had never seen them before now. What he perceived took his breath away, for they were each as big as a nuclear submarine. Where they came from, his guess, was no better than anyone else's, or hers.

'Sir. We've company.'

'What is it, Oberleutnant Finn?'

'Another ship. Heading this way.'

He looked at the radar screen, then picked up his binoculars, went outside onto the bridge.

'American.' He turned to Kriemhild. 'Coming our way. Recovery is going to take another hour. We're in international waters, do not have any scientific research permission to be here.'

'Permissions where the Order is concerned are neither here nor there. As Direktorin of the Order, they are mine to give.' She furrowed her brow raising her black mascaraed eyebrows. 'Verstehst du, was ich sage, Kapitänleutnant?'

'Understand perfectly, my lady.'

'My Queen, my Queen, Kapitänleutnant.'

'Yes, my lad– my . . . Queen.'

'Better, Kapitänleutnant Schulz. You have missiles aboard?'

'For defense, yes.'

'Defend me then. Sink the American.'

He was not about to obey any such order. For sinking a ship of the NASA line on the open seas was tantamount to a war cry. 'Not the best idea, my Queen. Ramifications could sink us instead,' Schulz said.

He thought he was taking his authority too far. Even so, he was Kapitänleutnant while at sea, what he said went. Or not, as in this case.

'*Kapitänleutnant*? I am executive power.'

'You want us fire on them first?'

'Such conventions of war do you proud, Kapitänleutnant. Were you expecting to negotiate? For they will have no appetite to make terms with us when they find out what we are here for. *Fire on them*. That's an order, Kapitänleutnant.'

Ahriman was in Queens alongside of her. 'Where's his guardian?'

She looked about herself once more. She wasn't expecting a confrontation with the sword-swinging-happy creature, even though they trumped spirit on spirit, for she was too late to save his life.

The fire alarm bell rang out loud across Queens. 'Now, girl. Now. Timing is everything.'

Kriemhild was dressed in the uniform of an Allgemeine SS officer. Kapitänleutnant Karl Schulz was not to make an immediate decision to fire on an American ship. A call came through, RV *von Reuter* was surfacing. A team of surface crew immediately tied it off. The robot arm carried a plastic bag.

Kriemhild looked, then staggered. She was losing her powers, becoming confused. The excitement, perhaps? Or the swell from the sea? Whatever it was, she had to turn away and support herself on the guardrail of the boat.

'Do you want this or not?' Shultz said annoyingly.

She turned on him. 'Do it quickly. Bring it here.'

A crewman took the bag from the robot's grab dumping it on deck. Sea water flowed out from inside. 'Careful with that, you idiot.' She bent and turned the hard drive out. Confusion or not, she had what she came for. Now she had all the bargaining power on earth at her disposal. And with O'Hare's guardian angel elsewhere in another time, Kriemhild was safe from a guardianship she had abandoned. The integration of both halves to take over the world would see Ahriman off her back for the rest of time. With him gone she no longer had a need for his magic of past ignorance, when science barely existed. She had it with those files. She was sitting on physics only scientist could dream of. Its words of revelations no longer being possessed by its Creator to be released drip, drip at a time as and when He felt man's research had come far enough for Him to be satisfied they'd put it to good purpose (another error of judgment). She was possessed of a creator's voice now. 'Didn't I tell you to take the American ship out, Kapitänleutnant?'

Oberleutnant Finn pointed. Schultz looked in his direction. The ship was not a NASA research vessel as he first thought, instead, an American Ticonderoga-class cruiser on Nato reconnaissance duties. She was armed with guided missiles and everything else needed for an afternoon's work that threatened America and the west.

The cruiser was on them now. Its commander hailed them to stop what they were doing. Kriemhild picked up the megaphone and shouted through it, 'Verpiss dich. This is a private research vessel operating out of Germany. You have no jurisdiction over us.' She took it away from her lips and turned to Schulz to fire on them.' The kapitänleutnant was not about to engage in any confrontation leading to a fire fight.

The cruiser was now alongside, its captain was coming aboard his vessel with a contingent of marines. Schulz saluted him. He was immediately pushed to one side. The captain was more interested in dealing with a Nazi officer than him. 'And what the fuck are you about, madam?' The Nato commander studied the woman wearing the uniform of an enemy from the second world war. 'Who are you people?'

She laughed. Her powers had returned. She hoped he had not figured her plan, to send him back from where he came, leaving her back in Queens in another time. She had brought her spirit from a dinner date to the middle of the Atlantic ocean, without any help from him. How it happened, she was not concerned. She stood upright and announced herself.

'I am Direktorin Elke Kriemhild, Queen for the New World Order. Are the Americans on litter patrol duties? We are on a scientific research program for the Order of the Most Divine Third Circle.' She was in confident mood to name the organization taking over the world. The thought in her head, timing was paramount now. She had both parts of the hard drive in her possession. She laughed. The fifteen-story building of Eduard Kerschbaumer und Bier in Queens had crumbled to dust taking O'Hare with it. Her alter spirit had drifted away from the scene as light snow in a breeze. She had changed into clothing more in keeping with her forefathers.

Hail Satan. Hitler's 1 000-year Reich was nothing to Satan's magic she had in her hands now. She opened them, palms up, expected torrents of flame extending to the heavens to burst forth. Nothing.

The Walmart bag, below the waves, brushed gently against the outside of the Sphere. Kriemhild was in another time.

'Kapitänleutnant Karl Schulz. Under United Nations Convention on the Law of the Sea, 1982, you are to hand over your vessel to me. Officers and crew are considered under arrest—

'And where's that Nazi princess disappeared?'

Should have left you dangling by your neck, Queenie.

–EVT CHRIIKUN broke free from the Sphere holding the three ExtraVersialTerrestrialist ships of the SENTINEL MOTHER invasion fleet. The container holding the keys for opening the files they had tractor beamed half across this ocean were immediately taken into their possession, its wrapping discarded into the sea. The data unlocked files from a source not currently known.

–EVT CHRIIKUN went to location. Harley Hare. Predator Guardian intervened, caused –EVT CHRIIKUN lockout. Predator Guardian downloaded into their system computer; coordinates showed a building Eduard Kerschbaumer und Bier in an area Queens. The building destroyed level to the ground held a man. –EVT CHRIIKUN sensed entity. Identity system computer showed file picture program Harley Hare, an aged and intellectual human male, as being source. No signal location guide. The obstacle to its knowledge, the firewall protection surrounding the sphere unlocked. Predator Guardian downloaded breadcrumb data with single access, excluding all other. –EVT CHRIIKUN allowed through. –EVT CHRIIKUN extracted Harley Hare from the building's war rubble, copied, downloaded codes from human brain, leaving Harley Hare sitting there, was gone.

A chanting signal came from the content of the hard drive removed from above them in the sea as –EVT CHRIIKUN downloaded its content data. The ExtraVersialTerrestrial copied the signal into their Identity earth computer. Processing it. A picture program of a human with the name of Barrie Mani Low came onto its screen. –EVT CHRIIKUN downloaded the image into their system for future reference as it played out its recording, ♫ *At the Copa, Copacabana, The hottest spot north of Havana* ♫.

The song echoed inside the hulls of the three ships rising from below the waves of the Atlantic Ocean in perfect alignment. Having all they had come to earth for, the ships turned west toward the co-ordinates of Becland . . . were gone.

She saw her lover, Bathilda Van Dijk, a grenade launcher over her shoulder, wearing the Stasi business dress of tight skirt with 22ct gold chain hanging from around her waist. Costing $20 000 from Totaram. She had gifted her. Her open blouse jacket showing a hint of a black bra, their contents spilling over had always turned her on. Her hair in the traditional plaited hairstyle common to 1930s German women she herself loved so much was the icing. Her mouth watered with desire for the woman she would love again. She watched in horror as Van Dijk's head twisted around in one direction three times. The complex structure of bones, muscle, nerves, blood vessels, lymphatics and all the other connective tissues becoming a knot of blue and red as her head came away from her body to fall onto the hangar platform, she wept. Briefly seeing her face she collapsed forward. Seated in the Bell, clutching a brown leather case, a young woman, bearing an uncanny resemblance to her father, seated among officers of the US Security service.

The culmination of 2 000 years of the Order; she had failed both them and Ahriman. A darkness descended and she . . . she, Direktorin Elke Kriemhild, was about to wander the detritus of useless spirits . . . [with] the rest of her kind, fallen from favor for her interference in the affairs of the Creator . . . torn from her current server, she was in shock. The realization powers granted her, no longer available, she was alone.

She stood inside the parapet and its partition bordering the temple precincts of this House of God in Canaan and shook in terror at the words in front of her. A sign she determined was not to be her destiny for eternity, hesitated. For at the entrance to this domain, she felt herself still flesh, still one with humanity, turned back.

Ahriman, part transcended from spirit to human, was of her same flesh, startled. She faced him square-on.

'Here! Loser! Have some of my, Malzeichen des Tieres,' then struck him hard, a punch to his face worthy of her time as the ex-German light welter-weight boxing champion of 1989, when she beat Silkie Kiss in the second round at the Ostseehalle arena in Kiel.

Ahriman recalled the voice of the dark shadow,

Tire yourself to eternity then.

The master deceiver, flipped, vanished. Before her, a man she recognized. A photograph, an article about him, in the rich-man's, *Forbes'* business magazine from the 1950s, Frederik Spannocs. A bruised, blooded and broken nose, sporting the infernal logo, mark of the beast below his chin, staggered, then went down as a sack tumbling off a shit truck onto the road. Confused.

The beast's mark, as old as time itself, in the throes of being partially branded to the top of her thigh, just two and a half sixes completed, was now disappearing, to be rendered null and void.

EPILOGUE ACCORDING TO CARTER

SHE RECEIVED A LETTER FROM CHARLIE. Then put it to one side to concentrate on another. A 2 000-year-old formal accusation against Jesus of Nazareth, showing purported evidence Rome was to use to criminalize, then crucify the man.

Father Joseph Donne, Dr. Artur Siefert in an earlier life, one of the leading lights in the field of historical religious documents.

And here she hesitated at the first of those names.

Ahriman-Spannocs, the demi-demon and anti-Christ-in-waiting knew it. All knew precisely what he wanted when those two sinners dressed in white suits, bearing badges of red crosses on their lapels, came for one document, and none other more valuable.

She never forgot them.

The one bearing the scar for her extinguishing a Marlboro into his eye to protect Father Joseph, the suffering he was going through to keep from them the combination of the lock containing Jesus's fake confession of pedophilia was painful to see. Only later, after forensic evidence was shown to have been altered with ink carbon dated back to around 200 BCE, did it become apparent why they needed it. Father Joseph, seeing the danger from the two men when they entered the library, hastily rolled up the parchment, combination locking it in the ark. For refusing to volunteer the sequence of numbers, they shot him with a single bullet into each kneecap, the pain spilling the numbers from him, then shot him in the head for the trouble he had caused them. Opening the ark they took it out and turned their attention to her. With no thoughts for her own safety, she remembered her still burning cigarette on the windowsill. Picking it out from the ash tray she pushed it into the man's eye. An action so rapid he did not have time to blink it closed. The one-eyed screaming cohort, raging all manner of obscenities, shot her in the chest. The bullet lodged close to her heart necessitated major surgery. She eventually recovered. Forgiving them in her turn.

She shuddered.

Those two differing in faith agents had their beliefs turned upside down. They found it difficult to ever understand their previously held beliefs based on the Hebrew or Christian bibles, any less than when they were children of God and Satan as nursery stories. Whatever stone Kriemhild was hiding under, Karla Kia had paid the price for her allegiance.

Carter had confirmed the 200 BCE carbon dating of the ink of the altered writing to the parchment to both Fitch and O'Hare as being correct and valid. Confirmation it was indeed altered before the birth of Christ. For it was not to be a problem for Satan x Ahriman. A multi-complex demi-god with identities in a singular form. None of whom reside in the oxygen of earth for long. For Angel or demon, both need dark matter of the universe to sustain themselves.

Whatever alter ego Satan chose to portray himself, his movements through Time–Universe was for purpose. She concluded the physics allowing him to come and go across Time–Universe (not Heaven, for Isle of Avalon was God's domain, whether He still resided there or not) was not for nothing. A self-guided bad judgment on His part? For black needs to continue black, for man to recognize white.

From documents held in the library, the evidence was showing God created the demigod as her bible read, giving him a window of physics eventually bringing Him down. For they had been, First and Last, enemies to each for the soul of man. A new world order eventually becoming a new universe for Satan x Kriemhild brushing away all was present and came before. Physics needed actors for a human perspective of understanding. A physics eventually playing out regardless of eggheads or demons.

Ahriman knew the First Coming of God through a mortal on earth was imminent. The physics of spirituality were, as far as Carter was concerned, the explanation for the mystery. Neither Fitch nor O'Hare had any other explanation, or answer. She had explained her version of the enigma inside a puzzle, leaving them to muse her being wrong with their own, when they concluded one. Not necessarily the right one.

Satan had overlooked an infinity sign on the end of the math equation. God, in His internal being, is raised above time; in His eternal absoluteness, He is throned above temporal development, saying,

For I testify unto every man heareth the words of the

prophecy of this book, If any man shall add unto him the plagues written in the book: and if any man shall take away from the words of the book of this prophecy, God shall take away his part out of this book of life, and from the things which are written in book.

 'So,' she said to O'Hare. 'No change will come from any future event?'

'Slightly disagree with your assessment of events past and future, Annie. For history, both good and bad will repeat, despite lessons of the past. For a mad dog, seven versts is not a long detour. Ha, ha, ha.'

ΧΧϚ

Mēthéna allogenē eisporeúesthai entòs tou perì tò hieròn trypháktou kaì peribólou. Hòs d'àn lēphthē heautōi aítios éstai dià tò exakolouthein thánaton.

Let no foreigner enter within the parapet and the partition which surrounds the Temple precincts. Anyone caught will be held accountable for his ensuing death.

ACKNOWLEDGEMENTS

The Three Monotheistic Religions: Children of One Father
PROFESSOR PAUL V. M. FLESHER,
Department of Religious Studies,
University of Wyoming.

Oxford History of the American West,
Edited by:
CLYDE A. MILNER, CAROL A. O'CONNOR,
MARTHA A. SANDWEISS, N.Y.,
Oxford University Press, 1994

Alistair Cooke's America, ALISTAIR COOKE,
Alfred A. Knopf, N.Y., 1973

A brief history of email dedicated to:
RAY TOMLINSON
awesome@phrasee.co

Judaism, C. M. PILKINGTON,
Hodder & Stoughton

Philosophy,

SIMON BLACKBURN,

Oxford University Press, 2005

'The dream of every lad ever threw a leg over a thoroughbred and the goal of all horsemen. There's only one Big Apple. That's New York.'

JOHN J. FITZ GERALD,

New York Morning Telegraph, 1920

ALSO BY GIL JACKSON

FICTION

The Seventh Gift

An FBI Charlie O'Hare Novel

Paperback: ISBN 978-1-8382326-3-4

Ebook: ISBN 978-1-8382326-2-7

The Sentinel Mother

An FBI Charlie O'Hare Novel

Ebook: ISBN 978-1-8382326-9-6

Direktorin Elke Kriemhild

An FBI Charlie O'Hare Novel

Ebook: ISBN 978-1-7391331-2-2

The Tinners Hut

A Barrister Phileas Cluff Novel

Paperback: ISBN 978-1-8382326-8-9

Ebook: ISBN 978-1-8382326-0-3

THROW ME *A-BUOY!*

If you like my style of novel writing, you can help me reach out to others with a few acts of kindness by reviewing my book.

Go to your favorite book platform where you bought the book, search for the title, and leave a review. It will help me, and I would appreciate it.

Perhaps you'd like to go further and subscribe as others to my email list. Here I regularly keep in touch and updating you with all my latest releases as they are published. There will also be FREE DEALS on my ebooks downloaded directly to your device. *The Mane Verses* is one such book. A Spine Tingler of a Horror. You will also find the second book in this series, *The Sentinel Mother*, doing the rounds on major platforms, currently FREE.

https://giljacksonbooks.com